'I know fine what you a
softly.

'What do you mean?'

'They gossip about y
poorer taverns such as t
folk, even the servant cla[illegible] about the Sinclair girl, who craves excitement, who means to kick over as many traces as she can, and the devil take the gossips. Was it not because you kicked over one trace too many that the perfumed young man reclaimed his ring, and your father punished you by sending you into exile in Scotland?'

'How dare you!' she gasped, feeling the colour spreading along her throat to her cheeks.

He raised an eyebrow at her. 'I dare because of my absurd pride. I will not be your latest escapade, Lucy Sinclair.'

Born of Afrikaans-speaking parents in Johannesburg, South Africa, Christina Laffeaty describes her education as 'erratic'. Between the ages of seven and fifteen she attended twelve different schools where her attendance depended on whether or not she was needed to help out with the ploughing or harvesting! She attributes the fact that she acquired any kind of education at all to her own obsessive reading.

She was nineteen before she learned English—from her husband, who brought her to live in England—and she started writing professionally shortly afterwards. Her work includes short stories for the BBC, the *Evening News* and various women's magazines; radio plays, serials and about sixty books. Mrs Laffeaty has a son and a daughter and lives in the West Country. *Love Undefeated* is her sixth Masquerade Historical Romance.

LOVE UNDEFEATED

Christina Laffeaty

MILLS & BOON LIMITED
15–16 BROOK'S MEWS
LONDON W1A 1DR

First published in Great Britain 1986
by Mills & Boon Limited

This edition 1986

ISBN 0 263 75481 2

Set in 10 on 11 pt Linotron Times
04–0986–72,500

Photoset by Rowland Phototypesetting Limited,
Bury St Edmunds, Suffolk
Made and printed in Great Britain by
Cox and Wyman Limited, Reading

CHAPTER ONE

LONDON WAS cloaked in a shroud of dull grey. Leafless trees lining the streets loomed starkly up from the February mist and were swallowed by it again as the carriage passed. Steam swirled like smoke from the nostrils of the horses and merged with the mist. The sound of a pie-seller crying his wares drifted on the air, eerily muffled and distorted.

Inside the carriage, Lucy Sinclair pulled her sable cloak more firmly about her and regretted for a brief moment that she had decided to follow the new, quite unpractical fashion for muslin worn over a transparent chemise and silk stockings. There was a good deal to be said for the comfort of worsted and flannel. Then she remembered, with a smile, the reaction when she had first appeared in the controversial new mode and she acknowledged to herself that panache was far more her style than was comfort.

As always, she had taken the lead in adopting the more daring of fashions created in Paris—which somehow crossed the Channel although England and France were still at war! The older ladies in London Society had been outraged and had called the new mode downright indecent, fit only for a French courtesan. The younger ones had tried to hide their envy by claiming that *they* would never sacrifice their modesty to the vagaries of fashion. The gentlemen of all ages had been entranced and had showered her with flattering compliments. But all of them had known that, whatever anyone did or said, Lucy Sinclair would go her own way, and that it would not be long before imitators followed where she led.

She reflected with pleasure on the extremely dashing bonnet which she had bought in Bond Street that morning. Of jade-green thread net with an upstanding poke trimmed with cascades of curled feathers, it was calculated to turn heads. It had been more than somewhat expensive at twenty guineas, but as the milliner had pointed out, it was something completely new and original, inspired by the latest Paris designs. Besides, Lucy could well afford it. Whatever his faults might be, her father was not in the least tight-fisted or mean.

Not for the first time, the thought led her to wonder whether his generosity with money was a conscious and deliberate substitute for love; an attempt to compensate for his coldness of heart. Materially he denied her and her mother nothing, but he was seldom to be found in the house in Cavendish Square. Such of his time as was not claimed by Westminster or his estate matters was spent in one of his clubs.

There seemed, to Lucy, to be no point upon which the interests of her parents touched. Hugh Sinclair, a Member of Parliament and a large landowner, was an austere, scholarly man given at times to a brilliant and cutting wit. He cared about his position in Society and his reputation in Westminster, but if he possessed any emotions about anything else, Lucy was not aware of it.

And poor Amelia, her mother, had no thought in her shallow head for anything but the trivia which made up her daily routine. Their marriage had been an arranged affair, Lucy knew. Hugh Sinclair had inherited land but very little money, while Amelia had been heiress to a great fortune founded on sugar in the Antilles. Apart from this coupling of money with land, it seemed to Lucy that her parents were glaringly mismatched. If her mother had not been stupid, she wondered, would she have minded the fact that there was no love in her marriage?

Lucy smiled wryly. Her mother would be astonished and shocked if she could read her daughter's thoughts. One was supposed to take one's parents for granted and not question their personal relationship. But Lucy's interest in her mother's marriage had sharpened ever since she had entered into a commitment to marry Victor Davenant.

Almost as if the thought of him had conjured up his physical presence, his curricle drawn by the familiar high-stepping bays approached from the opposite direction and she heard him shouting a command to her groom to stop. She lowered the window. Victor Davenant had handed the reins to his own groom and was strolling towards her carriage. She studied him dispassionately.

His driving coat with its profusion of capes was in the height of fashion and so, too, was the starched cravat around his neck. Of medium height and slight build, he was handsome in a classical manner, and he shared her taste for the outrageous and the flamboyant. His latest affectation was to drive around London with a matched pair of Italian greyhounds sitting one on either side of him. It was impossible, from his artfully groomed appearance, to guess his character, apart from his obvious love of show. His fair hair was brushed into carefully disordered locks, and as he removed his gloves, Lucy caught the familiar flash of diamonds upon his elegant hands.

She extended her own gloved hand to him and he took it with an exaggerated bow. 'My dear Lucy, I have just come from Cavendish Square, and when I was told that you had gone shopping, I hoped that I might meet you on your way home.'

'What did you want, Victor?'

'My mother hoped you might be persuaded to join her in a cosy, informal luncheon.'

His mother, Lucy guessed, wished to manipulate her and try to dictate all the terms of their forthcoming wedding, from the church at which the ceremony was to be held to the number of bridesmaids there should be and who were to be chosen to fill those roles. Clashing with Victor's mother would no doubt lend excitement of a sort to their marriage. She knew that she was more than a match for the woman, but she had little appetite for a verbal battle at the moment.

'Please make my excuses to your mother, Victor. I can feel one of my headaches coming on, and I think I had best spend the afternoon lying down in a darkened room.'

He accepted the lie with expressions of sympathy, and added, 'I shall give you my escort home. My groom can follow with my curricle.'

'Thank you, but there is no need.'

'I am anxious about your safety, my love.'

'Afraid that I might be set upon by footpads, Victor, and robbed of my dashing new bonnet?' She grinned derisively at him.

He took the remark seriously. She had noticed before that he had very little humour. 'No, of course not. But in this fog your groom might meet with an accident.'

'What nonsense! He is an experienced driver, and the fog is scarcely more than a mist.'

'It *was* a feeble excuse,' he conceded. He regarded her for a moment before going on, 'You know, of course, the real reason why I wished to accompany you. Mother has set her heart upon the ceremony taking place in the same church in which she herself was married, and she gives me no peace. I hoped you might persuade your parents . . .'

'It is to thrash out such details that you and your mother are to call upon us this evening,' she pointed out, bored with the subject. She did not very much care where the ceremony was to be held, except that it was important not to allow his mother to score too many victories too soon.

He shrugged ruefully, and released her hand. 'Very well, my dear. Until tonight.'

The carriage began to sway over the cobbled streets once more. Lucy stared unseeingly out of the window. The next few hours could be said to be the last she would be spending as a free young woman, for once the final details of the ceremony had been decided upon, the wedding day would be set and the date made public, and she would be irrevocably committed.

Viewed dispassionately, she could hardly have hoped for a better match than that of marriage to Victor. She did not love him, but she wanted children of her own, and whether one liked it or not, that necessarily involved a husband. And Victor promised to be an uncomplicated, undemanding husband. He was also wealthy and well connected, and Lucy did not feel at all daunted by his over-fond mother. Her own parents more than approved.

'My love,' her mother had fluttered, 'it is by far the best offer you have yet had! And just think, Lucy—the Davenant emeralds would pass to you! It seems like Fate, does it not? I cannot think of anything that would become you better, with that copper hair of yours, than the Davenant emeralds!'

Her father's approval had been equally characteristic: cold, and flavoured with his caustic observations. 'I know you have always thought yourself too good for any of your suitors, but you would be a fool to refuse

Davenant. You are not getting any younger, and at twenty-three you can expect few other offers. All the girls who came out with you have long since married. Unless you wish to be a lonely spinster, an object of pity, you had best take Victor Davenant and count yourself lucky.'

Lucy blinked fiercely as she remembered again how his words had wounded her. There had been no hint that he cared anything for her happiness. It had seemed that he was simply eager to have her respectably off his hands.

She wondered, a little dismally, whether it was this lack of love from her father which had made her search for it so restlessly, and which had caused her to turn down every offer of marriage she had received since she was seventeen. Men had protested their love for her, but none of them had ever struck an answering chord in her heart. And so, because there was no love in her life, she had filled it with fashionable crazes instead. She had hidden her vulnerability by presenting an outrageous, extravagant image to the world, flouting the social conventions, and astonishingly getting away with it. Old ladies might disapprove of her, and their daughters resent her popularity, but no social occasion was ever considered a success unless Lucy Sinclair was present.

But lately the need to have *someone* to love was proving too strong; a child of her own would fill it, and its father would be no more than a necessary means towards this end. And what matter if he saw her in much the same light as the Italian greyhounds perched beside him in his curricle—a fashionable accessory, adding to his air of distinction?

With a sigh, she abandoned her introspective thoughts as she realised that they had reached Cavendish Square. Armsworth, the butler, ushered her deferentially inside the house, volunteering the information that her mother was out and would be lunching with friends.

'In that case, I shall have something on a tray in my room,' Lucy told him.

She climbed the wide, curving staircase to her own suite of rooms. The walls of her private sitting-room were decorated with expensive paper in an ivory and blue design. A chaise-longue with gilded scroll-ends and deep blue velvet upholstery stood before the tall windows, which were draped in ivory silk and tied back with blue velvet. A secretaire, a satinwood sewing-table and some Hepplewhite chairs completed the furnishings, and the slightly cold effect of ivory and blue was softened by the ruby red of the carpet.

The sitting-room led directly to the bedroom. A large canopy bed with silk drapings of misty pink stood in the centre, and the dressing-table was prettily swathed in cotton lace over a rose satin petticoat. An ornate cheval mirror with a satinwood frame flanked it.

Lucy threw her bonnet and cloak on the bed and turned to the mirror, soberly studying her reflection. Her figure was tall and slim; her skin had an almost translucent milkiness against which her rich copper-coloured hair formed a stunning contrast. Long, heavy-lashed eyes of vivid green beneath straight dark brows had inspired many a fulsome compliment from would-be suitors.

Yes, she thought, her mouth twisting with wry humour, I shall look well beside the sleek Italian greyhounds . . .

She turned away from the mirror. Only too soon now, any compliments she received would be polite and conventional, for she would be married to Victor. She wished that the thought did not depress her so deeply.

Perhaps, if he had loved her, it might in time have been possible for her to cultivate deeper feelings for him. But then, she had decided to take him precisely *because* he did not love her, and she would therefore not have to feel that she was cheating him of anything.

She had a shrewd suspicion that he wished to marry her for the same reasons as she was prepared to enter into the match. It was necessary for him to settle down and produce an heir, and she was eminently suitable. Besides, she would complement his showy flamboyance, and they would no doubt come to be known as the Dashing Davenants. It was not a comforting thought.

At that moment her personal maid, Jane, entered with the boxes containing her purchases which Lucy had left to be carried into the house. Jane exclaimed over the bonnet, but Lucy had already lost her pleasure in it and responded abstractedly. Jane had just finished putting Lucy's things neatly away when one of the parlourmaids arrived with a tray, and the two servants withdrew so that she could eat her lunch in privacy.

She toyed with a piece of cold chicken, abandoned it and reached for an apple instead. But she had no appetite, and was staring with moody distaste at the large amount of food on the tray when Jane knocked on the door and entered the sitting-room.

'Oh, miss,' she reported, looking both flustered and excited. 'There is a person downstairs asking for you. Mr Armsworth says he thinks you had better see him.'

'What is his business with me?' Lucy demanded with a frown.

'He won't say, miss; only that it's very important he should see you.'

'What is his name?'

'Well, miss, he did tell us, but he is some kind of foreigner, and the truth is that none of us could quite make it out.'

'I cannot imagine what a foreigner would want with me,' Lucy said, and shrugged. 'Whoever he is, I don't wish to see him. Tell Armsworth to send him away.'

'He did try to do so, miss, but the person would not leave.'

'Good lord! Surely it is not beyond the servants to throw the man out! Armsworth must have known that I would not consent to see a complete stranger who does not even have the courtesy to send in his card!'

Jane spoke with awe. 'He is a very big, strong-looking man, miss, and—and not quite civilised looking, if you know what I mean. Mr Armsworth believes there would be a nasty scene if we tried to remove him from the house.'

Lucy nodded, her interest awakened. 'I suppose I had better see this man who is terrorising all of you! Tell Armsworth to send him up here.'

'Very well, miss. And Mr Armsworth said I was to tell you to have no fear, as he and the others would wait just outside the door, within call.'

'From all accounts,' Lucy said drily, 'that would hardly be adequate protection against so formidable a visitor.'

She waited with lively curiosity for the man to be ushered into the sitting-room. And as soon as he entered in the butler's wake, she could see why the servants had regarded him with both suspicion and respect.

He was tall; one of the few men Lucy had ever encountered who towered over her. His black hair was unfashionably short and fell in an unruly way over his brow. The clothes he wore were outlandish, to say the least. In one hand he held a kind of bonnet of dark green tartan, and in place of breeches he wore a kilted garment of similar tartan. His stockings reached to his knees, and inside the left one was tucked a knife. Flung across one shoulder in the manner of a cloak was a plaid, and she noticed that this curious garment was threadbare in places.

His features were strong and well defined, giving his face a ruggedly arresting look, and a pair of intensely blue eyes regarded her without any of the respect which she automatically expected from someone of his obviously low station in life.

His glance went from her to Armsworth, making it clear that he wished to speak to her in private. The butler stood his ground until Lucy said, 'If I should need you, Armsworth, I'll ring.'

Slowly, with reluctance, he bowed himself out, presumably to lurk with the other male servants just outside the door.

Once alone with the stranger, Lucy addressed him crisply. 'Having practically forced your way into my presence, might I know who and what you are?'

'Alistair Munro, tacksman, from nearby the clachan of Bencraig.'

His deep voice held an unfamiliar lilt, and he had a way of emphasising each syllable. No wonder the Cockney servants had found it difficult to understand him. Apart from his name, the rest of what he had said meant nothing to Lucy either.

'I have travelled all the way from Sutherland,' he went on, offering her his hand as he spoke.

Such was his presence that she found herself on the verge of taking it. She had to remind herself forcibly that he was no more than a Scottish peasant, in spite of his apparently arrogant conviction that they were equals. Why, he had not even made her a bow! Deliberately, she ignored his outstretched hand.

He raised his eyebrows, and his mouth curled in a half-smile. He withdrew his hand, examining it intently for a moment as if trying to discover what it was that had caused her to reject it.

The studied insolence of that small gesture angered her, and she said curtly, 'You had better tell me why you were so insistent upon seeing me.'

''Tis a long tale, ma'am.'

There had been something distinctly derisive about that '*ma'am*.' She compressed her lips. 'Then tell your tale, and have done.'

She sat down on the chaise-longue, but she did not invite him to sit also. He was presumptuous enough without being encouraged to make himself at home, and to take his time over the telling of his reasons for demanding an audience of her. He leant against the wall and folded his arms across his chest, regarding her with an expression that he did nothing whatever to conceal. It was one of mockery and disdain.

But when he began to speak, his words were strangely at odds with his expression. 'You have heard, perhaps, of what has been afoot in the Highlands?'

'No.' Lucy frowned. 'Why should I have done so?'

His mouth twisted bitterly. 'Mr Hugh Sinclair owns the Sutherland estate of Strathraora, which includes the clachan of Bencraig. Surely what happens there is of sufficient interest to him to discuss it with his family?'

'He owns many estates in various parts of the country,' Lucy defended her father. 'One cannot be concerned with all of them.'

He swept her a sardonic bow. 'Quite so.'

She contained her anger. 'I take it you have some grievance, Mr Munro, although why you . . .'

'With your permission, ma'am, I shall explain to you the matter which you are pleased to call my grievance!' His blue eyes sparked with passion, and it was abundantly clear that he meant to speak, with or without her permission. Once again his expression failed to match his voice, for it became almost lyrical as he continued in a manner which reminded her of an adult telling a story to a child.

'Our society in the Highlands has ever been a patriarchal one. The clans thought of themselves as the children of the chief; they were ever ready to fight for him, to work for him, to obey him in all things. And he, in his turn, might be a strict and even harsh parent at times, but he was a just one. As all good fathers should, he cared for the well-being of his children.'

In spite of herself she was beginning to fall under the spell of his voice. She fought it by saying impatiently, 'Will you please get to the point, Mr Munro? I fail to see how your Scottish tribal ways should be of interest to me!'

'Do you indeed, ma'am?' He was silent for a while, regarding her with a look which made her stir restlessly.

'Please bear with me a little longer,' he went on at last. 'Over the years, the system has been changing. The clans have remained true and loyal to their chiefs but the chiefs, alas, have lost interest in the fate of their children. They have forsaken the Highlands for the fashionable life in London; it has come to matter more to them that their daughters should marry well by finding husbands among the English aristocracy and that their sons should obtain commissions in fashionable regiments, than what has become of the tacksmen and sub-tenants and cottars who depend upon them.'

'Are you implying that landowners like my father have a duty to reside on their far-flung estates? That is not only impertinent but also highly unrealistic!'

'Lairds like your father, ma'am, have deserted the people by more than their physical departure! Of late years they have begun to argue that more money could be made from sheep than from the paltry rents which their tenants are able to pay them. And so, more and more people in the Highlands are being evicted from their homes in order that the land may be profitably turned over to sheep!'

Lucy was trying hard to understand a situation which

was totally alien to her experience. 'Presumably the lairds act within the law,' she began.

'Oh ay, ma'am.' His voice was low and bitter. 'The lairds are legally allowed to rob people of their self-respect, of their dignity, and to drive them like animals from their crofts into an alien land to starve!'

Lucy frowned. 'Are you saying that my father has behaved in such a manner?'

'Not yet, ma'am. But we in Sutherland have been sorely troubled by the way in which clans in other parts of the Highlands have been dispossessed by their chiefs over the years. Now Elizabeth, the Countess of Sutherland and your father's neighbour, has begun to pluck her clansmen up by their roots and cast them adrift. And we in Strathraora fear that the same thing may happen to our people.''

With an effort, Lucy pulled her wits together. She had been listening to him, half-mesmerised by his strange, lilting voice and the passion with which he described his people's plight. But it struck her that her father had too many other affairs preoccupying his mind to have given a thought to uprooting the people from his Scottish estate. 'You have no foundation for believing that my father intends evicting his tenants,' she said aloud.

'We do have reason to believe that your father relies on the judgment of his factor, and that factor is in favour of what he calls progress! We believe he has written to Mr Sinclair, advising the clearing of the land so that sheep may be brought in. And that is why each of my people sacrificed a few pennies—which they could ill afford—to contribute towards a fund set up to send a representative to put their case to Hugh Sinclair. As tacksman, I was the natural choice to be that representative.'

'If you have come to plead your case with my father,

Mr Munro,' Lucy asked, 'why don't you do so? Why do you waste your time with me?'

'Because, ma'am,' he replied harshly, 'I wrote to him, requesting an audience, but he refused to see me. He sent me a curt note, telling me to take whatever problem I might have to his factor in Sutherland. I hoped you might use your influence to persuade him to change his mind.'

She smiled wryly at the suggestion that she might have any influence over her father, and shook her head. 'I am afraid that I cannot help you.'

'Cannot, ma'am, or *will* not?'

'You are impertinent, Mr Munro!' she retorted. 'I have listened patiently to you, even though there is no reason why I should have done so . . .'

'No reason, ma'am?' he interrupted quietly. 'Have you no compassion at all for your own people?'

Lucy gritted her teeth. The man had an uncanny knack of putting her in the wrong. She thought of telling him that it would be impossible for her to speak to her father about the matter, for Hugh Sinclair would simply refuse to discuss it with her. But he would probably not believe her, for most people tended to assume that her father doted upon his only child.

In the end, Lucy said, 'I have never visited the Highlands, even though I was born there. Good heavens, it is not even as though Strathraora were our ancestral home! The land came to our family only when the father of the last Lord Sutherland lost them in a game of faro to a Sinclair. So it is quite unreasonable to expect me to think of the tenants as my people!'

He was studying her from beneath lowered lids, making it impossible for her to read the expression in his eyes. 'You would not consider them to be your people because of your position as their laird's daughter?'

'No, I would not! Any more than I would consider the tenants on any of my father's other estates to be my people!' She stood up. 'I am sorry, Mr Munro. There really is nothing I can do to help you. Now, I must ask you to leave.'

He did not move. 'Do you not concede, ma'am, that you owe *something* to your father's tenants? The rents they pay contribute, in no matter how small a way, to your pretty gowns, to the fripperies in this room . . . ' His glance went to the tray of food discarded by her, resting on the game pie, the sliced sirloin, the thinly-cut slices of buttered bread, all untouched. 'Ay, the very food your delicate appetite rejects, and which would feed a whole family of cottars for a day, has partly been financed by those people whose fate you dismiss so lightly!'

She bit her lip. 'I will not be made to feel guilty! There is nothing whatever I can do to help your people —if, indeed, they do need help!'

His mouth curved in a grimace of bitter irony. 'Supposing you *should* feel a belated stirring of guilt, and persuade Hugh Sinclair to grant me an audience, I may be reached at the Black Swan Inn this evening. But in the morning I leave London by the stage, for I can no longer afford the cost of bed and board.'

She recalled the way he had glanced at her unwanted lunch, and guessed that he had not been able to afford the cost of more than the most basic board for some time. She moved towards the door, and said, 'Before you go, I shall ask the butler to take you into the servants' hall so that a meal may be provided for you.'

Strong hands caught her by the shoulders from behind and spun her around. 'Indeed you will not,' Munro said with ominous calm. 'It is not for crumbs from your table that I have come here, grand lady!'

She stared into his face. How could this tacksman,

this threadbare tenant of her father's, succeed in making her feel as if she had committed an unforgivable social solecism by offering him a meal in the servants' hall? She groped for some way of humbling that absurdly proud spirit of his and then her anger faded suddenly. She was sharply aware of the fact that he smelled differently from any other man she knew. Instead of powder and pomade, he smelled of the country and of what she supposed vaguely must be heather and peat smoke, and she had a vivid mental picture of him striding through a glen with his plaid flying in the breeze.

She put out her hands and pushed him away. 'Please leave, Mr Munro. I shall tell my father of your visit, but for the sake of your people I shall refrain from giving him an account of your insolence.'

'Insolence?' He looked at her with blank amazement. Then he smiled sardonically. 'If it might lead your father to see me, then pray do tell him I was insolent!' He sketched a bow, tossed his plaid over his shoulder, and strode to the door.

She sat down after he had gone, torn between bewilderment, anger, pique and curiosity. He did not recognise that he had been insolent, of course, because he considered himself to be her equal. And yet he had nothing; he *was* nothing and no one.

She realised that the winter-short afternoon was drawing to a close and that it was growing dark. Simultaneously, she heard noises downstairs, and then her mother's voice drifted up to her.

'Thank you, Armsworth. Yes, a glass of mulled wine will be very welcome. We'll take it in the drawing-room. Is Miss Lucy home?'

Leaving her suite, Lucy descended the stairs. Plump, bird-witted Amelia Sinclair was handing the butler her cloak and gloves. She smiled when she saw her daughter.

'There you are, my love! Emily Brandon is an affected woman! I don't know why I accepted her invitation to luncheon. Really, the meal was fit for a City parvenu! Your father is taking dinner with us this evening. Isn't that nice? Ah, here he is now!'

'It is necessary that I should dine at home.' Lucy heard her father's dry, unemotional voice. 'The Davenants are arriving after dinner, remember, to discuss the arrangements for the wedding.'

Lucy wished he had not reminded her of her forthcoming wedding. She looked at him, trying to assess his feelings. Did he resent having to spend the evening at home, in a paternal role, instead of with his cronies?

Hugh Sinclair was a thin man with a habitual stoop, and his skin was pale from years spent incarcerated in a city. There was no expression on his face as he accompanied Lucy and Amelia to the drawing-room and listened to the artless prattle of his wife.

'Just think, Hugh, I was telling Lucy—an absurdly lavish luncheon, and everything served with such vulgar ostentation! I suppose the Brandons feel bound to let everyone know that they have twenty thousand a year. But one thing I will say—I desperately covet those Meissen vases of hers! Hugh, do you think, if I were to make Emily an offer . . .'

'By all means, my dear,' he said cynically, sitting down, 'if you wish to risk a rebuff.'

'No one could rebuff a hundred guineas! They would look marvellously well upon my salon table.'

Lucy broke into her mother's chatter. 'I met a man from Strathraora this afternoon, Father.'

Hugh Sinclair frowned. 'Alistair Munro? Don't tell me he had the effrontery to come here! I trust the servants threw him out!'

Before Lucy could speak, her mother prattled on, 'It is very tiresome indeed, being Scottish. People will ask one boring question about something called land clearances which has been going on up there. I'm sure I don't know what it is all about. Hugh, can you tell us?'

He shrugged. 'Until now, many of the glens have been cluttered with half-starved and useless inhabitants. Some of the landlords are clearing the land of their hovels and turning it over to sheep.'

Lucy frowned thoughtfully. 'I am sure *your* tenants do not starve in hovels, Father, and there will therefore be no need for you to turn them from their homes?'

'I have always borne the interests of my tenants in mind when I have considered changes,' he replied in a tone which made it clear that he did not intend discussing the affair with her.

She had done what she could in the matter. And her father, whatever his faults might be, was not forever counting pennies and considering where economies might be made or profits enhanced. And no matter what suggestions his factor in Sutherland might make, was it likely that her father, busy as he was, would give his attention to the making of sweeping changes on his Scottish estate? An estate which he had not visited since soon after Lucy was born.

No, she told herself, the people of Strathraora, Alistair Munro's people, were safe in their glens. There had been no need for him to come all this way to make his impassioned speeches on their behalf.

That her father was a generous man was illustrated when he began to outline to Lucy the marriage settlement which he intended drawing up for her. But she felt depressed as she listened to him, and her thoughts strayed continually to the arrogant Highlander who had nothing at all to justify such arrogance.

When they had drunk the mulled wine served to them by Armsworth, Lucy and her parents dispersed to their separate domains to prepare for dinner. As Jane helped her into a gown of ivory silk brocade worn over an underskirt looped with embroidered sprigs, it came to Lucy that seldom could a girl have taken so little pleasure in her own appearance on such a momentous evening in her life.

After the meal, she joined her parents in the drawing-room to await the arrival of the Davenants. Hugh Sinclair was reading a book and his wife was working on her embroidery, while Lucy gazed about the room and tried to cheer herself by thinking of the changes she would make in the Davenant home after her marriage.

Victor's mother, whether she liked it or not, would have to abdicate in favour of a new mistress. Lucy planned to sweep away all the gloomy old pieces which had come into vogue when the first Hanoverians ascended the throne, and replace them with elegant modern items of furniture which she hoped to commission, perhaps from Mr Pugin himself. That should give her an added interest . . .

At that moment, Armsworth announced the arrival of the Davenants. They entered, Victor's mother stout and imposing as she leant upon his arm. The fact that she had chosen to wear the Davenant emeralds for the occasion could only have meant that she wished to remind Lucy that she did not intend to give up any of her rights and privileges without a fight.

Lucy's gaze moved to her fiancé. His appearance was picturesque, if somewhat extreme, with his intricately tied cravat and the ruffles on his sleeves which spilled over his elegant wrists. She wondered how long it had taken his valet to arrange his hair so that it fell in such apparently careless locks over his brow.

She allowed the discussions to flow over her, taking little part. Mrs Davenant questioned several of the terms in the marriage settlement, and Hugh Sinclair justified them in his precise, unemotional way. There was a mild tussle between the two older women over the matter of Mrs Davenant's niece being invited to be a bridesmaid. Amelia Sinclair tied herself in verbal knots as she attempted to explain her objections without saying in so many words that the girl was too fat to be suitable. Lucy tried to derive some amusement from the situation, but she was aware, instead, of a growing depression.

'Now,' she heard Mrs Davenant say, 'we come to the question of the church in which the wedding is to be held.'

She was interrupted by a knock on the door, and then Armsworth entered. 'I am afraid, sir,' he told Hugh Sinclair, 'that the Scottish person has called again.'

'What? At this hour? The cursed impudence of the man! Throw him out!'

He was silenced by the appearance of Alistair Munro himself. He loomed over the butler, forcing him to stand aside with an authority which demonstrated the physical impossibility of Armsworth being able to eject him.

Lucy was aware that, for some unaccountable reason, her heart had given an odd little jerk and now it was beating rapidly and unevenly in her breast. She stared at the Highlander, but he did not even glance in her direction. There was no humility about him at all. Even the small bow which he made out of politeness to the ladies held no deference. He turned to Hugh Sinclair.

'I had intended to leave London in the morning, sir. But people have sacrificed money they could ill afford so that I might come here, and I decided I owed it to them to make one last effort to gain an audience with you.'

Lucy saw that her father was regarding him grimly. 'You—and they—have wasted both your time and your money. Any matters regarding my Sutherland estate are to be referred to my factor, Mr Buchanan. That is my last word upon the subject.'

Alistair Munro's knuckles gleamed white as he clenched his hands in anger. 'With respect . . . ' he began in a voice which held no respect whatever.

'My patience is exhausted, Munro! You've made an accursed nuisance of yourself since your arrival in London, trying to badger me at my club, even attempting to waylay me on my return from the House! And now you have twiced forced your way into my home! I will not stand for any more! If I do decide to make changes on my estate in the North—or on any of my other estates, come to that—it will be done with a due regard for the law. The people will have no legal cause for complaint.'

Munro's eyes blazed with anger so intense that Lucy caught her breath. He looked down at his hands for a moment as if he were struggling with an overwhelming desire to strike Hugh Sinclair. Then he allowed them to drop to his sides.

'You talk of *legal* cause for complaint!' he said in a blistering voice. 'Ay, and have the lairds not ever acted within the law as they plucked their tenants from their crofts? And should a law exist to stand in your way, 'tis the very law-makers like yourself who remove it!'

Hugh Sinclair spoke coldly. 'You do the cause of the people who have sent you here little good with your display of impertinence. Now get out, before I send for a constable!'

Unhurriedly, with a deliberate gesture, Munro drew his plaid across his broad shoulders and strode to the door, his head held high, and Lucy noticed that something about him forced an involuntary small bow from Armsworth as the Scot passed him.

'Well!' Mrs Davenant broke the silence which followed his departure. 'What a strange, violent creature!'

'Quite barbaric,' Victor drawled, fastidiously rearranging the ruffles of his sleeves. He shuddered, and then gave a little titter. 'My dears, those *clothes*!'

Now I know why the Scot is proud for all his poverty, Lucy thought, staring at her fiancé. He is a real man. A strong, caring, passionate man with an inborn sense of his own worth. Not a fashionable fop who needs to bolster his own self-esteem by drawing attention to himself with a pair of Italian greyhounds . . .

'Now, let us return to the matter of the church,' Mrs Davenant was saying. 'Lucy, dear, I beg you to consider the merits of St James's . . .'

'No.' She had spoken without consciously reaching a decision, but as she went on she knew instinctively that the decision had been the right one. 'I do not wish to marry Victor—in St James's or anywhere else.'

Slowly and deliberately she removed the diamond engagement ring from her finger and held it out to him.

CHAPTER TWO

Lucy spent a restless night, alternating between staring wakefully at the ceiling and dozing fitfully, her sleeping moments troubled by tangled dreams.

Once, she dreamt that she found herself wandering on the crest of a hill, blinded by fog, and when the fog cleared she saw with a shock that a deep gorge yawned at her feet. She turned her head, and found Alistair Munro leaning against a rock, his arms folded across his chest, watching her with mocking, insolent eyes. Then he stretched out a hand and pushed her into the gorge.

She awakened, her heart hammering, her throat dry, and gradually relaxed as she recognised that it had only been a dream. The gorge, she supposed, must represent the way in which her mind interpreted her own uncertain future now that she was not to marry Victor after all. And while the Highlander was not actively responsible for what she had done, there was no denying that he had been the influence behind her decision.

She watched the morning light peep into the room through the slight gap between the curtains, and thought of the ghastly scene which had taken place the evening before.

At first, everyone had thought she was joking. Then they had bombarded her with demands for an explanation, which she had been unable to give. At that point Victor had turned on her with unexpected venom. 'You'll not make a laughing-stock of me and escape unscathed!' he'd snarled. 'You think you may do whatever you wish and Society will always smile indulgently at your latest antics! But not this time!'

His mother had entered the fray against Lucy. 'At last people will see you for what you really are. To play fast and loose with men's affections, as you have been doing for years, is one thing. But when it comes to wearing a man's ring for six months, and then calling everything off at a whim and totally without explanation—well, you will be exposed as a wanton, fickle little baggage! And there is not a thing Victor or I will say in your defence! After tonight, your reputation will not be worth a fig!'

But what had hurt more than the attack upon her by the Davenants had been the reaction of her own parents. Hugh Sinclair had looked at her, white with rage. Then he had picked up the document detailing her marriage settlement and flung it at her, before walking out of the room.

'*No one* will ever offer for you again after this!' her mother had wept. 'The Davenants will see to it that your name is made mud. Oh, what harm you have caused to everyone, you wicked child!'

With condemnation and recriminations ringing in her ears, Lucy had fled to her suite. And there she had faced squarely the reality of what she had done.

It was quite true that no other man of her acquaintance was likely to risk being humiliated as she had humiliated Victor. She could live with Society's outrage; it would not last for ever. But what *would* last was the knowledge that her father cared more to have her respectably off his hands than he did for her personal happiness, and that her mother was solely concerned with what people would say. And by jilting Victor Davenant last night, Lucy had almost certainly condemned herself to spinsterhood and a lifetime spent under her parents' roof.

Yes, that bottomless gorge in her dream had not been so very fanciful after all . . .

She sighed, and leant out of bed to reach the bell-pull. A short while later Jane entered with a porcelain jug filled with hot water, and on her heels came a chambermaid who drew the curtains back and made up the fire.

'I'll breakfast in my room,' Lucy told Jane as she swung her legs out of bed.

'Begging your pardon, Miss Lucy, but the master said I was to tell you to join him and the mistress.'

Well, she told herself resignedly, she could not have hoped to hide from her father's anger indefinitely. She washed, and then allowed Jane to help her into a morning gown and dress her hair, and afterwards she went downstairs, steeling herself.

Hugh Sinclair's expression was more grimly austere than usual as he looked up at her from the breakfast table, and Amelia had been weeping again. Lucy helped herself to scrambled eggs and kidneys and sat down, waiting for the storm to break over her head.

But she ought to have remembered that, with her father, a storm was more likely to take the form of a hard frost. In chilling tones, he addressed her.

'Perhaps you will now be good enough to explain the reason for your latest wayward folly.'

'Was it folly?' she countered. 'You heard the things the Davenants said, Father. For myself, I can only be grateful that I shall not have a husband and a mother-in-law capable of such venom . . .'

'Can you blame them? I cannot!'

'Oh,' her mother wailed, 'there will be such a scandal, and I shall not be able to hold up my head again . . .'

'It will pass, Mother.'

'Will it?' her father put in grimly. 'Do not be too sure.

The Davenants are an old and respected family, and you have greatly insulted them by waiting until such a late stage before changing your capricious mind. Why did you do it? Why did you allow all the discussion about arrangements for the wedding to continue, making fools of all of us, if you had intended breaking off the betrothal? Was it deliberate, to amuse yourself at our expense?'

'No.'

'Then *why*? And do not insist again that you do not know!'

She looked down at her plate. 'I—It is difficult to explain. It had something to do with Alistair Munro . . .'

'With Munro? How could a common tacksman have influenced you?'

'I don't know,' she repeated helplessly. 'At least—I only know that he made me realise the difference between himself and Victor.'

'It would scarcely take a giant intellect to perceive the difference between them! One is a gentleman of breeding and wealth, and the other does not and never will have more than two farthings to his name!'

'I—I think you must have taken complete leave of your senses, Lucy,' her mother accused, pressing a handkerchief to her eyes. 'Jilting Victor, and then claiming it was because of a Scottish peasant . . .'

'I am sorry to have caused all this fuss and distress,' Lucy told her parents in a quiet voice. 'But I cannot pretend to be sorry that I returned Victor's ring. I looked at him last night, and I could not help comparing him with the Highlander. Victor would never fight passionately to help anyone but himself. He is interested only in what touches his own desires and needs. There is nothing behind his foppish façade. He is selfish, immature and superficial; a hollow sham who cares only about outward appearances.'

'And Alistair Munro,' her father queried with cold sarcasm, 'tacksman on my Scottish estate, somehow caused the scales to fall from your eyes so that you perceived all these hitherto hidden faults in Victor Davenant?'

'Well—yes.'

Amelia began to weep more bitterly than before. 'Everyone has been waiting to hear when the wedding was to be, and many of my friends have ordered special gowns for the occasion. How am I to face them?'

'If it would help,' Lucy suggested, 'I could take Jane with me, and go and stay in Bath for a while. You could then tell people that my behaviour was caused by an affliction of the nerves, and that I have gone to take the waters on medical advice.'

Lucy saw that a cold smile was playing about her father's mouth as he considered her suggestion. 'Yes,' he nodded at last, 'it would be a good thing for you to leave London as soon as possible. But since you find Scotsmen so praiseworthy and superior, a visit to my Sutherland estate would be more appropriate than Bath.'

'But, Hugh,' her mother objected. 'Lucy cannot travel all that way with no one but Jane to accompany her!'

'Precisely, my dear. You will go with her.' He added smoothly, 'In that way, you will be spared the need to face people in London for a while.'

Lucy knew instinctively that he did not only wish to punish herself, but that he was seizing on the excuse to rid himself of his irritating wife for a while.

Amelia gave a little shriek of dismay. 'Oh Hugh, no! Not that dreadful, desolate place!'

'It has been decided, my dear. The more I think about

it, the more sensible a solution it appears.'

'But *no one* goes to Scotland!'

'All the more reason for Lucy to do so. Added to her recent behaviour, it might persuade people that she has suffered some kind of brainstorm. Anyone who visits Scotland in February can hardly be said to be in possession of all her wits. She may even wring some sympathy from people who would otherwise have condemned her roundly. So I suggest that you and she start preparing for the journey without delay.'

Lucy kept her eyes cast down so that her parents would not recognise the excitement which was coursing through her. It would be an affront to her mother, who felt nothing but dismay, and it might cause her father to change his mind if he realised that what he regarded as punishment was, instead, something to be looked forward to.

A visit to Scotland would be a new experience, she told herself. A mental picture of Alistair Munro filled her mind, but she drove it out determinedly. He had nothing whatever to do with her eagerness to visit Sutherland. He was only a poverty-stricken peasant, after all, and as such did not merit a second thought from her. She had been born in Scotland, she reminded herself, so it was only natural that she should wish to visit her birthplace. And by the time she returned, London Society would have grown tired of talking about the abrupt cancellation of her marriage to Victor.

In the meantime, it was impossible not to be aware that Society was agog with curiosity. Card after card was carried in by Armsworth, announcing callers who had obviously come to find out all the details of the quarrel between the Sinclairs and the Davenants. Lucy and her mother pleaded indisposition, but even the stage of siege in which they were living did not reconcile Amelia to the thought of the long, uncomfortable journey to remote Sutherland. She was triumphant when what seemed to her to be a valid objection presented itself.

'We shall have to cancel the visit, Hugh!' she announced. 'Lucy's maid Jane has offered her resignation. She says she cannot put such a great distance between herself and her sick mother. She is an excellent maid and would be hard to replace, and in order to keep her we shall have to change our plans!'

'Nonsense, my dear. Allow the girl to remain behind and make herself useful here. Lucy can share the services of your abigail.'

'I'm sure Harriet would resent such an additional burden . . .'

'I'll ask her,' Lucy put in.

Harriet, her mother's abigail, was quite happy to attend to Lucy's toilette as well, and Amelia was forced to drop that particular objection. But as the preparations for their departure to Scotland swept the household up in a fever of activity, she tried other ways of delaying the journey, appealing to her husband who was spending far more time than usual in Cavendish Square.

'I cannot possibly leave,' she told him, 'until the new gowns I have ordered arrive from the seamstress!'

'My dear, you will have no need for smart gowns in Strathraora House,' her husband said firmly. 'No one but the servants and Neil Buchanan will be there to see you.'

Amelia's eyes filled with tears at this bleak forecast, and then they took on a triumphant look. '*Servants*! Lucy and I cannot stay at Strathraora, Hugh, when the only staff are a housekeeper and a gardener! If we really must go, we shall have to wait until servants have been sent up there to prepare the house for us!'

Lucy, watching them, saw an odd gleam enter her

father's eyes. 'There is no need for that, Amelia. I shall send Armsworth with you. He will engage a staff from among my tenants when you arrive in Sutherland. A girl will also be taken on to act as Lucy's maid.'

'Oh, but you cannot send Armsworth! You have no notion how quickly servants take advantage of a butler's absence to neglect things!'

'I am closing the house,' he told her, 'and dispersing the servants to my various estates to make themselves useful there. I shall move into my club until I have made my own arrangements to depart for Sutherland.'

'Oh!' Amelia's astonishment equalled that of Lucy. 'I had no notion that you meant to travel to Strathraora also!'

He gave Lucy a look of cold displeasure. 'I cannot put my head outside this house without being accosted by some bore whose womenfolk have charged him with the task of ferreting out the details of the cancelled wedding. I have decided, therefore, that I might as well give my attention to my Scottish estate.'

'Then why can you not accompany us,' Amelia argued, 'instead of following on later?'

Lucy saw her father close his eyes briefly. The last thing he would wish, she knew, was to be cooped up inside a carriage with her mother for a long journey.

He patted Amelia's shoulder. 'I have several things to attend to in London before I shall be able to leave. As I shall be travelling much more lightly than you, I expect to reach Sutherland not long after you have done so.'

Dolefully, Amelia resigned herself to leaving for Sutherland, and dabbed at her eyes with a handkerchief. 'That cold, bleak house,' she said with a shudder. 'I shall probably take a chill, and very likely die there.'

This mood of self-pity and despair still prevailed when they set off the following morning, but it was, Lucy decided, an impressive retinue which proceeded north. She and Amelia rode in Hugh's best travelling carriage, driven by his coachman, with the groom sitting up beside him, heavily armed in case of highwaymen. Behind their own vehicle followed another, conveying their luggage and Armsworth as well as Harriet.

While the carriage clattered along London's crowded streets, Amelia was preoccupied with the fear that they would be overturned by one of the sporting curricles or chaise-and-fours which overtook them. But soon London had been left behind, and there were no other diversions to occupy her attention.

She sank into a mood of melancholia, her handkerchief never far from her eyes. 'I have a presentiment,' she said over and over, 'that I shall not live to see my home in Cavendish Square again.'

Lucy leant back in her seat and watched the countryside rolling by, withdrawing into her own thoughts. She was disturbed and angry with herself to find that Alistair Munro's image continued to stray into those thoughts, and she tried to dismiss him by telling herself repeatedly that he was nothing but a threadbare, poverty-ridden tenant of her father's.

As they overtook other slower vehicles, she gave mental thanks for the fact that their own carriage and constantly changed team were capable of covering more than forty miles in a day. But gradually the boredom of the routine—the many halts for fresh horses, the overnight stops at posting-houses—began to wear away at her nerves, and she would almost have welcomed the sight of the highwaymen which, in between predictions of her own death in Scotland, her mother was constantly forecasting.

In places the road was pitted with holes and sloughs, and at one spot it was impassable because of a tree which had blown down, so that the two coachmen were forced to turn the vehicles round and make a detour through a small village whose inhabitants had never before seen such fine carriages, and who lined the narrow streets to watch their passing.

The weather had turned noticeably colder as they proceeded north. The sun shone, eerily translucent, through the frozen mist that overlaid the air, and the horses blew steam from their nostrils. Lucy was grateful for her large fur muff and the copper foot-warmer on the floor of the carriage, and she hoped devoutly that there would be no heavy snowfalls to delay them further.

She heard the coachman shout to his horses to slow down, and simultaneously the familiar blast from the horn carried by the mail-coach told her that they were approaching a turnpike. A glance through the window showed that there were other vehicles besides their own and the mail-coach waiting to pass through the turnpike. Sheer boredom made her alight from the carriage and brave the bitter weather outside while they waited.

The reason for the delay became apparent as she walked along the row of stationary vehicles. The pike-man had obviously been trying to fight the cold and the tedium of his occupation with alcohol, for he was moving clumsily, with a staggering gait, collecting toll-money and opening the gate for each vehicle to pass through, while the coachmen's angry shouts rained upon his head. Lucy's glance moved away from the turnpike, and she felt her heart turn over in her breast.

Behind the mail-coach, the ordinary stage was waiting with its passengers. Alone on its open top, his plaid drawn across his shoulders and his black hair blown awry by the wind, sat Alistair Munro.

The unexpected sight of him, and her own reaction to it, filled her with dismay. She stared up at him and received a slight, ironical bow in return. If he was surprised to see her, he gave no sign of it.

The bitter weather seemed not to affect him. He sat there, completely unprotected from it except by his plaid, as if contemptuous of the less hardy souls inside the coach, supremely confident that his own strength and force of character could challenge the elements. There was something just as arrogant in this defiance of the weather as there had been in his manner towards herself and her father.

'I hope it snows!' she taunted him. 'That would soon send you scuttling inside the coach! I wish I could be there to see you beat an undignified retreat from your lofty position!'

A smile tugged at his lips. 'You would not see that, even supposing it were to blow a blizzard.'

'My goodness, what confidence in your own powers of endurance! No doubt you think a common chill would be too daunted to attack you?'

He laughed aloud. 'No such thing,' he said ruefully. 'It costs more, do you see, to ride inside the coach.'

'Oh . . . ' She was seized by a sudden, disarming tenderness. She stared up at him, reflecting that the stage-coach was slow and that he had been travelling on its open top for several days longer than she and her mother had been on the road. But before she could say any more, the stage began to roll towards the turnpike gate. Her own coachman called respectfully to her that she had better resume her seat.

'Simpson, do you know which posting-house the stage uses?' she asked impulsively.

'Yes, miss. The Three Feathers.'

'We'll stop there tonight.'

'But, miss, it isn't at all the sort of place you and madam would use . . . '

'I am sure that respectable rooms could be found for us. We'll stop there.'

As she took her seat, she told herself, the man is

Father's tenant, and we therefore have some responsibility towards him. He cannot be allowed to make the rest of this long journey sitting in the open. I shall pay the stage-coachman to let him ride inside, and if Alistair Munro's ridiculous pride causes him to continue riding on top—well, then, he deserves to contract pneumonia!

Darkness had fallen when they drove with a clatter into the courtyard of the Three Feathers. It was clear from the way in which the attendants ran to them that the posting-house was not accustomed to catering for travellers who arrived in imposing carriages like Hugh Sinclair's.

But the two best rooms in the house were speedily cleared of their less important occupants to make way for Amelia and Lucy, and a private parlour was placed at their disposal.

Amelia sank into a chair. 'I cannot think why we had to stop here. This is a dreadful place, Lucy!' she complained peevishly.

It was only the knowledge that she had said precisely the same thing of every other posting-house at which they had stopped that kept Lucy from feeling guilty. She soothed her mother, and made sympathetic noises about the headache which she claimed their surroundings had somehow induced.

'I know the dinner will prove to be uneatable, even if I hadn't always had the most delicate of appetities,' Amelia went on. 'It is hardly worth having covers laid for me. I think I shall retire to bed and eat a little something from a tray. Could you ask the parlourmaid to attend to it when she comes? Just something light, Lucy. Harriet, have you prepared my bed? Take me to it, if you please.'

Lucy smiled ruefully to herself after she had been left alone in the parlour. Her poor, brainless mother was determined to make the worst of the journey with her many grievances and her imaginary headaches. No wonder Hugh Sinclair had manoeuvred matters in such a way that he would not be called upon to travel with them, and so be subjected to his wife's air of martyrdom.

The parlourmaid entered, and shyly took Amelia's order. 'And yourself, miss? Will you be dining alone?'

'Yes . . . ' Lucy stopped. Once again impulse took hold of her. 'An—An acquaintance of mine is travelling by the stage. A tall gentleman in a plaid.'

'Yes, miss, I have seen him in the taproom.' The maid's expression suggested that she had not only seen him, but had been greatly impressed by his presence.

'Please ask him to join me here,' Lucy said.

The girl gave her a curious look and nodded. As soon as she had gone out of the room, Lucy regretted her impulse. She would have liked to call the maid back, but she was aware that such behaviour would have seemed even more odd. Her heart beating uncomfortably fast, she waited.

A few minutes later, Alistair Munro's large frame filled the doorway. Again, as in Cavendish Square, she had an impression of some untamed quality in him, something that made him seem hopelessly incongruous in that prim little parlour. She could imagine him striding through heather with the wind in his face, attending to whatever a tacksman's rural duties were. Yet, at the same time, he had a kind of grace which set him apart from an ordinary man of the soil. And always there was that indefinable hint of arrogance, as if he knew himself to be the equal of anyone and better than most.

He sketched a bow. 'The maid told me that you wished to see me, Miss Sinclair.'

'Yes. I—wished to invite you to dine with me.'

To her surprise and relief, he did not question her motives, but said simply, 'Thank you.'

He sat down, and they made polite conversation while the maid served the meal. Afterwards, Lucy watched him eating. Only someone who knew how very straitened his circumstances were would have been aware of the fact that he was ravenous, for he had the table manners of a gentleman.

She had to break the silence, driven by curiosity. 'Why did you accept my invitation to dinner, when you reacted so violently that last time I offered you food?'

He looked up, that cool gaze fixed upon her face. 'Since you can be on your way to Strathraora only because I influenced you in some way, it would have been churlish of me to refuse your invitation.'

She felt a flush staining her face. There was no limit to the man's superior estimation of himself! With an angry laugh, she said, 'You did not decide to accept because your dinner would otherwise have been a crust of bread and a jug of ale in the taproom?'

He speared a slice of roast beef, a slight smile curving his mouth. 'That question deserves no answer. Since you merely asked it in order to provoke me, I shall ignore it.' Relentlessly, he went on, 'You made it clear, in London, that you had no interest in your father's Scottish estate, and you have not visited it since early childhood. You expressed no intention of going there at that time, so I can only conclude that you are here because of me.'

She ground her teeth. 'You flatter yourself! If you wish to know the truth, I am being sent to Scotland as a *punishment*! I displeased my father . . .'

'Ah . . . ' He gazed at her left hand, and nodded slowly. 'It would have something to do, perhaps, with the bonnie, scented, young man I saw in your father's house. Well, you'll not find many diversions at Strathraora, I fear.'

'It would be interesting, Mr Munro, if not diverting, to

discover whether *all* Highlanders share your unfounded arrogance!'

He looked straight into her eyes. There was a gleam of derision in his. 'If I have arrogance, it must have been bequeathed to me by my forefathers. I am descended from one of the clan chiefs, and indeed I am distantly related to Elizabeth, Countess of Sutherland.' The derision in his eyes deepened. 'And where do you come by your arrogance, Miss Sinclair?'

She almost choked on a mouthful of food. The unbelievable effrontery of the man! It seemed impossible to teach him his place, for he simply would not acknowledge that his place was anything but her social equal. Just because of some distant link with the Countess of Sutherland, he regarded the difference in their status as laird's daughter and impecunious tenant to be irrelevant!

She looked at him with glittering eyes, wanting to wound him. 'No doubt it was the noble blood in your veins that madc you feel you could carry off a visit to London in those outlandish clothes you choose to wear!'

Once again he melted her anger and disarmed her completely by glancing ruefully at the frayed ruffles on his sleeves, and saying, 'They do not seem outlandish in Strathraora. Besides, they are the best I own.'

She was overwhelmed by the same tenderness she had felt when he openly admitted that poverty forced him to ride on the open top of the stage, and she wanted to do something for him.

'Mother and I have more than enough room for you to spare in our carriage,' she offered impulsively. 'Leave the stage and join us.'

She could see by the tightening of his lips and the haughty tilt of his head that he suspected charity. 'You would be doing me a service,' she went on quickly.

'Mother sleeps for most of the time, and there is no one with whom to talk.'

He smiled then. 'Thank you. But I doubt if Mrs Sinclair would welcome such an arrangement.'

'Leave her to me,' Lucy said with confidence, and rose. 'I shall bid you good night now, Mr Munro.'

As she moved the heated brick from her bed and slipped between the sheets, she was aware of excitement coursing through her. It was, she told herself, because the journey had been so very dull this far, and because at least Alistair Munro's company would be something to look forward to.

The next morning, as they went out into the courtyard where the carriages with fresh teams of horses were awaiting them, Lucy saw Munro talking to a groom and she led her mother to his side. Amelia was in the middle of describing the disturbed night she had endured, and she allowed herself to be steered across the courtyard without protest.

'Mother,' Lucy broke into her tale of woe, 'you remember Mr Alistair Munro, do you not?'

'Why, yes . . . ' Amelia blinked up at the Highlander.

'I have invited him to share our carriage.'

'Oh!' Amelia's voice was faint with horror.

'The stage has not yet left,' Munro said. 'If it is inconvenient, I shall continue my journey on that.'

'Well . . . ' Amelia foundered. 'It is not precisely *inconvenient* . . . That is to say . . . ' She stopped, and Lucy knew that she had calculated aright. By springing the news on her in the man's presence, her mother was unable to voice the nature of her objections.

'It is quite convenient,' Lucy said firmly. 'Shall we get aboard the carriage?'

Her mother sat rigidly in her seat once they had set off, regarding Alistair as though he were some dangerous creature who was only waiting for her to doze off before he murdered all of them and stole the carriage.

'Mr Munro is related to the Countess of Sutherland, Mother,' Lucy volunteered with deliberate casualness.

'Oh!' A look of relief swept over Amelia's face. 'Well, of course, that . . . What I mean is, all families have their poor relations. How extraordinary of your father not to have mentioned the connection!'

She relaxed visibly in her seat. Clearly, she had decided that a relation of the Countess of Sutherland could be trusted, no matter how shabby his clothes or untamed his looks. After a few minutes she had fallen asleep.

Lucy looked up to find Alistair Munro shaking with suppressed laughter, but he did not offer to share the joke with her. Perhaps it was simply her mother's attitude which amused him, she decided.

'Please tell me something about life at Strathraora, Mr Munro?'

His voice took on its pronounced lilt as he began to talk. Lucy learnt the history of the clan system, and how the chief's tenants in times gone by had been regarded as his warriors, to be called upon to fight for him whenever the need arose.

'Even supposing he had not a penny in his sporran,' Munro went on, 'rich was the chief who could call on five or six hundred fighting men with their broadswords. Below the chief came his tacksmen, who were generally his blood-kin, and they were granted a lease by the chief. In their turn they leased land to sub-tenants by goodwill. There they grazed their cattle and grew their oats and barley. Below the sub-tenants in status came the cottars, who were landless and worked as servants and as blacksmiths, as herdsmen or armourers. But when the call to arms came, all left their tasks and rallied to fight under the chief's command, the tacksmen as officers, the . . .'

He never completed the sentence. The carriage jolted suddenly and Lucy, caught unawares, found herself sliding across the seat. Her mother made a sound of irritation in her sleep but did not wake.

Lucy had been thrown against Alistair Munro. His hands reached out automatically to steady her and lingered on her upper arms. Through the material of her sleeves, the warmth of his fingers seemed to her fancy to be burning into her flesh. Her cheek brushed against the slight roughness of his chin. She jerked her head away, disturbingly aware of his strength and of some powerful physical male magnetism which she could no longer pretend to ignore. She found herself looking into his eyes.

He did not let her go, even though the carriage was now moving along smoothly. His eyes were veiled, and something about the curve of his mouth made her heart beat erratically.

'The—The carriage is steady now,' she pointed out in a breathless voice.

'Ay,' he agreed softly.

'So—you may release me now.'

He let her go, and she regained her own corner of the seat and stared out of the window. But after a while, something compelled her to look at him. He was watching her, a hint of a smile twisting his lips.

She felt her colour rising. 'Why do you stare at me like that?' she demanded.

'I was merely thinking,' he murmured, his eyes mocking her, 'that beneath your fine clothes and your grand manner you are but a small wee thing.'

She was glad that they reached the posting-house at that moment, and that the halting of the carriage had woken her mother, so that it was not necessary for her to reply to that impudent statement.

That evening Amelia joined them for dinner, and steered the conversation to Alistair's connection with Elizabeth, Countess of Sutherland. Amusement leapt into his eyes, but he explained gravely, 'Many tacksmen, like myself, are blood-kin to the clan chiefs. As you have said yourself, ma'am, we are their poor relations. Well enough born, but with not a penny to our names.'

'Well,' Amelia declared charitably, 'everyone cannot be rich, I suppose.'

'How kind of you to say so, ma'am,' he murmured.

Lucy found that her thoughts were wilfully straying along a path of their own. Apart from being kin to the Countess of Sutherland, had he not said that a tacksman was immediately below the clan chief in status? Why, that put him roughly in the same class as an English knight! And one would not automatically regard a knight as unacceptable, simply because he lacked a fortune . . .

Her heart began to beat a tattoo in her breast as she recognised to what her thoughts were leading. She argued angrily with herself. The clan system no longer existed; he had said so. The chiefs no longer required the clans to fight for them, and therefore a tacksman was no more than a tenant, only slightly above the status of a servant—whether or not he was related to the noble Sutherlands.

The trouble was, she decided, Munro's own inflated view of himself tended to colour one's judgment in spite of oneself. It had been ridiculous to think of him as a possible . . . Deliberately, she stopped short of formulating in her mind just what role she had contemplated casting him in.

But as she prepared for bed later, she could not help remembering that moment when the movement of the carriage had flung her against him and the weakness which had overcome her at his touch. She had never felt like that with any other man before. She had never been so *aware* of another man before . . .

A laugh escaped her as she recalled something else. She was considerably taller than most girls, and quite as tall as a good many men, and her deep-bosomed figure had often been described by her admirers as being Junoesque. No one had ever before called her 'a small wee thing'. Her laughter died, and she gave a wistful sigh instead. It was oddly comforting to be thought of as small and, by implication, in need of protection.

The next morning Alistair's manner was impersonal as they continued their journey. Amelia followed her usual habit of falling asleep, and Lucy thought it was no wonder her mother complained of sleepless nights, since she made no effort to stay awake during the day.

The carriage was now slowly moving north, and Alistair pointed out the sights to Lucy. He explained that a group of women and children at work in a valley were cutting peats for the fire, and his face took on an austere, gaunt look as the carriage passed grassy plains teeming with flocks of sheep.

'The new clansmen of the chiefs,' he said bitterly.

'Had there not been sheep in Scotland before?' Lucy wanted to know.

'Oh ay. Each crofter kept a few sheep for their wool and their milk, and of course in time their mutton. But the pride of the people lay in their cattle, until the lairds began to argue that an area of land could produce twice as much mutton instead. And so came the invasion of sheep from the Cheviot hills. They thrived where black cattle starved, and because the crofters and cottars took up space which could more profitably be occupied by sheep, the people were ruthlessly removed.'

His voice took on a note of love and hopeless pity as

they approached the Highlands. He might have been talking of a young woman whose death had left him bereft.

'Look round you, Miss Sinclair. The land in this glen once supported five clachans in which hundreds of clansmen lived. Now there are but four human beings: four foreign shepherds from England with their dogs, tending some three thousand sheep.'

Lucy said nothing. She found herself almost overawed by their surroundings, and also strangely saddened, as if the people who had been driven from this land had left an aura of their despair behind them. There was an undefinable melancholy in the beauty of the high, scowling hills and of the narrow valleys and frozen burns.

She looked at the man beside her. His expression had become stark and withdrawn, shutting her out. She felt an overwhelming impulse to remove that brooding look from his face and to make him aware that other things existed apart from these hills and glens and their reminder of wrongs perpetrated on a once proud people.

'How very much colder it is here!' she said, and added lightly, 'Mr Munro, I cannot believe that you do not feel the chill also, even accustomed to it as you are. If that absurd pride of yours would allow you to admit it, then pray feel free to share my travelling rug.'

He turned his head to look at her. His gaze moved to the travelling rug which covered the lower part of her body. Belatedly, she realised that if he were to share it he would have to sit very close to her indeed.

'I know fine what you are about, Lucy Sinclair,' he said softly.

'What do you mean?'

'They gossip about you in London: ay, even in the poorer taverns such as the Black Swan. Forbye Society folk, even the servant classes talk about the Sinclair girl, who craves excitement, who means to kick over as many traces as she can, and the devil take the gossips. Was it not because you kicked over one trace too many that the perfumed young man reclaimed his ring, and your father punished you by sending you into exile in Scotland?'

'How dare you!' she gasped, feeling the colour spreading along her throat to her cheeks.

He raised an eyebrow at her. 'I dare because of my absurd pride. I will not be your latest escapade, Lucy Sinclair.'

He had, she thought in deep mortification, taken all her half-formed, confused feelings and longings and translated them, in his blunt way, into something which could not have been more unflattering to her. And she could not refute his accusation, because if she did so she would have to admit . . .

She shook her head at herself. No, she would not take the thought to its conclusion. It was, literally, unthinkable.

Because she had to say something, she spluttered inadequately, 'Kindly call me Miss Sinclair when you address me!'

He threw back his head and laughed so loudly that Amelia awoke with a startled sound.

CHAPTER THREE

SHE HAD never encountered a man like him before. He recognised no unwritten laws; he conformed to no prescribed standards. He said what he thought, simply and bluntly, and in doing so he was able to reduce her, Lucy Sinclair, to a speechless, awkward young girl fresh out of the schoolroom.

Lucy watched her mother glance out of the carriage window, and give a shudder. 'This awful, bleak landscape . . . I had hoped never to see it again.'

' 'Tis a sentiment shared by many a laird and his lady,' Alistair observed with a hard note of cynicism in his voice. He added with deliberate emphasis, 'I understand that *Miss Sinclair* has been banished to Scotland as a punishment, but it does not seem just that you should be forced to share her exile, ma'am.'

'No, indeed it is not!' Amelia agreed with bitterness. 'And were you not a connection of the noble Sutherlands, Mr Munro, I would not have suffered your daily presence, for I hold you partly to blame for the whole sorry business!'

'I?' he queried, his eyebrows lifting.

Lucy winced, and cast her mother a pleading glance, but Amelia did not seem to recognise it as such, for she continued broodingly, 'The wilful child broke off her engagement when matters had reached a very advanced stage, and the only reason she would give was that *you* had influenced her in some way! It would have been such a suitable match, too . . .'

'My apologies, ma'am,' he told Amelia gravely, but there was secret laughter in his eyes as they rested upon Lucy.

Amelia settled down to resume her nap, and Lucy shot Alistair a defiant look. She said tartly, 'Pray do not allow your already high self-esteem to become even more inflated. I could think of no easy reason to explain my change of mind, and so I pretended it had something to do with your entirely coincidental arrival at the house.'

'Quite so,' he murmured.

'Well, it *was* so! Even you cannot seriously imagine that I would break off my engagement to a gentleman of birth and breeding because of a chance meeting with one of my father's tenants!'

'No, indeed. I understand fine. Having thrown everyone into an uproar by ending your engagement, you thought you would shock them further by bringing my name into the affair.' He sketched a mock-humble salute. 'I am honoured to have been of use to you, Miss Sinclair.'

She gritted her teeth and stared out of the window, ignoring him. Then she beheld a sight which transcended her own confused feelings of anger and pique.

A party of ragged people were toiling across a valley, their heads bowed against the wind. In the distance the air was blackened by smoke. Everyone in the party was carrying something, and a young boy drove a pony before him. Its back was hollowed by the load which it carried. A small girl struggled with a creel which she tried to keep balanced upon her back. She fell under the weight of it, and its contents of potatoes spilled out over the frozen earth. The child was crying with cold and hopeless frustration, but Lucy noticed that she hunted for the last of the potatoes before she struggled on to catch up with the others.

Lucy realised that Alistair had been witnessing the scene also. There was no sign of his earlier mocking amusement. His face was harsh and his eyes burned with a bitter and hopeless anger. 'They are crofters who have been dispossessed by their chief,' he said. 'Those are their houses burning. There is nowhere for them to go. They have been driven out to make way for sheep.'

Lucy said nothing. The scene haunted her, and her heart went out to those hopeless travellers into nowhere.

'Now that you have seen to what they have been brought,' she heard Alistair go on harshly, 'perhaps you will, from the depths of your own good fortune, do something to help your people in Strathraora. If you were to write to your father of what you have witnessed . . .'

'My father would not deal so unfairly with his tenants! As for my writing to him . . . There will be no need, because he will witness conditions for himself.'

Alistair caught her wrist in a hard hold. 'Your father is to visit Scotland? Why did you not tell me that before?'

'Did I not? I dare say I forgot to do so . . .'

'You *forgot*!' His voice was angry, and the pressure on her wrist increased. 'You knew about the fear and the despair of my people, and you forgot to tell me something so important! Why is he visiting his Scottish estate? He did not have it in mind when I spoke to him! Indeed, he told me to deal with his factor, Neil Buchanan!'

'It was a sudden decision,' Lucy explained. 'The thought only occurred to him once he had made up his mind to send me to Scotland.' She added, 'You are hurting me, Mr Munro.'

The pressure of his fingers slackened, and she heard him draw a sharp breath as he stared at her wrist. Angry red weals marked the skin where he had gripped it. 'I am sorry,' he said. 'Why did you not speak out before?'

She looked into his eyes, and all the thoughts which she had been suppressing rushed overwhelmingly to the forefront of her mind, like an overflowing river bursting its bank.

I remained silent, she acknowledged to herself, *because you were touching me. Even in anger and causing pain, I wanted you to go on touching me. I would sooner be hurt by you than be caressed by any other man.*

Aloud, she said, 'It doesn't matter. And—I am sure my father will be as shocked as I have been when he sees how the landowners have been behaving.'

'I wonder,' was all Alistair said. He glanced out of the window. 'Tomorrow we reach Strathraora, and the clachan of Bencraig.'

The posting-house at which they put up that night was noticeably more austere than any of the others along the way had been. Travelling gentlefolk were obviously rare here, and the inn's usual clientele probably consisted in the main of tenant farmers who stopped there on the way to or from a market.

The carriage bearing the luggage, with Armsworth and Harriet, the abigail, had arrived there first. The butler came out into the courtyard to meet them, and addressed Amelia apologetically.

'It's a poor sort of place, madam, with no private parlour, and the only food to be had is peasants' fare. I knew it would not do, so I have arranged for you and Miss Lucy to be served a dish of coddled eggs in your bedrooms. It was the best I could manage, for eggs appear to be the only commodity they have in plenty.'

Dismay, followed by numbing disappointment, swamped Lucy. This was to have been the last evening spent in Alistair's company, and the thought of being cheated of it was not to be endured. She *needed* this evening: needed it to convey to him, as subtly as possible, how she felt about him. Once they arrived at Strathraora it would probably be too late, for they would inevitably slip into the roles of tenant and laird's daughter, and a pattern would be set which would become difficult to break.

'Whatever the nature of this peasants' fare,' Lucy said, 'it must surely be preferable to coddled eggs. And there must be a room of some sort in which we could sit down to eat.'

They had entered the squat building and stepped straight into the taproom. 'This is the only room for public use, Miss Lucy,' Armsworth told her.

A few gnarled old men sat nursing jugs of ale and staring curiously at them. Lucy ignored them and gazed around the badly-lit room. A small voice of common sense told her to bow to circumstances and dine in her room, but the need to have this last precious evening with Alistair made her ignore the voice.

'Please ask the landlord to come over to us,' she commanded Armsworth. 'If this place serves as a posting-house, it must be prepared to cater properly for travellers!'

'For goodness' sake, Lucy,' her mother protested peevishly, 'why make so much fuss? It is such a dreadful place that we may as well submit to coddled eggs served in our rooms, and the men may eat in the taproom.'

'I have no wish to spend the evening shut up in my room, and I loathe coddled eggs.'

The landlord was accompanying Armsworth to where they stood. Lucy explained what it was she wanted, and Alistair added something in the Gaelic. The landlord answered him in the same tongue.

'He says,' Alistair translated, 'that the only room which could be put at our disposal is his family's own parlour. He wishes to know whether that would suffice.'

'Please tell him it would.'

The landlord bowed politely and went off to give orders to have the room prepared for them. Amelia continued to complain about the shortcomings on the inn and Lucy responded mechanically, while Alistair said nothing but stood with his arms folded across his chest.

At last the landlord appeared and announced that they were to follow him. They were shown into a drably furnished room, displaying clear signs that it had been hastily vacated and tidied. The floor was of uneven flagstones, and neither the few scattered cotton rugs nor the sluggishly drawing fire did anything to soften the chill which overlay the room. Her mother, Lucy thought with relief, would not wish to linger here after dinner, but would retire to bed and leave her alone with Alistair.

She noticed that the landlord had, naively, caused places to be laid for all of them at the table, including Armsworth. The butler had noticed it too, for he coughed and addressed Amelia.

'With your permission, madam, I'll withdraw to the taproom, unless you wish me to wait upon you.'

'What a dreadful room!' she interrupted. 'It does not offer the slightest comfort! Harriet, help me to my bedroom, if you please, and Armsworth, tell the landlord that I wish for coddled eggs to be sent up to me.'

When the two of them were alone in the parlour, Alistair pulled out a chair for Lucy, but neither of them spoke while the landlord was serving their meal. Dinner consisted of vegetable soup thickened with barley and accompanied by coarse bread. Lucy toyed with the food, her heart hammering as she mentally rehearsed a seemingly innocent remark which would convey to him that she not only regarded him as far more than her father's tenant, but also as far more than an 'escapade' with whom to kick over the traces.

'You do not find peasants' fare to your taste, I see,' he broke the silence abruptly.

She looked up, startled, into his unsmiling face. 'I am not hungry.'

'Then why,' he demanded with a blistering note in his voice, 'did you insist upon turning the landlord's family from their parlour, so that you might sit and play disdainfully with your food?' He pushed his chair back and stood up. 'For myself, I do not intend to go on sitting here with you, while the landlord's wife and children are doubtless shivering in some unheated back room. I shall take my dinner in the taproom.'

'Please sit down . . . ' she began, dismayed.

'The devil I will!'

She knew that she had thoughtlessly ruined everything. It would not be possible, after this, to meet his eyes in a revealing look or to make remarks which said one thing and meant another. The waste of the evening, and shame at the recognition of her own selfishness, made her seek relief by whipping up her temper.

'After all the hospitality you have received from us, the least you owe me is your company—such as it is! So sit down, Mr Munro, because I refuse to be abandoned, to dine alone!'

She saw his hands go to the fur-covered pouch which he wore attached to his belt, and which he had told her was called a sporran. He withdrew a handful of coins and flung them on the table.

'That should suffice to buy me an evening's freedom!' he snarled. 'It is all I have, but I consider it to be cheap at the price!' Then he turned and strode towards the door.

Rage coursed through her. No man had ever treated her like this, nor spoken to her in such a manner, and she would not allow Alistair Munro to do so. She pushed her chair back with the intention of going after him and forcing an apology from him. But a leg of her chair caught against one of the uneven flagstones and it tipped over on its side with herself thrown in an ungainly heap on the floor.

He had stopped and turned, but he uttered no words of concern nor made an attempt to help her to her feet. A sound of pain escaped her as she tried to rise.

'I—I have twisted my ankle,' she was forced to admit. 'If you would be so good as to give me your arm up the stairs . . .'

He stooped, and helped her to her feet. Instead of allowing her to lean upon his arm while she hopped from the room, he picked her up much in the way as he would have picked up a sack of potatoes, slinging her over one shoulder, and made for the stairs. She gritted her teeth. She was powerless to free herself from this undignified position, and any scene she created would only serve to highlight the ridiculous aspect of her dilemma, for a woman and several children had appeared and Alistair was exchanging words with them in the Gaelic.

Obviously he had been told which was Lucy's room, for he turned left along the landing, opening the door of the second room he came to. A candle had been left burning upon the wash-stand, and as he lowered her to the floor, Lucy saw that its light was creating mysterious hollows of Alistair's eyes. Although he had set her on her feet, he did not release her. Her heart had begun to beat stormily, and all feelings of rage and humiliation had disappeared.

He said something in the Gaelic—then his mouth was on hers in a kiss which was unlike anything she had ever experienced. Even Victor had reserved his passionate kisses for her hands, and had only occasionally brushed her mouth with his. But this man knew no restraint: he cared nothing for the conventions or for the dictates of polite behaviour, and while Lucy felt herself carried along upon a tide of helpless passion, part of her mind was warning her to take care, that there were many difficulties in the way, that if she wanted him she would have to fight her parents and even be prepared to cross over into his world.

When he lifted his head at last she saw that his eyes were glinting at her, and that a smile played around his mouth.

'How d-dared you,' she said in a small voice, for no other reason than that she could think of nothing else to say.

She waited for him to reply, '*I dared because I could not resist you.*' Instead, he laughed aloud. 'Come now,' he said mockingly. 'Was not that what you were about all this time? The perfumed London dandies had begun to pall, and you had a mind to see if Highland crofters were more diverting. Perhaps you will stop playing games, now that your curiosity has been satisfied.'

She felt as if he had struck her. She said indistinctly, 'I shall see to it that my father learns of your disgraceful behaviour!'

He shrugged. 'Be sure to tell him also how much you enjoyed my disgraceful behaviour, Miss Sinclair, until you suddenly remembered that you were the laird's daughter.'

He moved to the door, and she watched him with a mixture of anger and self-disgust. He turned in the doorway, and murmured derisively, 'Do not feel too much shame at your own behaviour, Miss Sinclair. Remember my kinship with the Countess of Sutherland, and remind yourself that the social gulf between us is not so very wide after all.'

She sat down on the bed when he had gone, violent emotions clashing inside her. He must have knocked on Harriet's door before going downstairs, for a few minutes later the abigail entered to help Lucy undress for bed. Her injured ankle showed no signs of swelling, and she decided that no great harm had been done.

But once she was alone and lying wakefully in bed, the thought came to her—*No harm might have have been done to your ankle, Lucy Sinclair, but the episode has not left you unmarked . . .*

She sighed, and turned over. It was no wonder that he assumed she regarded him as a diversion. He must believe that he had nothing to offer her, nothing to make her wish to throw in her lot with his. And, in truth, he *had* nothing to offer . . . If only he were not her father's tenant. If only the two of them were equal in wealth and property and social standing. For she wanted Alistair Munro in a way which she had never wanted any man before, and at last she was admitting it to herself in so many words.

Her mind began to turn over ways and means of accomplishing the thing she wanted. One of the main stumbling-blocks would be parental opposition, but if she could win her mother over to her side before her father arrived . . .

Alistair's connection with the Countess could be used to this end. Her mother was a snob, and if Lucy harped on the kinship sufficiently, Amelia might come to disregard the fact that he had no money and no land of his own. It helped, too, that Alistair was well spoken and that he behaved more arrogantly than many gentlemen.

Then there was her father. If he had loved her, it would have been more difficult. But as it was, would he not be relieved to have her off his hands once he had given the matter thought? He would be the first to admit that they could no longer hope for a match of any brilliance for her, now that the scandal she had created in London would have scared off other suitors. In the circumstances, was it not more than likely that her father would accept—if not with enthusiasm, then at least with resignation—a marriage between herself and his tacksman?

That left only the gulf of the two different worlds in which she and Alistair lived. Could she become accustomed to having no money? If it came to that, why *should* they be penniless? Her father, she argued, had been prepared to be generous in the matter of her dowry when she was planning to marry Victor. If he might be persuaded to be equally generous again, she and Alistair could live comfortably upon little more than the invested proceeds of her dowry. Besides, her father could easily find a position for Alistair as land-agent in charge of one of his many estates . . .

Excitement tore through Lucy. Yes, the thing was possible. If her mother could be counted upon to add her voice, her father would give in for the sake of peace, if nothing else. Lucy's last thought, before she fell asleep, was of Alistair dressed in fashionable tight-fitting breeches and a satin coat, with lace ruffles at his throat as he awaited her at the aisle.

In the morning, Alistair did not allude by as much as a secret, mocking glance to that scene between them the previous evening, and even her slight limp brought no change in his expression. Lucy studied him with a heightened awareness, and her heart beat tempestuously. As soon as they had resumed their travel, she began her campaign to draw her mother over to her side.

She turned in her seat and addressed Alistair. 'Does your kinswoman, the Countess of Sutherland, reside on her Scottish estate?'

'She is more usually to be found in Stafford House, in London.'

'I am told it is a magnificent house,' Amelia put in enthusiastically, 'and filled with art treasures.'

'Have you ever been inside it, Mr Munro?' Lucy asked, guessing full well that he had not. The important thing was that his kinship with the nobility should be stressed within her mother's hearing.

An ironical smile twisted his mouth. 'Indeed I have not. Perhaps I had best explain the precise nature of my connection with her ladyship, before your mother gains too lofty a notion of my social status.'

Lucy put her hands up to her bonnet, pretending to pull it straight, so that he would not notice the colour which had swept into her face. Could he possibly have guessed what she had been about?

She heard him address her mother. 'You see, ma'am, my great-great-grandmother was the illegitimate daughter of the clan chief. She was ugly as sin, and with a foul temper to boot, but the chief felt that he ought to do something for her, so he offered a reward to any of his men who would marry her. It wasn't until he promised her bridegroom the status of tacksman that Robert Munro offered for her. He, poor man, came to regret his bargain, for after several stormy years she poisoned him in a fit of temper.'

'What a disreputable story!' Amelia exclaimed, and added reflectively, 'Not that the blame for it can be laid at your door. But still . . .'

'Quite so,' he agreed blandly.

Lucy clenched her hands into fists and stared out of the window. His many references to his kinship with the Countess had clearly been meant to mock them, not to impress them. No wonder he had looked so amused when her mother accepted his presence in their carriage purely on the strength of it.

Another far more devastating thought struck her. Had he purposely chosen to spell out the crude reality of his connection with the Countess of Sutherland to nip in the bud her own attempt to turn it to advantage?

Surely she was not as transparent as that? Because, if she were, it meant that she, Lucy Sinclair, had just undergone a unique experience. She had been rejected by a man.

'We have now entered the glen of Strathraora,' she heard Alistair say, and his voice was totally different this time; warm and caressing. 'Yonder is the clachan of Bencraig.'

What he called a clachan was revealed to be a township of small rudely-constructed houses huddled within a long and narrow valley. The wan winter sun swept the snow-covered summits of the surrounding hills and lent a strange brilliance to the air. As they drew nearer, Lucy saw that the clachan straddled one side of a burn which lay frozen in its twisting course. Peat smoke rose pungently into the air from a hole in the roof of each of the houses in the township.

As Lucy watched through the carriage window, a girl emerged from one of the houses and strode towards the byre which adjoined it, and began to drive some sheep across the valley. From that distance it was impossible to see the girl's face, but her figure in its homespun petticoat and white jacket gave an impression of litheness and vitality.

She stood still for a moment, her head thrown back, and Lucy saw her free her hair from its confining snood. It streamed behind her in the breeze like a soft black cloud. There was something ingenuously abandoned in the gesture, as if she took an unashamed delight in her own beauty.

Lucy turned her head, and found that Alistair, too, had been watching the girl. His mouth was curved in a smile, and there was a tenderness in his eyes that hit her with the force of a blow to the midriff. Every instinct told her that the girl in the glen meant something to him. How could she have been such a fool, not to suspect for a moment that she might have a rival?

'I should,' Alistair said, confirming her intuitive knowledge, 'be obliged to you if you would ask your coachman to set me down here.'

Filled with a welter of emotions such as she had never before experienced, she rapped on the glass and signalled to the coachman to stop. Alistair swung himself from the carriage and began to hurry with long strides along the glen and towards the girl.

'Fiona!' his voice reached Lucy. 'Fiona, *mo ghaoil*!' Without having any knowledge of the Gaelic, she knew that he had used an endearment towards the girl.

Lucy watched him sweep Fiona from her feet. He stood laughing down at her, his arm about her waist. Then the carriage swept past them and they were lost to sight. Lucy sank back into her seat, responding mechanically to her mother, whose melancholia had deepened now that their journey was almost at an end.

'I'm sure I don't know how I am to survive the winter here!' Amelia was wailing. 'Mark my words, I shall succumb to the cold of that draughty house. Already I feel so pulled down by fatigue, since I had no sleep whatever on this dreadful journey. And to think of what awaits us at Strathraora House . . . ' She shuddered.

Lucy forbore to point out that her mother had done very little *but* sleep the days away, and murmured something soothing.

All the time she had been hatching her pathetic schemes, she thought with painful disillusionment and loss, Alistair had been comitted to someone else. How her friends in London would laugh if they knew that proud, popular Lucy Sinclair was eating her heart out for a man who belonged to a rustic shepherdess . . .

'You will not feel quite so complacent about this visit, once you discover the bleak discomfort of Strathraora House,' her mother said. 'And to think that, but for your irresponsible behaviour, we would have been snug at Cavendish Square and planning to attend all manner of functions . . . ' Amelia dissolved into tears.

Lucy did what she could to comfort her. From what her mother had told her in the past, she knew that Strathraora House was a palace compared to the humble little cottages in the clachan, and she was aware for the first time of how relative were people's ideas of comfort. To the women in the clachan, life in the big house would no doubt seem like unbelievable luxury.

A thought struck her, and she voiced it aloud. 'Mother, why do you suppose Father has decided to visit Scotland, rather than one of his other country estates? Do you think it is because he wishes to decide whether or not to drive his tenants from the land and bring in sheep?'

'I'm sure I don't know,' Amelia sniffed indifferently, preoccupied with her own misery. 'I should think the people would be glad to leave those wretched hovels.'

It would have been useless to point out to her mother that even a wretched hovel was better than none at all. Lucy changed the subject. 'When Father arrives, it would be better not to tell him that we invited Mr Munro to ride in the carriage.'

'No, I dare say he won't care for it. Indeed, if I had known how disreputable his connection with the Countess of Sutherland was, I would never have agreed to it, although I admit that he conducts himself like a gentleman . . . ' Amelia leant forward and stared broodingly out of the window. 'There it is,' she changed the subject with a sigh. 'Great, gloomy place—just as I remember it. And to think that I am unlikely to leave it alive again . . . ' Tears welled into her eyes once more.

The lodge gates had been opened for them by a man who, Lucy supposed, must be the gardener. The carriage moved slowly along an avenue, and she had her first view of Strathraora House. For once, she thought, her mother had not exaggerated. Large and grey and rambling, with numerous shuttered windows, the house brooded dourly against a background of hills.

The carriage stopped outside a flight of stone steps leading to the massive oak front door. The groom jumped down, and he had just lowered the carriage steps when an elderly woman came hurrying from the house. She bobbed a curtsy.

'Ah, Mrs Bannerman,' Amelia greeted her with a sigh. 'I had my butler send word to you last night that we would be arriving, but doubtless you have been unable to provide much for our comfort.'

'No, ma'am. A pity it is that I had no earlier warning, for I might then have called on folks from the clachan to help me set the house in order.'

The second conveyance drew up outside the house, and Armsworth and Harriet joined them. The butler addressed Amelia in a soothing voice.

'The master gave me instructions to engage servants from among his tenants, madam. I shall see to it immediately. Miss Lucy and yourself should go inside the house now, out of this bitter cold, while I have the luggage attended to.'

'It will be no warmer inside,' Amelia predicted dolefully, 'than it is out here.' But she began to climb the steps to the house, with Lucy holding her arm. They passed through the vast Gothic doorway into a large stone-paved hall.

The walls were hung with faded tapestries and old weapons and oil paintings. The subjects of the paintings were almost unrecognisable through age and long years of neglect. In the large fireplace a log fire smouldered sullenly, giving off scarcely any heat.

'Nothing has changed,' Amelia said dejectedly.

'Come, Lucy, we may as well go up to our bedchambers.'

The staircase, of black oak, was uncarpeted. Most of the rooms were shut up, Lucy noticed, and curiosity moved her to open one or two doors. Ponderous furniture was draped in white covers, adding a ghostlike air to the general gloom. The housekeeper, who had accompanied them up the stairs, explained that she had had time only to clean and air rooms for their own use.

In Lucy's room, she found the furniture to be solid, probably centuries old and most certainly valuable, but also depressing to the spirits. A fire was drawing sluggishly in the grate and she tried to coax it with the bellows, but it resisted all her efforts and continued to give off more smoke than heat. She gave up in resignation and sat down on the bed, blowing on her fingers to warm them.

Her father had meant this visit to be a punishment to her, and a punishment it was indeed proving to be, she thought dismally. Alistair Munro, for whose sake she now admitted that she had been eager to make the long journey, was bound to a beautiful girl called Fiona. If, indeed, he were not already married to her.

A knock on the door broke through her thoughts. It was Harriet. 'I came to see whether you needed assistance in changing out of your travelling clothes, Miss Lucy. I understand a maid is being chosen for you from among the local people, and she will deal with your unpacking later.'

Lucy drew her cloak more firmly about her. 'Thank you, Harriet, but I cannot bear even to contemplate changing my clothes in this bitterly cold room! I shall wait until something has been done about that wretched fire.'

'That is what the mistress decided also.' Harriet nodded, and withdrew.

Lucy moved to the window after she had gone, and returned to her former train of thought. Why had it never occurred to her before that Alistair might be married? She remembered how he had kissed her the night before, and told herself that no married man would have behaved like that. But, then, the kiss had been meant to punish and humilate her. Besides, he did not behave in any way like other men. He made and followed his own rules. And was not that precisely why he had intrigued her in the first place, so that she had allowed him to acquire a dangerous and foolish fascination for herself?

As she stood by the window, she noticed that Armsworth had lost little time in recruiting staff from the clachan, for he was returning to the house with some dozen men and women. In the hope that they might do something about the inadequate fire in the hall, Lucy left her cold bedroom and went downstairs.

Armsworth was with her mother, apologising for the rawness of his new staff. 'I chose them from among the list drawn up by the master, madam, but I fear they are not accustomed to service, and even I cannot hope to train them properly.'

'It is all of a piece,' Amelia responded wanly. 'I never expected to be other than wretchedly uncomfortable here in every way.'

The new servants were, presumably, waiting in the nether quarters to be briefed upon their duties by the butler, and there seemed little likelihood of any of the fires being cosseted into giving off some heat. Judging that it was indeed probably less cold outside in the winter sun than within the walls of the large house which had been unoccupied for so long, Lucy slipped out by the front door.

She strolled aimlessly towards what she assumed must be the stables. As she approached, a man emerged and swept her a bow. He seemed to have newly arrived, and she studied him. He was, she supposed, about thirty years of age, and he looked the type who would run to fat later. He was clearly a man of some standing, for his clothes, although rustic, were well cut and his tweed top-coat looked new. His face could have been said to be handsome, but his grey eyes were a shade too bold for her liking, and she instinctively distrusted his somewhat narrow, thin-lipped mouth. It suggested a cruel streak in his nature, but at the moment it was curving in an overly ingratiating smile.

'Your servant, ma'am!' he said, extending his hand. 'I take it you can be none other than Miss Lucy Sinclair? I am Neil Buchanan, and we are by way of being distant cousins.'

'Oh . . . ' Her father's factor. She took his hand, and frowned as he brought it to his lips. 'It is news to me, Mr Buchanan, that we are related.'

'Indeed we are, Miss Lucy! May I call you that? Your father and I are second cousins. I had word that you would be arriving today, and I hurried to bid you welcome.'

'Thank you. You had better come to the house, Mr Buchanan. I believe preparation is being made for luncheon of some sort.'

'Please call me Neil,' he urged, casting an appreciative sideways glance at her. 'I already feel as if we are old friends as well as cousins.'

Lucy remained silent. She would, she told herself, reserve judgment on Neil Buchanan until she had learnt more about him, and try not to be prejudiced because of his too easy, too early familiarity.

It did not take long for her to make up her mind about him. They had strolled to the house, and when they entered by the front door she realised that, in spite of the rawness of the staff, a great deal of improvement had been made in the comfort of the house. The staircase had been polished and the fire in the hall had been built up to a comforting blaze.

A ruddy-faced young man, looking uncomfortable and ill at ease in the uniform of a footman, approached them uncertainly. 'Will I open the door of the dining-room for you, miss?' he gulped.

Before Lucy could reply, Neil Buchanan burst into a guffaw. There was something cruelly mocking about the laughter, and the awkward young footman's face crimsoned. He seemed to be on the verge of tears as Buchanan spoke to him in the Gaelic, and it was clear that he was taunting the young man about the incongruity of his footman's livery.

Lucy compressed her lips and turned her back on Neil Buchanan. 'What is your name?' she asked the footman gently.

His Adam's apple worked. 'M—Macleod, miss.'

'Very well, Macleod. You may open the door for us, if you please. And, by the by, if it was you who persuaded that previously wretched fire to burn so beautifully, then I congratulate you!'

He flushed again, but with pleasure this time, and darted forward to open the dining-room door for them.

As they entered, Buchanan said with a chuckle, 'I never thought I would see the day when Willy Macleod exchanged his ragged trews for a footman's finery!'

'I dare say he did not either,' Lucy returned shortly.

Amelia was standing by the long refectory table, lifting up the lids of dishes and peering with a kind of gloomy triumph at their contents. 'I knew it,' she said. 'Mutton stewed to a mush, and plain boiled vegetables with not so much as a simple sauce dressing them. And the second course will be no better.'

'Mother!' Lucy interrupted. 'This is Mr Neil Buchanan, Father's factor and, it appears, his second cousin.'

Buchanan made Amelia a deep bow. 'I dare say you will not remember me, ma'am. I was still in short coats, the last time we met.'

Amelia wrinkled her brow. 'I believe I do remember. Your father owned a piece of land some ten miles from here?'

'That is right, ma'am. I inherited it after his death, but the land is poor and yields little, so when I wrote to my Cousin Hugh, offering my services as his factor, he very kindly appointed me to the post. And I flatter myself that I have been carrying out my duties with efficiency and enthusiasm.'

'Yes, well . . . ' Amelia responded vaguely. 'We had better sit down, before this dreadful food becomes completely inedible.'

During the meal, Buchanan paid a good deal of flattering attention to both Amelia and Lucy, and it was obvious that he was trying to ingratiate himself with them. When he realised that Lucy had no intention of calling him by his first name, he began to address her as Miss Sinclair, but that did not make his compliments any less fulsome.

She cut him short in the middle of one by saying, 'By the by, I believe we forgot to tell you, Mr Buchanan, that my father will shortly be joining us here.'

'Is that indeed so!' The factor looked both eager and thoughtful. 'I wrote to him some while ago, suggesting certain changes about the estate, but I have received no reply. It is very good news that I shall be able to discuss matters with him in person.'

Lucy gave him a grim look. She remembered that Alistair had said the factor favoured the bringing in of sheep. 'Don't be too sure, Mr Buchanan, that my father will agree to the changes you have in mind. He has no need of the extra revenue sheep will bring in.'

'It is not only a question of profit, Miss Sinclair, but also one of progress.'

'*Progress!*' She thought of the wretched band of dispossessed people they had passed on the road, and reflected that they would not regard their altered circumstances as 'progress'.

'The people,' Buchanan went on, 'are as miserable a bunch of starvelings as one may wish to meet, Miss Sinclair. It is difficult to see what use they will ever be to themselves or others, and while they occupy the land, with their feckless ways, no progress will ever be made!'

Lucy could only hope devoutly that her father would not share his factor's view of the sub-tenants and cottars, or that even if he did, he would count himself wealthy enough not to seek extra revenue at their expense.

To change the subject, and because she could not resist the perverse desire to bring the conversation around to Alistair, she asked, 'Tell me, Mr Buchanan, exactly what is the role of a tacksman?'

'He is a tenant farmer, Miss Sinclair: the only one who has a written lease. Normally, he contents himself with sub-letting pieces of his land and making sure that rents are collected when due. But in the case of Alistair Munro, he has appointed himself a kind of leader of the people. This will make you laugh—he has had the presumption to teach some of them to read and write!'

'It does not make me laugh at all, Mr Buchanan,' Lucy told him coldly. 'It is to Mr Munro's credit that he has done what he could to educate his people.'

She escaped from the dining-room as soon as she decently could, leaving her mother to recount all her woes to Neil Buchanan. Her own dislike of the factor had been growing steadily, and she did not look forward to his arrival each day to check on estate matters and generally to inflict himself upon them.

When she arrived in her bedroom, she found that a young woman was standing by the window, staring outside. She turned, and for a moment Lucy was startled into speechlessness by her beauty.

Her features were regular, her complexion that of a healthy child. Grey eyes veiled by long lashes surveyed Lucy expressionlessly. It was impossible to see her hair, for it was tucked away inside a starched cap. A uniform had been found for her, and even though it fitted none too well, it was obvious that her figure was shapely. But in spite of the servility suggested by the uniform, there was nothing humble about the girl. Her full lips were proudly set, and she held her head high.

Lucy smiled at her. 'I take it that Armsworth has engaged you to be my personal maid? Tell me your name.'

The girl's voice was clear and far more cultured than Lucy would have expected. 'I am a Macleod.'

Lucy frowned. No doubt the girl's apparent insolence stemmed from ignorance of the ways of serving the gentry. 'When you speak to me,' she said kindly, 'you must address me as *miss*.'

'Very well, miss.'

Had there been something sarcastic in the girl's voice? Lucy could not be sure, and decided not to pursue the matter. She said lightly, 'There is already a Macleod in the house, a young footman. I assume he is related to you, but in any event, to avoid confusion you had better tell me your first name.'

'It is Fiona, miss.'

Lucy stared at her. Fiona—the girl Alistair had hurried to meet upon their arrival. The girl to whom he had called out an endearment, and had swept into his arms.

Lucy wished that she had not recognised so clearly the pang which shot through her, or that she had been capable of self-deception. Instead, she faced the truth squarely. She was in the ignominious position of feeling bitterly jealous and envious of her own maid.

CHAPTER FOUR

FIONA HAD, at least, answered one question for Lucy. She was not married to Alistair, and a swift glance at her ringless fingers revealed the absence of a formal engagement. There was still hope, then. How could she herself ever have been poor-spirited enough to accept that Alistair, the only man who had ever claimed her heart, belonged irrevocably to someone else? She would fight for him, and if humanly possible she would win!

But what malicious fate had caused Fiona Macleod to be chosen as her maid from among all the young women there must be in the clachan? Aloud, Lucy asked, 'Have you any experience at all of this kind of work, Fiona?'

'No, miss.'

'Well, you will be required to look after my clothes and see that everything is kept freshly laundered and in good repair. You will be responsible for ensuring that there is hot water in the pitcher, mornings and evenings, so that I may wash. I don't expect you to be able to dress my hair in elaborate styles, but you will be required to brush it in the mornings and again at night . . .'

Lucy stopped. Fiona's face had been growing steadily redder. Surely she could not be flushing with anger at the list of her duties? She must have had some notion, no matter how vague, of what being a lady's maid entailed. Her eyes were downcast, so that it was impossible to read her expression, and Lucy decided that the flush must have been caused by agitation. Fiona was obviously overawed at the thought of her unfamiliar new duties.

Deciding that some mundane task would help the girl to settle down, Lucy said, 'First of all, Fiona, please do something about that wretched fire.'

'No!' Her head had jerked up, and anger was flashing in her eyes.

Lucy stared at her, taken aback. 'What do you mean —no?'

'I wasn't hired as a skivvy! I don't rake out fires!'

Lucy had never before met with open insolence in a servant, and for a moment she did not know how to react to it. It was all too clear, now, that the girl had been listening to her list of duties with anger. For some reason she resented having been chosen as Lucy's maid.

She had obviously conquered her temper, and was trying to make amends, for she said, 'I'll fetch someone to re-lay the fire, miss . . .'

'No.' It had just dawned on Lucy that she had been handed the opportunity to extricate herself from the undignified situation of having a maid with whom she was in competition over a man.

'I ordered *you* to attend to the fire, Fiona,' she went on, 'and you refused very rudely. I realise that you are quite unused to being in service, but you must know the difference between impertinence and respect. It is clear that you resent having to serve me. You are dismissed.'

For a moment the girl seemed to be on the point of a furious outburst. Then she swallowed visibly. 'I—promised my mother I would serve you, miss.'

'In that case, you have not kept your promise, have you? You refused to obey the very first order I gave you. I am sorry, but it is clear to me that you and I shall not deal together well.'

Fiona said nothing. With her lips firmly compressed

and her head held high, she marched out of the room.

Lucy sat down on the bed, frowning to herself. Perhaps it was true that most Highlanders shared a stiff-necked pride which made them reject a subservient role, and yet there had been something personal in Fiona's insolence. It had seemed as if she resented not just serving someone else, but serving *Lucy* in particular. And yet they were strangers to one another . . .

There was a possible answer. The girl must be just as jealous of her as she herself was of Fiona. Alistair would have told her that he had shared the Sinclair carriage for most of the journey, and some sixth sense must have warned Fiona that something had passed between them. She probably felt herself at a disadvantage. The very fact that she was jealous gave Lucy hope, for it must mean that Fiona was not at all sure of Alistair.

A knock on the door broke into her thoughts. It opened at her invitation, and a woman entered, bobbing a curtsy. 'I am Kirstie Macleod, miss,' she told Lucy quietly. 'The mother of Fiona and Willy.'

Lucy studied the woman, liking what she saw. There was a quiet dignity about the small, neat figure in her shabby petticoat, in the lined face and grey eyes which looked as though they had seen too much sorrow and hardship.

'I have come to attend to your fire, miss,' Kirstie went on. 'And also to speak to you about Fiona.'

'She told you that I had dismissed her, and why?'

'Ay, miss. But I'm thinking perhaps you did not understand the way of it. Fiona knew fine the fire would have to be raked out and re-made. It would be dirty work, and she would not be in a fit state to attend to your fine gowns afterwards.'

Lucy chewed at her lower lip. 'You plead your daughter's case well, Kirstie! But, with respect, I do not believe that was what she meant at all. She was inexcusably rude.'

'She knew that *I* had been given the task of cleaning the bedrooms and attending the fires, miss, and she wished to explain that she would fetch me . . .'

'Then pray do something about the fire, Kirstie, for I am freezing,' Lucy put in, hardening her heart. She did not want the beautiful Fiona back as her maid, reminding her that they were rivals.

Kirstie gave a resigned sigh, and went to kneel by the fire. Lucy watched as she raked over the half-burnt embers and began to arrange small pieces of coal inside the grate at intervals, applying the bellows to encourage them to burn. The woman's hands were misshapen, and it was obvious that they caused her pain.

She paused in her efforts with the bellows, and looked up. 'It was your father's wish that Fiona should be given work at the house, miss. I am thinking it will anger him when he arrives and finds that he has not been obeyed.'

'My father's wish?' Lucy echoed in astonishment.

'Ay, miss.'

'My father has never taken any interest in the hiring of domestic staff! And how can he even have known of Fiona's existence?'

'The way of it, miss,' Kirstie explained quietly, 'is that I served Mr Sinclair and your mother well, many years ago, and when he gave his butler instructions to hire people from the clachan, my name was mentioned. The butler was also told that if I had a family, they were to be offered work.'

Lucy gazed at her in surprise. She would not have expected her father to remember the name of any servant for long, no matter how well she might have served him. 'I shall explain to my father that Fiona was not suitable,' she said at last. 'In truth, her services are not needed. We shall be living quietly here in Strathraora, and my mother's abigail could easily attend to my needs also.'

Kirstie put the bellows down and rose. She looked directly into Lucy's eyes. 'You do not understand how it is with us, miss. Forbye a few sheep, our only wealth is half a dozen head of cattle. A month or so past they strayed on to the new sheep pastures belonging to the Countess of Sutherland. Her factor's men impounded them, and will not let us have them back until fines have been paid. By working here, we had the chance to earn the money for those fines.'

Lucy shifted uneasily. 'You will still have your wage, and that of your son, Willy. And—And I would willingly make up the amount which Fiona would have earned.'

It was a small price to pay, she told herself, not to have the girl underfoot. Instinct told her that she and Fiona could never have a comfortable relationship.

Kirstie inclined her head. 'That is kind of you, miss, but it is not only a matter of earning money. While we work here we are fed good, wholesome meals each day. How can I eat meat and potatoes with an easy heart when I know that Fiona, by her own folly, has to make do with naught but a bowlful of boiled oatmeal at home?'

Lucy looked away, feeling ashamed now. Having Fiona serve her had been distasteful, uncomfortable and embarrassing as far as she was concerned, but for the girl herself it would mean the difference between eating well and merely subsisting. And Kirstie, Lucy guessed, possessed her own share of pride but she was willing to sacrifice it for her daughter, and beg on her behalf. This dignified old woman could not be allowed to debase herself further.

'Tell Fiona to attend for duty in the morning,' Lucy said. 'We'll start afresh.'

'Thank you, miss.' Kirstie's voice was quiet.

When she found herself alone again, Lucy sat deep in thought. Kirstie Macleod had given her a brief glimpse of the reality of the crofters' lives. She had also revealed an unexpected side to Hugh Sinclair. Who would have thought that he would remember Kirstie after all those years, and take the trouble to ensure that she and her family would be offered employment at the house, and thereby earn some extra money? Surely, she considered, in view of this, he would be far more likely to improve the lot of his tenants than to wrest from them the little security they already had. It was beginning to seem that he had a hidden core of softness in him that was perhaps brought out only by people who shared his Highland roots.

In the meantime, it appeared that she and her mother had a duty to do what they could for the people. Lucy thought of the luncheon prepared by Mrs Bannerman and the way in which her mother had disparaged each course. How lavish even one of those courses would seem to a crofter whose family had nothing to eat each day but boiled oatmeal . . .

On a sudden impulse, she left her room and went in search of her mother. Amelia was seated in a chair by the fire in her room, with several shawls draped about her while Harriet brushed her hair. In a silver-backed mirror which she held in her hand, she was critically watching the abigail's handiwork.

'I have just been speaking to a woman called Kirstie Macleod . . . ' Lucy began, but she was interrupted by the sound of breaking glass. The mirror had slipped from her mother's hand and had shattered on the floor.

'Harriet, gather up the pieces,' Amelia ordered, her voice agitated. 'The mirror was part of a matching set. If you had not pulled my hair, I wouldn't have been startled into dropping it!'

'I am sorry, madam.'

Lucy waited until the fuss of the broken mirror had died down, and Harriet was once more brushing her mother's hair, before she repeated what she had said.

'Do you remember Kirstie Macleod, Mother?'

'Such outlandish names these people have,' Amelia shrugged.

'She says she served you and Father so well years ago that he made a point of telling Armsworth to offer herself and her family employment.'

'Have done, Harriet!' Amelia waved the abigail pettishly away. 'Instead of soothing it, you have made my headache worse with your pulling and tugging. Just arrange my hair in a simple braid. After all, who is there here to see me but the servants?'

'Speaking of servants,' Lucy persisted, 'do you remember Kirstie Macleod?'

Amelia closed her eyes. 'I have tried my best to forget everything about this awful place. And it was a long time ago, during the first years of my marriage to your father, when your grandfather insisted that we live here. He was absurdly sentimental about his Scottish origins.'

Lucy frowned. Was her mother being deliberately evasive about Kirstie? Surely not. It was more likely that she had forgotten the woman and was bored by the subject.

'Do you remember Kirstie Macleod?' Lucy repeated.

Her mother made a petulant gesture. 'Who is this wretched woman, and what has she been saying to you of such importance that you continue to pester me about her?'

'She is one of the sub-tenants, and presumably a widow, since she made no mention of a husband. Who she is is not important. But I gathered from her that there is a great deal of hardship in Bencraig, and I felt we ought to do something for the people.'

'It is the duty of that charming young man, Neil Buchanan, to attend to matters of that kind.'

How like her mother, Lucy thought sourly, to have been taken in by the factor's ingratiating manner. Aloud, she said, 'I cannot imagine him caring whether the people starved or not, provided they paid their rent when due. What I have in mind, Mother, is offering a modicum of food to those who are in real need.'

'Oh, do as you please, Lucy,' Amelia said fretfully. 'But, I warn you, *everyone* is likely to claim grinding poverty when they smell the offer of charity.'

'No, they won't,' she corrected, excitement quickening inside her. 'I mean to ask Mr Alistair Munro who the families are who need help.'

She did not like to examine her own motives too closely, for she could not deny that, right from the moment she had first conceived the notion of helping the crofters, Alistair's part in the scheme had leapt to her mind. In any event, she asked herself defiantly, what did it matter which was her main desire—helping the crofters, or having a legitimate excuse for calling on Alistair? In the end, they would benefit.

She remained for a while in her mother's room, and listened patiently while Amelia bemoaned the lack of amusement at Strathraora House. As soon as she judged that she had done her duty, Lucy excused herself and slipped from the house, making for the stables.

From one of the grooms she learnt that there was no suitable horse for her to ride. She looked at him in dismay. 'If you are thinking that I cannot cope with anything but a plodding old hack, let me assure you I am a very experienced horsewoman! There must be a mount I could use.'

The man shook his head. 'There's no' but horses for the pulling of a plough or a carriage, miss.'

She cast a frowning glance about her. The short winter

day was fast drawing to a close, with mist rising from the glens to hang in frozen vapour upon the air. By the time a carriage had been prepared, it would be too late to set out in search of Alistair's home. She thanked the groom, and returned to the house. In her room, the fire was now burning cheerfully and Harriet was waiting to help her to change for dinner.

With distaste, Lucy discovered that Neil Buchanan had been invited to share their meal. 'How splendid you are looking, Miss Sinclair!' he exclaimed, his gaze boldly examining her. 'Forgive me if I stare, but our glens are not accustomed to such beauty!'

She bit off an irritated retort. There was nothing subtle about the man—he was making it as plain as possible that he aspired to the hand of Hugh Sinclair's daughter.

She said lightly, 'The glens are well accustomed to feminine beauty, judging by the looks of my maid, Fiona Macleod.'

Something in the factor's expression told her that he had, at some time, turned his attention to Fiona. But he merely said, 'She is a wild one, that girl, for all her mother believes she has been tamed.'

Lucy wanted to continue discussing Fiona, in the hope of discovering the precise nature of her relationship with Alistair. But Amelia protested in a plaintive voice, 'Do we have to talk about the servants throughout dinner? Mr Buchanan, pray tell me whether there is any possibility whatever of some kind of social diversion in this bleak place.'

'Indeed, I believe something could be arranged, ma'am.' He went on to explain that the wealthier, more important landowners were wintering in London, but that a few families of the lesser gentry were forced to remain in Scotland throughout the year, since they possessed no London homes. Curiosity alone would persuade them to accept any invitation from Strathraora House.

'They will be dreadfully provincial and dull,' Amelia sighed, 'but better than nothing. We shall have to arrange an informal supper and dance.'

Neil Buchanan nodded, and turned to Lucy. 'The kind of function your mother has in mind, Miss Sinclair, would be described hereabouts as a *ceilidh*.'

'Would it?' She looked at him, wondering whether he might be of practical use to her. 'I wish to acquire a horse for my own use, Mr Buchanan. Do you know where a suitable one might be purchased?'

'There are regular horse-sales held in the market town each week. I would gladly undertake to choose a mount on your behalf.'

'Thank you,' she said shortly, irritated by his patronising manner. 'I am a very good judge of horseflesh, and would not dream of having anyone else choose a mount for me.'

'In that case, it would give me pleasure to escort you to town, Miss Sinclair,' he returned, apparently unaware of her snub.

She made an evasive response, and took the first opportunity to escape. She knew that Neil Buchanan was watching her departure with frustration, and she took pleasure in the knowledge that he would be forced to retire to the drawing-room with her mother and listen to an endless list of complaints about the shortcomings of life in Sutherland.

The next morning brought the kind of weather to the glens which lowered even Lucy's spirits and made her inclined to share her mother's gloomy opinion of Scotland. A wild, icy rain lashed the landscape, promising to savage it all day and making it impossible to set foot outside without becoming drenched to the skin.

Soon after Lucy awoke, Fiona entered the room,

bearing hot water in a copper jug. The girl's beautiful face was carefully blank, and she bobbed a small curtsy after she had set the jug down.

'Good morning, Fiona,' Lucy said, deliberately ignoring what had previously passed between them. 'Would you be so good as to hand me my robe?'

Fiona said colourlessly, 'Very good, miss.'

She helped Lucy to dress, afterwards, and arranged her hair in a simple but effective style, gathering it at the top of her head and securing the locks with a ribbon. Her manner was punctiliously correct and neutral as she worked.

It was only later, when she was tidying the room, that her careful mask slipped slightly. Lucy saw her pick up the tablet of perfumed soap and hold it to her nose. In her expression was something almost like hunger, mixed with frustration.

She yearns for luxuries and pretty things, Lucy thought as she went downstairs to breakfast. And she likes me no better than she did before, even though she is careful to hide her feelings. *Why* does she dislike me? Surely it cannot simply be because Alistair travelled in our carriage?

The thought of Alistair caused her heart to turn over painfully. There seemed no prospect of seeing him, because the foul weather showed no sign of changing. In the days that followed, Lucy was unable to do anything about consulting him in the matter of her scheme to help the crofters. And whatever his duties as tacksman were, they did not bring him to Strathraora House.

At last, after three days, the morning dawned fine and clear, the air crisp with cold. When she had breakfasted, Lucy returned to her room, where she found Fiona engaged in some mending. It was not so much that she had been well schooled in her duties by her mother, Lucy felt, watching her. The girl derived a sensual pleasure from examining and handling fine fabrics.

'Fiona,' Lucy said, 'please leave what you are doing, and go and ask your brother to take a message to the stables. I want one of the grooms to bring a pony and trap to the house. Tell Willy that I shall not be requiring a driver.'

'Very well, miss,' she replied tonelessly, laying the sewing aside.

When she returned to the room, Lucy said, 'I shall require my sable cloak, please.'

The maid kept her eyes downcast as she fetched the cloak and helped Lucy on with it. Her voice seemed to be carefully controlled when she spoke. 'You will be needing me to go with you, miss.'

Did the girl simply long for an outing, Lucy wondered, any kind of diversion, or had she guessed that a visit to Alistair was proposed? Had some possessive, feminine sixth sense warned her? Taking her maid with her, Lucy conceded, would be the proper thing to do in normal circumstances. But these were not normal circumstances; one did not take as a chaperon the very girl one hoped to oust from the affections of a man. After all, it was not as if there was anything questionable about her visit. She wished to see Alistair for a valid and practical reason.

'No, Fiona,' she said aloud. 'I shall not need you. You may continue with your mending.'

Whatever reason the girl had had for wanting to be taken along, she could not hide her reaction at being refused. In the mirror, Lucy saw her head jerk up, and for an instant hostility and resentment smouldered in her eyes. Then it was gone, and she said in a neutral voice, 'As you wish, miss.'

Lucy went downstairs, and Willy Macleod sprang forward to open the door for her. He stammered the information that the pony and trap were awaiting her, eager only to serve her in any way he could.

'Thank you, Willy.' Lucy could not help contrasting his attitude towards her with that of his sister.

A short while later she was driving away from Strathraora House. The hills seemed to huddle protectively about her as the pony trap moved along the valley. She skirted the clachan with its humble dwellings, asking directions of her father's sub-tenants. They removed their hats and humbly touched their foreheads as they told her how to reach the house where the tacksman lived.

Lucy turned into a lane which took her past yet another small township, and after a while she passed through a gateway and along a drive up to a stone-built farmhouse. Cows grazed along the grassy slope of a hill, and inside the dry-stone walls of a paddock a horse was spiritedly kicking up its heels. A parcel of arable land lay fallow, waiting for spring, and from the chimney of the farmhouse smoke curled into the air.

There was no one in the outbuildings, and Lucy turned to the house. Her knock was not answered, but the door was not quite closed, for it moved on its hinges at her touch. She pushed it open. She entered a living-room, from one corner of which a flight of stairs ascended towards the top of the house. Beyond the living-room a door stood ajar, showing her what appeared to be a kitchen, and she crossed towards it, her footsteps silenced by a faded hooked rug on the floor.

Now she realised why her knock had gone unanswered. Anyone visiting the house would automatically come to the kitchen door, for this was clearly the hub of the dwelling. Alistair was seated by a table in the far corner, and was so engrossed in whatever he was doing that he remained unaware of her presence.

Her mouth was dry, her heart racing, and all she

could think of was the moment when he had kissed her in the posting-house. Then she realised what it was that so absorbed him.

Frowning in concentration, he was mending a rent in his plaid, and she heard him mutter what sounded like a curse in the Gaelic as the needle obviously stabbed his finger. Now, mixed with her physical awareness of him, was a shattering wave of tenderness for his poverty, and for the circumstances which forced him to mend his own clothes. She had to restrain herself from going over and taking the work from his hands.

He sensed her presence and looked up. If he experienced any pleasure at the sight of her, his scowl gave no indication of it. 'What are you doing here?' he demanded.

'*You* forced your way into *my* home on two occasions,' she retorted, trying to make her voice crisp. 'However, I did knock, but you did not hear me.' She moved towards him, looking at the plaid which he had thrown on the table, and stifled a compassionate smile at sight of the clumsy stitches with which he had drawn the edges of the tear together. 'Do you live here alone? Is there no one who could do your mending for you?'

'I live alone,' he answered shortly. 'As for my mending—Fiona would do that, were she not occupied as your maid.'

Lucy's nails bit into the palms of her hand with the effort to disguise the devastating jealousy which shook her. *That I should have come to this*, she thought with painful disbelief. *That I should feel like this because my maid has the right to darn a man's threadbare clothes, and not I . . .*

Aloud, she tried to speak lightly, as if she were displaying no more than a casual interest. 'Are you betrothed to Fiona, or is there merely an understanding between you?'

'I am promised to her.'

'I—see. I take it that quaint term means you are betrothed?'

He looked steadily at her. '*You* were betrothed to yon scented dandy in London, and you broke it off at a whim. *I* am promised to Fiona, and a promise cannot be broken. There is a difference, you see.'

How implacable he sounded—how firmly immovable in his resolve. 'Do you—love Fiona?' Lucy asked with difficulty.

His lashes veiled his blue eyes. 'I am promised to her,' he repeated. 'That speaks for itself.'

Lucy turned her head and pretended to study the plates on the shelves of the dresser so that he would not see the desolation in her eyes. So much for her resolve to fight for him, and for her conviction that Lucy Sinclair would somehow always be able to get what she wanted in the end!

'I called to see you,' she changed the subject when she could trust herself to speak, 'because I wish to plan some kind of scheme for the provision of food to the most needy in Bencraig . . .

'The people, Miss Sinclair,' he interrupted harshly, 'would sooner be certain of having oatmeal every day than be offered meat for today and the open road and starvation tomorrow!'

'Why do you cling to your suspicions that my father means to drive the people from the land? He may have many faults, but he has always been a generous man. Were it not for his long absence from his Scottish estate, I am sure the people's lot would have been improved by now. In the meantime, I wish to do something for them.'

'So you have a fancy to play the Lady Bountiful. Why call on me, Miss Sinclair? You need neither my permission nor my help.'

She chewed at her lower lip. 'I do, however, need you to tell me who are in the most need.'

'Is that the way of it?' His voice was coolly mocking now. 'Indeed, they are all in like need. So if it pleases you to call on them with charitable gifts, you will not require a guide.'

This man, she thought with painful humiliation, could read her like a book. He knew precisely what she was about, and what had inspired her wish to help his people. She wanted his approval, his involvement and —most of all—an excuse to seek his company. And he was making it clear that he was not prepared to give her any of it.

She drew herself up to her full height. She was Lucy Sinclair, and this penniless Highlander might have the power to break her heart, but he would not be allowed to grind her pride into the dust.

'I am not asking for your help, Mr Munro—I am commanding it! You will accompany me to the market town next week, and buy meal for distribution among the people. You have a clearer knowledge of how much is required by each household and how much should be bought. I also need you to help me to buy a horse for my own use and bring it back, so be ready to go with me . . .'

'I will not, then,' he interrupted, his voice dangerously calm. 'Find another lackey, Miss Sinclair.'

Fury seized her. 'You are a tenant, Munro, and I am the laird's daughter! You will do as I ask!'

He gave her a long, disconcerting stare. 'I have told you before, Miss Sinclair, that I'll not play your game.'

'This is no game!'

'Oh ay,' he acknowledged, rubbing his chin reflectively and looking into her eyes. 'I'm thinking it has ceased to be a game. But 'tis a dangerous business for all that, playing with fire.'

Their glances locked, and a strange, electrifying moment passed between them, a moment of unspoken but acknowledged truths. 'I'll not deny,' he went on softly, 'that I've been sore tempted more times than I care to recall. Ay, and once took the first foolish step towards yielding.'

Her heart jerked, and she moved closer to him. '*Yielding* . . . Was that what you did in the inn, the other evening?'

'Ay. And the danger, Lucy Sinclair,' he said in a low voice, 'is to what it might lead. So no more yielding.'

She spoke unevenly. 'Are you—afraid of discovering—that you do not love Fiona after all?'

He folded his arms across his chest as if to restrain himself from touching her. 'I have told you,' he said brusquely, 'I am promised to Fiona. Nothing can alter that. So it is not for the burning of my own fingers I care—or yours, for that matter. I care about keeping my word to wed Fiona.'

Lucky, lucky Fiona, Lucy thought desolately. *In worldly terms she might have nothing, but I would change places with her if I could.*

She tried to salvage some dignity and pride by saying sharply, 'I don't know how we strayed into this ridiculous exchange of riddles about burnt fingers. I called on you to seek your help in buying meal for the crofters, and . . .'

'We both know fine why you came,' he interrupted bluntly, robbing her of even a semblance of protective pretence. 'You are the laird's daughter, as you reminded me a few moments ago. So behave like the laird's daughter, and stop offering me temptation.'

CHAPTER FIVE

As Lucy drove herself back to Strathraora House in the pony and trap, she reflected with bleak amusement that Victor Davenant and his mother would have derived the greatest satisfaction from her present situation. She, who had thrown over with scarcely a qualm one of the most eligible bachelors in London Society, had tried to steal from her own maid a threadbare tenant, and she had failed. How they would laugh if they knew!

Anger rose inside her, creating an anodyne which served to dilute her pain. Because of Alistair she had broken her engagement to Victor; because of Alistair she had willingly allowed herself to be sent into exile in Scotland. She was now to be forced to spend the rest of the winter here, eating her heart out for a man who clung stubbornly to his obligation towards Fiona?

Lucy frowned to herself. *Obligation.* That was precisely the impression which Alistair had given regarding his relationship with Fiona. He had refused to say in so many words that he loved the girl; he had talked of being promised to her, as if he had a duty and a responsibility towards her.

Lucy thought back to the day when he had left their carriage and hurried across the glen to greet Fiona. He had swept her from her feet, but he had not kissed or even embraced her as a lover would have done. His manner had been more indulgent and affectionate than passionate. And surely Fiona was beautiful enough to inspire passion in any man?

It was beginning to seem that Alistair knew he had made a mistake in betrothing himself to the girl. He no longer loved her, but because he had entered into a commitment to marry her, he would honour it, come what might.

As it was still early, and luncheon would not be for some time, Lucy drove straight to the stables, deciding to walk the rest of the way to the house. She bit off an irritated sound when she recognised the bay stallion being rubbed down by one of the grooms. It belonged to Neil Buchanan.

She had no desire for his company this morning, and decided to enter the house unobtrusively by the back way. As she was walking through the kitchen garden and was about to skirt a sheltering wall against which fruit trees had been trained to grow, she heard Fiona's voice coming derisively from the other side.

'*You?* She fancies herself far too high and mighty for the likes of you!'

Lucy froze as instinct warned her that she herself was the subject under discussion. 'Don't be too sure.' It was Buchanan's voice that answered Fiona. 'I've pumped the butler, and it seems clear to me that there was some kind of scandal in London, and that she was sent to Scotland in disgrace. With nothing much to do here, and no one else to turn to for companionship . . .'

Lucy heard Fiona laugh bitterly. '*Her* you'd marry, of course!'

'Of course. But don't brood, my lovely. I'd see to it that you gained by the marriage, too.'

Their voices faded as they moved away. Lucy leant against the wall, frowning into space. It had come as no surprise that Neil Buchanan harboured ambitions to marry her. What had been a revelation were the many intangibles raised by that overheard snippet of conversation. If Fiona believed that Lucy would consider herself too good for the factor, then it followed that she would never even have thought of her mistress in connection with Alistair. And that, in turn, meant that her hostility stemmed from something quite different.

There was also, Lucy thought, the way in which Fiona and Buchanan had spoken together. As if they were, somehow, involved with one another. And had there not been more than a suggestion that Fiona would be jealous and resentful if Lucy did marry the factor?

Changing her mind about slipping unseen into the house, Lucy altered course and approached the front door. It was opened to her by Willy Macleod, who swallowed nervously and said,

'Oh, miss, the factor has just this moment called, and I have put himself in the drawing-room. 'Twas the mistress he wished to see, but herself not being down yet, I was not sure . . .'

'You did right, Willy. I shall go and keep him company until my mother comes down.'

If there is anything between Fiona and Buchanan, she was thinking as she moved towards the drawing-room, and I can bring it to light, Alistair would no longer feel that he is committed to marrying her. He would be free.

The factor jumped to his feet as she entered the room. She tried to keep her expression neutral and not to give any hint that she had overheard a part of his conversation with Fiona.

'Good morning, Mr Buchanan. I understand that you have called to see my mother.'

He bowed over her hand. 'Yes indeed, Miss Sinclair. I have brought with me a list of people to be invited to that *ceilidh* she wishes me to arrange.'

Lucy sat down. 'Mother will welcome the diversion of planning an entertainment.'

'And so, I venture to suggest, would you. There is not a great deal to do in Scotland during the winter.'

She hid a grim smile. He was counting, was he, on boredom driving her into his arms! Aloud, she said, 'I am more easily able to amuse myself than my mother is. I am interested in the people here, for instance. Take Fiona Macleod. She may be desperately poor, and yet she is not in the least servile. What did you mean, by the way, when you called her a wild one the other day?'

'Well . . . ' he hedged. 'Merely that she is too beautiful for her own good.'

'Because she is poor?'

'Because she resents being poor, and she feels her beauty entitles her to something better than she has.'

'You seem to know a good deal about her innermost thoughts,' Lucy murmured.

She saw him flush. 'It is a matter of intelligent deduction, Miss Sinclair. A wealthy acquaintance of mine told me that when Fiona was barely fifteen, she tried to seduce him into running away with her to Edinburgh.'

With an effort, Lucy hid her contempt. Whatever there was between him and Fiona, they were close enough for him to have confided in the girl. And yet he did not scruple to blacken her character.

'That sounds like malicious tittle-tattle to me, Mr Buchanan,' Lucy said. 'And even if it were true, Fiona was no more than a child at the time. Most of us do foolish, reckless things when we are young.'

'Your charitable nature does you credit, Miss Sinclair,' he responded ambiguously.

Her mother entered the room at that moment, and Lucy left them together. In her room, there was no sign of Fiona, but Kirstie was engaged in rubbing beeswax into the surface of the dressing-table. Lucy sat down and watched her at work.

Kirstie looked uncertainly at her. 'Will I go and call Fiona to put away your stole and gloves, miss?'

'It doesn't matter. Where is Fiona?'

'With the weather improving, miss, she thought she would launder your clothes.'

'She certainly cares most devotedly for my clothes,' Lucy observed.

'I—hope she has been giving satisfaction, miss?' Kirstie inquired with a note of anxiety in her voice.

Lucy nodded. 'It must be very difficult, at times,' she probed, 'to have a daughter as beautiful as Fiona. I gather, from something the factor said, that you've had trouble in that direction, Kirstie.'

'It ill behoves him to blabber about it!' the old woman returned fiercely. 'Trying to turn my poor girl's head with the offer of work as his housekeeper! Fine I knew what he really had in mind, for all she believed it would end in marriage!'

Lucy sat in thoughtful silence. From what she had overheard, Fiona had known full well that Buchanan would not offer her marriage. She had, indeed, sounded resentful about it. So she must have been fully aware that the factor wanted her as his mistress, and from the way in which Kirstie had spoken it seemed that Fiona would have accepted his offer if her mother had not put her foot down. Did Alistair know about the incident, Lucy wondered.

Kirstie went on, almost as if she knew what was in her mind, 'But now my girl is safe, for Alistair is promised to her, and she will always mind him.'

There was that word again—*promised*.

Lucy was still musing about it when Fiona herself entered the room, and Kirstie spoke to her in the Gaelic. The older woman's voice held a warmth and tenderness which gave Lucy a wistful feeling. For all her own advantages, no one had ever cared about her as much as Kirstie obviously cared about her daughter.

Fiona answered her mother in the same tongue, and then switched to English, addressing Lucy. 'Will I help you out of your travelling dress, miss?'

'Thank you, Fiona.'

Kirstie picked up her cleaning materials and left the room with her painful, awkward gait. 'I like your mother,' Lucy said impulsively.

'Do you, miss?' Fiona's voice was expressionless. 'We cannot choose our mothers, can we? Nor yet their fortunes either.'

It was a curious response, and a somewhat chilling one, for it seemed to suggest that if Fiona had been given a choice she would have exchanged Kirstie's devotion and poverty for Lucy's own wealthy, shallow mother.

Then it was time to do down to luncheon. As Lucy had feared, her mother had invited Neil Buchanan to share the meal with them. But distasteful though his presence was, at least it had succeeded in diverting Amelia, who had lost her melancholia and appeared quite animated as the two of them discussed arrangements for the planned *ceilidh*. Her mother, Lucy thought, was like a child whose fit of the sullens had temporarily been dispersed by the novelty of a new toy.

'Goodness knows how the servants will cope with such a large number of guests,' she was saying. 'You don't think we are being a trifle ambitious, Mr Buchanan, inviting so many people?'

'They are almost all of them related to one another in some way, ma'am, and every one of them will be expecting to be invited. As you may remember from your last stay here, the Scottish clan spirit is very strong, and it would be regarded as an unforgivable slight if any of their family connections were left out.'

'Oh, those Scottish tribal ways! I had quite forgotten how they can hate one another like poison, but let an outsider offer one of them an insult and they are as united against him as a pack of wolves! Very well, then, let them all come. The servants will just have to cope.'

'May I suggest, ma'am,' Buchanan said, 'that you press all the younger people from the clachan into service on Saturday evening? I shall arrange it for you, if you like.'

'Very well, Mr Buchanan. Now let me see—what about musicians?'

'There is no shortage of fiddlers and pipers hereabouts, ma'am.'

'Fiddlers and pipers!' Amelia sighed deprecatingly, and then stiffened as she glanced again at the list of guests. 'You have included the name of Alistair Munro!'

Lucy's heart gave a jerk of excitement. She heard Buchanan explain, 'He has important family connections . . .'

'I know,' Amelia interrupted tartly. 'An ancestor of his married into the Countess of Sutherland's family. It is not only a distant connection but also a thoroughly disreputable one, and . . .'

'With respect, ma'am, Munro's position as tacksman alone makes it necessary for you to invite him. But he is also related to many of the other guests, and they would expect to see him here.'

Amelia made a gesture of irritation. 'Scotland is a barbaric place, with barbaric customs! Very well. I shall just have to resign myself to the thought of entertaining tenants as well as provincial farmers.'

For the first time Lucy was experiencing some interest in the forthcoming *ceilidh*, and she made a mental inventory of her wardrobe, glad now that she had taken the precaution of bringing several gowns suitable for a festive occasion.

But the following afternoon Alistair called at Strathraora House, and Lucy was present during his interview with her mother. He placed his gilt-edged invitation card on a table, and said, 'I thank you for this, ma'am, but I'll not be coming.'

Sick disappointment coursed through Lucy. She was aware that her mother was struggling between relief and indignation at having her invitation turned down by a mere tenant. 'And why, pray, won't you be coming, Mr Munro?' she demanded.

'You did not invite Fiona, ma'am.'

'Certainly not! She is a servant!'

'Oh ay, ma'am.' His voice was expressionless.

'Well, so she is,' Amelia floundered. 'And she will be needed to wait upon my guests, besides.'

'I'll not put her in the position of having to wait upon *me*,' Alistair said uncompromisingly.

He nodded and turned away, and Lucy stared after him. What a fool she had been! Of course Alistair would not attend a function to which Fiona was not considered good enough to be invited.

All her pleasure in the forthcoming *ceilidh* was gone, and she felt nothing but irritation in the days that followed, for everyone in the house seemed to be occupied in some way in preparing for it. Servants swept and polished and cleaned silver, while in the kitchens Mrs Bannerman, with several helpers from the clachan, embarked on an orgy of baking and roasting.

Neil Buchanan was an almost daily visitor, flinging himself enthusiastically into the arrangements for the festivity. 'I cannot help feeling,' he commented when he joined them for luncheon one day, 'that it is a pity my Cousin Hugh has chosen to remain austerely aloof from the occasion.'

'What do you mean?' Amelia demanded with a frown. 'How can he be keeping aloof when he is not here?'

'Oh, did I not tell you? I was sure I had! Forgive me, ma'am. The truth of the matter is that Cousin Hugh has arrived and is staying at my house.'

'At *your* house? Why has he not come on here?'

'He called on me on his way to Strathraora in order to discuss estate matters, ma'am. But when I mentioned the *ceilidh* to him, he decided to defer his homecoming until—as he put it—all the fuss was over.'

'How very disobliging of him!' Amelia lamented.

It was no more than Lucy would have expected of her father. He did not feel sufficiently warmly towards her mother and herself to have hurried to join them, and the last thing he would wish to find himself caught up in was frenzied preparation for a party.

Lucy excused herself and escaped from the house by going for a walk in the gardens. She wished her father had not chosen to stay with Buchanan, for the factor would, without a doubt, have been urging him to clear the people from the land and bring in sheep. But then, she told herself, her father was not a man who would allow himself to be persuaded by others. He made up his own mind.

When she returned to the house Buchanan had left, and her mother was waiting for her, unusually pink in the face. 'By the by, Lucy,' she said with a pretence at casualness, 'I have decided to invite Fiona to the *ceilidh* after all.'

'What?'

'Mr Buchanan feels it would cast a cloud over the evening if Alistair Munro does not attend, and since he will come only if the wretched girl is also invited . . . And, besides, matters are quite different here, you know. One is expected to treat the oddest people as if they were on an equal footing. And as Mr Buchanan points out, it is not as if any of the other invited guests will be out of the top drawer. The girl is well spoken, and seems to have been nicely brought up.'

Lucy was thinking that her mother was trying to convince herself of the rightness of her action, rather than explain it. Amelia went on, 'I dare say the girl will not have something suitable to wear, so it would be a kindness on your part if you were to lend her one of your gowns.'

Neil Buchanan, Lucy said to herself with a thoughtful frown, must have been extremely persuasive to have brought about her mother's change of heart. Why did he consider it so important that Alistair should attend the *ceilidh*? Or—could it be that he had, from the outset, wanted *Fiona* to be invited? He would have guessed that Alistair would refuse to go if she were excluded. There was certainly something more here than met the eye, but she decided not to examine it too closely. It was sufficient that Alistair would be coming to the *ceilidh* after all, even though it would be on Fiona's arm.

'Will you lend her a gown?' Amelia was asking.

A wry smile twisted Lucy's mouth. It was, indeed, an ironical situation. 'Yes, Mother, I'll lend her something suitable. Does she know that she is to attend the function?'

Amelia nodded. 'She is in your bedroom, waiting for you.'

It was obvious that Fiona regarded her invitation to the *ceilidh* as a personal triumph, for although she cast her eyes down when Lucy entered the room, a smug little smile continued to play about her mouth.

Lucy said expressionlessly, 'Let us look through my wardrobe, and choose a gown for you to wear tomorrow night. Fortunately, there does not appear to be much difference between us in size.'

Fiona's lovely face took on a look of excitement as the two of them examined the row of gowns hanging in the cupboard. 'This apricot silk is very bonnie . . .'

'It would not suit you, Fiona. The colour would make your skin appear sallow. This simple white gown would be precisely right.'

Fiona made no comment, but it was clear that she was disappointed and that she did not think much of a plain gown of white silk, with its high waist and long sleeves, its only adornment a single narrow flounce round the hem.

But Lucy knew that, with her dark hair properly dressed, the gown would set the girl's fresh beauty off to perfection, whereas a more sophisticated one would have tended to detract from it. Once again, the irony of the situation struck her. Here she was, conscientiously trying to show off her rival in the best possible light!

'The gown needs letting out slightly at the waist,' Lucy said critically when Fiona had tried it on. 'You may attend to it now.'

'Yes, miss. Thank you.'

'I'll ask my mother's abigail to dress your hair tomorrow night. She can help me with my toilette first, and then attend to yours while I go down to join my mother in receiving the guests.'

Fiona nodded, almost giving the impression that she was hugging herself with suppressed excitement.

The following evening Lucy stood beside her mother as they greeted their guests. Intermittent snow-flurries had deterred no one, and every guest who had been invited arrived at Strathraora House. Lucy studied them, thinking how very different they were from the kind of people her mother would normally expect to entertain.

With the exodus to London of all the great land-owners, these yeoman farmers clearly considered themselves to be the new gentry, and they seemed determined not to be patronised by the Sinclairs. They might not be rich enough to become absentee landlords, but the fact that they had money was proclaimed by the personal appearance of the women. Their gowns, a season or two out of date in style, were nevertheless of the richest fabrics, and each of them seemed to be wearing every piece of jewellery she possessed.

But even though Lucy studied them as she smiled and murmured a welcome, there was only one guest in whom she had any real interest. And he, she knew, would be waiting until Fiona was ready to be escorted into the hall. Harriet was attending to the girl's toilette, and Lucy had given her detailed instructions on how Fiona's hair was to be dressed. Simplicity was to be the keyword.

Lucy's own copper hair had been twisted into a knot on top of her head, from where it fell on either side of her face in apparently careless ringlets. She wore a gown of sage-green satin trimmed with a lighter shade of velvet, and her only jewellery was a pair of emerald earrings.

Her heart gave a painful lurch as she saw Alistair arrive with Fiona on his arm. He was dressed in his best kilt, and he wore his plaid and his shirt with its frayed ruffles as proudly as though there were no difference between it and the silk stockings, the watered silk waistcoats and swallow-tailed coats of the other male guests.

Then Lucy caught her breath as she studied Fiona. Harriet had worked wonders, and the girl looked quite stunning in the unadorned white gown, her black hair pulled away from her face and secured with a white ribbon. In that company of predominantly over-dressed, over-bejewelled women, she stood out like a perfect white rosebud among overblown blooms.

Lucy welcomed her, and then held out her hand to

Alistair. He bowed over it, and raised his head, gazing into her eyes. 'I do not know what you have sought to achieve by inviting us,' he murmured, 'but . . .'

'Neil Buchanan insisted that your presence here tonight was essential.'

'Is that indeed so . . . ' Looking thoughtful, he took Fiona'a arm and led her into the salon where the musicians were striking up a tune.

As the evening wore on, Lucy found Fiona's behaviour more and more puzzling, especially in view of her earlier excitement. At first the girl had attracted admiring glances from every male in the room, but as she settled herself into the background they lost interest in her. Beautiful she might be, but tonight she lacked animation and confidence in herself. Perhaps she was overawed by her surroundings . . .

Lucy declined to take part in the reel which had just started, and made her way to where Fiona was sitting against one wall, looking sullen and ill at ease. Alistair stood beside her with his arms folded, making no attempt to disguise his boredom. If most of the other guests were connections of his, he seemed to take no pleasure in their company.

'Will you not join the dancing?' Lucy asked them.

Alistair shrugged. 'Fiona does not care to do so.'

Lucy bit her lip. 'I see . . . Perhaps she would care for a glass of wine, however, I know I would. Mr Munro, if you would be so kind?'

He nodded, and moved away. When he was out of earshot, Lucy said, 'Why do you not dance, Fiona? You are looking very beautiful, you know.'

'Am I, miss?' The girl's voice was resentful and bitter.

'I assure you of it! What is the matter? Are you not pleased with the way you look?'

'Since you ask, miss—I look what I am, someone in the plainest of borrowed gowns, and with not so much as a brooch to her name. I had thought there might be some silk roses to wear in my hair at the very least. As it is, everyone is laughing at me. I will not make a further show of myself by dancing.'

What a fool I was, Lucy berated herself. I should have allowed her to wear the apricot-coloured gown, and told Harriet to arrange her hair in fussy curls. What would it have mattered if it had made her look too bold and a little sallow? *She* would have believed herself to be beautiful, and she would have sparkled with confidence. I do not like the girl, and I bitterly begrudge her Alistair, but tonight she is our guest, and I can take no pleasure in any guest feeling out of her depth.

Alistair returned with two glasses of wine, and Lucy said lightly, 'See if you can persuade Fiona to dance, Mr Munro.' She was unable to stop herself from adding, 'But even if you cannot, perhaps *you* will take the floor a little later?'

He gave her a look which she had no difficulty in recognising. It was the look he had worn when he had said to her, '*I know fine what you are about, Lucy Sinclair*.'

Her colour high, she moved away. The fiddles were being tuned up again for another dance, and she felt a hand on her elbow. Neil Buchanan said, 'I have requested the musicians to start up a waltz, Miss Sinclair. Would you do me the honour of dancing with me?'

'Why not?' She gave him a brittle smile, set her wine glass down, and moved into his arms.

After a moment it became clear that they were the only ones to have taken to the floor. No doubt, Lucy thought, the steps of the waltz were unfamiliar to people more used to dancing reels. Knowing that every eye was fixed upon them, a wild recklessness took hold of her. She moved closer to Neil Buchanan, smiling up at him, and allowed his lips to brush her cheek.

She glanced under her lashes at Alistair. His mouth was grimly set, his eyes smouldering as he studied them from the other side of the room.

That's right, she thought with bitter pain. Suffer, as you make me suffer. Stay there by the side of Fiona, to whom you are 'promised', and make believe you are in the factor's shoes. For I know now that you want me as much as I want you, but you are too proud and unyielding to do anything about it . . .

The next moment it seemed that he *had* decided to do something about it. She saw him push past Willy Macleod, who had entered with a tray of glasses, and move inexorably towards where they were dancing. She felt herself being jerked roughly from Buchanan's arms. Then she was ignored as Alistair loomed over the factor. The music slowed and faded as Alistair aimed a single powerful blow at Buchanan's jaw. The factor slumped to the floor.

After the first stunned silence, the room was filled with a confusion of voices. Lucy blinked at Alistair. 'You should not have done that,' she faltered. 'It was my fault! I encouraged him.'

'You think I would trouble to knock him down because you chose to play wayward games with him?' Alistair glanced with contempt at the body of the factor on the floor. 'When Willy had told me what had been done, the smile on Buchanan's face became an affront to every man, woman and child in the clachan!'

'Please—tell me what happened?'

Alistair jerked his head in the direction of the prone factor. 'When he regains consciousness, ask *him* to explain to you the real reason why this *ceilidh* was held tonight.' He turned away and pushed a path for himself through the crowd.

With shock, Lucy heard the musicians begin to play

again, but this time it was not the waltz or a reel which their fiddles and pipes were executing. They were playing a lament.

Now, suddenly, she did not need anyone to spell out to her what Alistair had meant, or the true reason why he had knocked the factor down. Instinct told her that tonight the people of Bencraig had been betrayed. When the lament had died down, the many whispers in the room confirmed what she already knew.

While Alistair was safely out of the way, neatly manoeuvred into attending the *ceilidh* so that he would not be able to plan any resistance, the sheriff's men had arrived at the clachan and served Writs of Removal on the crofters.

The people were to be moved on, and Bencraig cleared for the bringing in of sheep.

CHAPTER SIX

WHILE THEY SAT at the breakfast table, Lucy allowed the flow of her mother's grievances to wash over her.

'That poor, dear Mr Buchanan—he could have been seriously injured in such a vicious and unprovoked assault!'

'It was hardly unprovoked, Mother!'

Amelia made an irritable gesture. 'Some silly trifle which I confess I don't understand. But it could not possibly have justified such violence, to say nothing about the entire evening being ruined!'

It would, Lucy felt, be useless to try and explain to her mother that the 'silly trifle' meant that the crofters were to be plucked from their roots. Amelia would continue to attach greater importance to the fact that the *ceilidh* had broken up in disarray soon after Alistair had taken Fiona's arm and swept out of the house.

Her father had never witnessed the reality of the crofters' lives at first hand. He had been relying solely on Buchanan's view, and the factor regarded them as being of no use to anyone, responsible for their own poverty and deserving no pity. Would not her father withdraw those Writs of Removal when he saw the desperate need of the people? He had so much already, with his various estates scattered around the country and his business interests in London, that he could at worst afford to ignore his Scottish sub-tenants, and at best do something to help them, surely?

'I had a presentiment,' her mother's voice forced its

way through her thoughts, 'that Munro would ruin the evening! He should never have been allowed to attend.'

'Have you not yet grasped the fact, Mother, that you were cynically manoeuvred into inviting him? That the entire *ceilidh* was used, by Buchanan and by Father, for their own ends? Did you not even suspect that something was afoot when you were persuaded to ask Fiona?'

'Mr Buchanan said it was necessary. He said your father wished it.'

'Because both of them knew it was the only way they would get Alistair to attend! Only by Fiona begging and badgering him would he be certain to be safely out of the way when the Writs of Removal were being served!'

Buchanan himself, she recalled, had admitted without a sign of remorse that it had been necessary for Alistair to be otherwise occupied when the sheriff's men arrived at the clachan.

'Cousin Hugh and I planned it so,' he had said, rubbing his bruised jaw. 'Well, the Writs have been served and there is nothing Munro can do about it now. It is too late to get the crofters to resist. There will be nothing for them but to leave when the notice period has expired.'

Lucy made a sound of revulsion as she remembered the smugness there had been in his voice. Speaking half to herself, she said, 'Father cannot, in all conscience, drive the crofters from the land . . .'

'I am sure I don't know why you should care, Lucy. I hope you do not mean to turn into one of those depressing spinsters who are forever occupying themselves with the misfortunes of the poor!'

'Perhaps I am, for I do care.' She changed the subject. 'Should we not get ready for church, Mother?'

'Oh dear . . . I remember so well how the Scottish ministers like to sermonise for hours! And they are not even the kinds of prosy sermons that send one mercifully to sleep, but thunderings about hell-fire and brimstone . . . ' Amelia's brow cleared as she seized on a reasonable excuse. 'No, of course we cannot attend the service, for your father will surely be arriving some time today.'

Lucy did not comment. She excused herself and went to her room, where she found Fiona draping the white silk gown over a chair. 'I am sorry I am late, miss,' the girl said tonelessly. 'I forgot your gown, and had to return home for it. I shall take it in at the waist again as soon as I have time.'

Lucy was on the point of offering the gown to her as a gift, when she remembered how Fiona had despised it. 'There is no hurry,' she said instead.

'No, indeed, miss.' For an instant bitterness flashed in Fiona's eyes, and then she veiled them with her lashes. 'The Writ of Removal allows us to remain in the clachan for several weeks more.'

Lucy started. She had completely overlooked the fact that the Macleods would be one of the families affected by the Writs. Alistair's position was secure, for he had a lease. But Kirstie and her son and daughter would have to leave their home. What would happen now? Would Alistair marry Fiona without further delay, and take them all in?

Lucy tried to ignore her own agony at the thought, and consider the matter dispassionately. Surely Alistair could not afford to make himself responsible for the Macleods. His small piece of land had barely been able to support himself alone, so how could it support four adults?

'I shall do everything in my power to have those Writs withdrawn, Fiona,' Lucy promised.

The girl looked neither grateful nor impressed, but merely asked, 'Will I help you to change for kirk, miss?'

'We are not attending morning service. You may go home, Fiona; I shall not be needing you today.'

Lucy was trying to concentrate on the book she was reading, later, when the sound of hurrying footsteps reached her, and then her mother's head appeared round the door.

'Oh, Lucy, do come down! Your father has arrived at last. I saw his carriage through my bedroom window!'

The two of them reached the hall just as Hugh Sinclair entered the house. He greeted Lucy and her mother in his usual unemotional way, merely brushing the cheek of each with his mouth.

'Father,' Lucy began, 'if you would spare me a moment . . .'

'Yes, I wish to speak to you, too, but all in good time.' There was a preoccupied note in his voice; clearly his mind was on his own affairs, and Lucy could not help concluding, with a sinking heart, that his expression of cold remoteness offered very little hope for the crofters and their fate.

'It was most unhandsome of you, my love,' Amelia reproached him, 'to stop with Mr Buchanan instead of coming straight on here.'

'We had business matters to discuss. Besides, I was kept informed of your well-being.'

'*Well-being*!' his wife echoed bitterly. 'Oh, you are trying to mock me! When you have heard all that I have been forced to suffer . . .'

'Later, Amelia, later,' he interrupted with barely concealed impatience. 'I have urgent letters to write. If you will excuse me, I shall go straight to my study. Please see that I am not disturbed.'

He handed his greatcoat to Willy Macleod and strode towards the gun-room and study. Lucy knew that her mother's face mirrored her own frustration, but she was also aware that Amelia would now be seeking some other audience for her many complaints. Hastily, Lucy escaped by slipping out of the house.

It was a cold, bright day. From the direction of the clachan, peat smoke rose in the air, and faintly in the distance could be heard the sound of a piper playing a lament. Lucy listened to the sad air, and remembered the desperate little band of homeless refugees that their carriage had passed on the way to Strathraora: people who had also been served with Writs of Removal.

She came to a decision and returned to the house, making her way to her father's study. Whether he wished it or not, he would have to grant her an audience immediately.

He was seated behind the desk and engaged in writing, but he laid his quill down and gave her a resigned look. 'I had thought it was too much to ask for a little peace! But now that you are here, Lucy, sit down and tell me how you feel about Neil Buchanan.'

She stared at him, taken aback. '*Feel* about him? I don't like him!'

'That does not appear to be the impression you have given him. He felt sufficiently encouraged to ask my permission this morning to declare himself to you.'

Lucy opened her mouth to protest angrily, and then she remembered that she had flirted with the factor in a foolish attempt to arouse Alistair's jealousy. She looked away. 'He is mistaken. I do not care for the man at all.'

'You could do worse, Lucy.'

She made a sound of revulsion. 'No, Father! I know he is related to you, but I find the thought of him as a suitor quite repellent!'

'You are not in a position to be choosy,' he reminded her coldly. 'Buchanan may lack wealth, but socially he is perfectly acceptable, and if you married him I would be prepared to turn over to him all revenue from my Scottish estate.'

Marriage to Neil Buchanan, she thought with a chill feeling in her heart, would also mean that she would have to make her home in Scotland, where her father would hardly ever have to see her. Was not that perhaps Hugh's overriding motive in favouring a match between them?

She pushed the matter to one side, and said, 'Father, I wished to speak to you about those Writs of Removal which you caused to be served on the people of Bencraig. You cannot be cruel enough to turn them from the land and make them homeless!'

He frowned at her. 'I shall deal fairly with my tenants. But Neil Buchanan's reports have convinced me that the future of my Scottish estate lies with sheep, and so the people will have to be moved.'

Her heart plummeted. 'Alistair Munro says . . .'

'That trouble-maker! Indeed, he will pay dearly for assaulting my factor! And do not ape his sentiments to me, Lucy.'

'Very well, then, go and visit the people in the clachan yourself, Father! You will discover how they are suffering even without the threat of eviction hanging over their heads!'

He shrugged. 'If they are suffering, as you say, then any change in their lot can only be an improvement.'

'You cannot uproot the people and cast them adrift . . .'

Her mother entered the study at that moment, and said plaintively, 'Oh, Lucy, you are not mounting that boring hobby-horse again! She read us all a lecture last evening, Hugh, after that dreadful, uncivilised Alistair Munro knocked poor, dear Mr Buchanan to the ground . . .'

Lucy ignored Amelia and appealed passionately to her father. 'I have witnessed people who had been dispossessed, wandering aimlessly . . .'

'The people of Bencraig will not wander aimlessly. I have told you, their lot will be improved. Now they are so wretchedly poor that Buchanan tells me they live for part of each year on nothing but nettle broth.'

Amelia shuddered. 'For myself, I declare I would sooner starve!'

Lucy was frowning at her father. 'You say the people will not have to wander aimlessly. What, then, is to become of them?'

'They will be allowed to take up a free gift of land which I have acquired for them by the sea. There, they will be able to turn to the bounties of the ocean, instead of scratching a miserable existence from the soil.'

'And they will be so much healthier by the sea!' Amelia exclaimed. 'The benefits of ocean air are well known.'

Hugh Sinclair picked up his quill again, the gesture dismissing both his wife and daughter. As they left the study together, Lucy closed her ears to her mother's chatter and thought about her father's plans for the crofters.

It was true that they would be better off by the sea than they were here. But would the Macleods, too, move to the coast, or was Alistair's marriage to Fiona to be brought forward?

Lucy had been so absorbed in thinking about him that it did not come altogether as a surprise to see him standing in the hall, speaking to Willy Macleod. Amelia shuddered at sight of him and hurried away, pointedly failing to acknowledge him.

Lucy moved towards him, her heart beating a slow tattoo of pain and loss and longing. How powerful and indomitable he looked, for all his shabby clothes! He did not wear the expression of a man who had called to plead his cause, but of one who had come to make demands.

'I intend speaking to your father.' He confirmed her

thoughts in a curt voice. 'Willy is about to announce me.'

'Come into the drawing-room while you wait.'

'I do not intend to wait meekly!'

'Please?' She touched his arm, and after a moment he shrugged and strode with her towards the drawing-room.

'Well, Miss Sinclair,' he demanded, looking down at her with a hard little smile. 'I am thinking it was not to congratulate me for knocking down the factor that you have brought me in here.'

'No . . .'

He laid his hand on her throat, tilting her chin with his thumb. She stared at his mouth with a hopeless, shamed longing, the blood pounding in her veins. Almost as if she had no control over her own limbs, she moved towards him.

'If it would help my people to make love to you, Lucy Sinclair,' he said softly, 'I might try to forget honour and integrity. But it would not.'

His hand had dropped to her shoulder, pushing her away without gentleness. 'Now I intend seeing your father.'

She swallowed hard. 'I—have something to tell you. You would ruin everything by angering my father and storming into his study. Already he has threatened action against you for having knocked down his factor.'

'Ruin everything?' Munro echoed. 'Is there indeed anything at all left to be ruined? What greater harm can Hugh Sinclair do to the people?'

'You misjudge him. He has plans to improve their lot.'

He regarded her with raised eyebrows. 'Has he, then? What are those plans?'

'My father intends making the people a gift of land

by the sea. They will be able to earn a better living as fishermen.'

The words died in her throat as she saw his blazing look of anger and contempt. 'Is this your notion of revenge because I spurned you?' he growled, taking her in a rough hold and pulling her against him. 'Then see if you prefer the alternative!'

His mouth fastened on hers in a kiss of such savagery that it was akin to a physical assault. Indeed, so passionate was his rage that she sensed he would have knocked her down instead, had she been a man. And even though the kiss lacked any semblance of a caress, she found herself responding to it. The knowledge shamed her so deeply that she found the strength from somewhere to push at his chest, and she tried to gather the remnants of her pride by saying,

'Pray remember who I am, Mr Munro!'

'Ay, I'll do that! You are the laird's daughter, who thinks it a fine jest to talk of the people making a living *from the sea*!'

'It was no jest! They will be better off as fishermen.'

'By God, you do mean it!' He shook his head in a gesture of angry despair. 'What do my people know of the sea, of fishing, when they have been used to living by ploughing and reaping the soil? How could they compete with expert fishermen from the South, who have already made our fishing grounds their own?'

She caught her lower lip between her teeth, registering the fact that it had been bruised by that savage kiss. 'That had not occurred to me,' she said slowly.

'It could not have failed to occur to your father'—Munro's voice was grim—'he is not a fool. Well, now I intend seeing him and making demands of my own!'

He strode out of the room, and she sank into a chair, staring in front of her. Whatever demands he were to make, her father would not accede to them. How could she ever have thought Hugh Sinclair might be swayed by compassion or reason into changing his mind? He must have decided, a long time ago, exactly what he meant to do about his tenants in Scotland. The fact that he had already bought land by the sea to which to move them pointed to that.

A while later, more composed, she walked slowly past her father's study. Munro's voice came from within, sounding hard and implacable. She could not make out what he said, but it astonished her that her father had consented to the interview at all, and that he was apparently listening to his demands.

Lucy was even more astonished later on, when Neil Buchanan joined them for luncheon and she heard her father tell him, 'The Writs of Removal are to be withdrawn.'

'But, sir,' the factor protested, 'the sheriff's men were due to come and oversee the burning of the pasturage . . .'

'Send word for them not to set out.'

'But what has made you change your mind, Cousin Hugh?'

'The Writs of Removal are not important. A Warrant read to the people at a later date would be equally legal and binding.'

'With respect,' the factor protested, 'we cannot delay. May I remind you that we had planned every move to dovetail precisely . . .'

'Have done, Buchanan!' Hugh Sinclair interrupted roughly. 'I've changed my mind, and there's an end to it! The crofters wish to go on starving in their hovels, so let them!'

Now what on earth, Lucy wondered, could Alistair have said to her father to make him change his mind? The fact that he *had* done so emboldened her to say, 'Since you acknowledge that they are starving, can you not do something to improve their lot, Father?'

He gave her a look of such cold dislike that she caught her breath. 'All I intend doing about the wretched crofters is to forget their very existence.'

'Lucy planned to buy meal and distribute it among them,' her mother observed.

'It is easy to be charitable with someone else's money!' he snapped.

Lucy flushed. 'Since you would not have objected to my charging the purchase of a new gown or bonnet to your account, Father, I did not think you would mind . . .'

'Well, I do mind!' He pushed back his chair. 'Since it is obviously impossible to enjoy a meal in peace and quiet, I shall have something on a tray in my study!'

'What on earth,' Amelia wondered aloud after he had stormed out, 'could have happened to put your father in such a temper?'

Lucy made no reply. She still felt astounded by that crude reminder that any act of charity on her part would necessarily have been financed by her father. It was almost as though he had secretly been keeping an account of what she had cost him over the years, and resented her for its total . . .

'I cannot understand it,' she heard Neil Buchanan mutter. 'The crofters were to have been moved on, and sheep runs created. The profits would have been enormous. And now this complete about-face . . .'

There could be only one logical answer, Lucy was thinking. Her father had changed his mind, against his will, because of something Munro had said. He must have threatened Hugh Sinclair in some way, but what possible threat could a tacksman hold over his laird?

A shaming thought struck her. Had Munro told her father how she felt about him, and threatened to take advantage of those feelings if he did not relent? It would explain why her father's anger seemed to have been directed against herself.

She had no appetite for her food, and she feared that Neil Buchanan would try to engineer a situation in which they could be alone together. She rose from the table, pleading a headache, and climbed the stairs to her room. As she pushed open the door, a slight sound from within reached her, and she frowned. Kirstie must be late with her cleaning today . . .

But it was not Kirstie who was inside the room; it was Fiona. The girl stood before the large looking-glass, staring at her reflection with an enraptured expression, too preoccupied even to notice Lucy's entrance. She has loosened her hair and pinned it in disordered locks on top of her head with Lucy's diamond clips, and she was wearing the apricot-coloured silk gown which she had wanted so much to borrow for the *ceilidh* last evening. It did not make her look sallow after all, for excitement had brought vivid colour to her cheeks, and her eyes sparkled.

Lucy was too stunned by the flamboyant beauty of the girl to be angry. She closed the door behind her and saw Fiona stiffen. The girl turned slowly. The colour had left her face, and she kept her eyes cast down.

'I'm sorry, miss. I have not harmed the dress.'

'I'm sure you haven't, Fiona. But what are you doing here? I told you I would not be needing you today.'

'I thought you might change your mind, miss.'

The glibness with which the lame excuse was offered made Lucy's anger rise. 'No, you did not, Fiona! You thought I would still be at luncheon, and that you could safely amuse yourself by parading in my clothes! Because I lent you a gown for a special occasion does not mean that you are free to try on my possessions whenever the mood takes you.'

The girl's head jerked up, and there was a glitter of

hatred in her eyes. 'Oh, you lent me a gown right enough! The plainest, drabbest gown you possessed! I must not be allowed to outshine you, must I? As I could so easily have done, had I had your chances! *It isn't fair*!'

Lucy felt her anger turn to pity. It must indeed be hard to be beautiful and poor, and know that one's beauty was doomed to go unsung by the world. 'Since you are clearly so besotted with the apricot-coloured silk,' she said, 'you may keep it. I shall overlook your behaviour this time, but . . .'

With a passionate gesture, Fiona pulled the gown over her head, so that the diamond clips fell to the floor. 'I take no charity from you!' she shouted. 'Do you think I want your fine clothes? I merely wished to prove to myself that I could look better than you!'

Lucy said sharply, 'You are being inexcusably insolent! Keep the gown, and if you wish to keep your post also, remember your place in future . . .'

A wild burst of laughter cut through her sentence. '*My place*! You think my place is to bow and scrape to you, to fetch and carry for you, to cast my eyes down and be humble—all because you are so far above me! Well, my grand lady, hear this. *You are no more highly born than I*!'

Lucy stared at her. 'You are hysterical!'

'Do you think so? Then ask Amelia Sinclair . . . Ask her whose daughter you really are!'

CHAPTER SEVEN

THE RECKLESSNESS seemed to have left Fiona, and her face turned very pale. 'I—I am sorry, miss. I did not mean it. I talked nonsense. I was angry, you see, because—because you sent me home . . .'

'Why should that make you angry?' Lucy asked mechanically.

'Because it is cold at home, and there would be nothing but oatmeal to eat, miss. If I were not on duty, I could not share the warmth of the fires here, or the servants' lunch . . . ' Her voice cracked, and she continued in a scared whisper, 'Please forget what I said.'

'I doubt if I could forget it, Fiona—spiteful nonsense though it was. Now, I don't care where you go, but please leave my room.'

With agitated movements, Fiona pulled her own gown over her head and scurried to the door. Lucy sank down on the bed after she had gone, and frowned into space.

That ugly scene had upset her, for never before had Fiona given such complete expression to her hostility and resentment. In her passion, she had abandoned any pretence at respect. It was clear, now, that what lay behind her attitude was envy and a burning sense of injustice. But Fiona must be more than a little unbalanced if she could sustain such a personal and overwhelming hatred for everyone who had been born to advantages which had been denied to her.

'Ask Amelia Sinclair . . . whose daughter you really are.'

What an extraordinary thing to say, when one thought about it. What a bizarre taunt to pluck out of thin air. She stirred restlessly. It was nonsense, of course. Fiona herself had said so, once she had calmed down. All the same—why choose that particular combination of words to express malice? It would have been far more understandable if Fiona had said something like, 'I saw the way you were looking at Alistair last night, but he is mine!' It would have been more hurtful, more natural, and patently true.

Lucy rose, and picked the diamond clips up from the floor, dropping them inside her open jewellery box. She glanced at the discarded apricot-coloured silk gown, and shuddered. Whether Fiona wanted to keep it or not, she knew that she herself would never be able to bear the sight of it again, for she would always remember Fiona standing there with it in her hands, her face contorted as she gave vent to her bitterness and spite . . .

'Ask Amelia Sinclair . . . whose daughter you really are.'

Lucy shook her head impatiently, trying to dislodge from her mind the memory of the words and their implication. She would have to decide what to do about Fiona. Now that her father had decided so astonishingly to allow the crofters to remain on his land, the servants recruited from the clachan would expect to keep their employment while the house was occupied. But she did not think she could continue to have Fiona waiting on her after the things that had been said.

'Ask Amelia Sinclair . . . whose daughter you really are.'

That insinuation was like an evil seed which had been planted in her brain and which insisted on flourishing.

There was, Lucy decided, only one way in which to tug it out by the roots. She would do exactly what Fiona suggested, and put the strange question to her mother. Amelia would think she had taken leave of her senses, but it was the only way in which to have the taunt exorcised.

Briskly, Lucy descended the stairs. Neil Buchanan, she was relieved to find, had obviously grown tired of her mother's chatter and had made himself scarce. Amelia was alone in the drawing-room, an unopened Bible resting on her lap and her fingers drumming a monotonous tattoo on the table beside her.

'How dull the country is!' she greeted Lucy. 'Nothing whatever to do, and no one worth calling upon! And your father has locked himself in his study. It really is most shabby of him, considering he has only just arrived.'

'Mother,' she interrupted, 'will you tell me something?'

'If it is about those wretched crofters again, Lucy, I neither know nor care what is to become of them.'

'Whose daughter am I—*really*?'

The Bible fell with a clatter from Amelia's lap. Lucy felt the room tilting about her, for her mother did none of the things she had been expecting. Amelia did not stare in astonishment, or frown in perplexity, or look blank at the absurdity of the question. Instead, her face crumpled and her mouth began to tremble uncontrollably. It was like watching a long-established building rocking on its foundations before crashing to the ground.

'Mother?' Lucy spoke sharply, her voice pitched too high.

'I . . . Who . . . ' Amelia moistened her lips. 'It is a lie!'

A drumming sound reverberated in Lucy's ears, and

after a moment a detached corner of her mind registered the fact that it was her own heartbeats she could hear.

'*You* are not my mother, are you?' she asked with difficulty.

Amelia's mouth worked, but no sound came. She was shaking as uncontrollably now as if she had the ague.

'Who am I?' Lucy cried. Amelia shook her head, and stretched out her arms in a beseeching gesture. Lucy turned and, like a sleepwalker, began to make her way to her father's study. No, not her father. She could not possibly be Hugh Sinclair's daughter either, now that she knew Amelia was not her mother. In this moment of devastating revelation, Lucy finally understood the reason behind the coldness with which he had always treated her. She was not his flesh and blood.

She knocked on the door of the study, and heard him growl, 'Go away! I gave orders not to be disturbed!'

She continued pounding on the door, and after a while the sound of his chair being scraped back reached her. The door opened, and he stood regarding her with a grim expression.

'If I can get no peace in this house . . . ' he began.

Through frozen lips, she said, 'I want to know whose daughter I am.'

He had grown still, his eyes wary. 'I don't know what you think you may have overheard, but . . .'

'Don't try to fob me off! I asked—Mother—the same question. Go and take a look at her! She is shaking like an aspen with the shock of it!'

Hugh Sinclair expelled his breath in a resigned sound. 'So . . . I always knew this grotesque deception was the height of folly! I should have realised there was a danger in sending you to Scotland.'

'I was born here,' she said slowly, mechanically, and then her voice rose. 'Who were my parents?'

'We cannot talk here,' Hugh Sinclair told her sharply.

He took her arm and steered her towards the drawing-room, closing the door behind them.

Amelia, her arms clutched about her breast, looked beyond Lucy and fixed piteous eyes upon her husband. 'Hugh, someone—someone has tried to make mischief, telling lies . . .'

His curt laughter cut through her stammered sentence. 'It's no use, Amelia. She knows.'

Her mouth dry, Lucy said, 'I know nothing, other than that I am not your daughter. Who am I? And why have you pretended to be my parents?'

Even now, part of her longed to have one of them say, 'We always *felt* as if we were your parents.' But the man she had thought of as her father moved to the window, and began: 'The story started twenty-three years ago, when Amelia and I were living at Strathraora . . .'

'I know,' Lucy said, when he paused. 'At Strathraora, where I was born.'

'That was not true. You were born in Ross.'

'Oh . . .'

'The night before we were due to leave Sutherland for the South,' Hugh Sinclair went on, 'a young woman and her baby were brought to the house. They had been found on the road, the woman in a state of collapse. She had walked all the way from Ross with the child. After her husband's death she had been unable to pay the rent, and had been dispossessed of her cottage. The woman was ill, and seemed likely to die.'

He turned and looked at Lucy without emotion. 'The child was pretty and remarkably healthy. Amelia decided that she wanted her. The widow, fearing that she would die, agreed to let her keep the child. We did not know, until months later, that she had recovered, but she agreed to let us keep the child. She had been nursed back to health by a woman in Bencraig, and later she married the son of that woman. She, and the man who had first brought her to the house, were sworn to secrecy, for I had no wish to be pestered by other women seeking to be rid of unwanted children. Amelia and I travelled on to London with the child. You were that child, Lucy.'

Amelia had begun to cry. Lucy stood up and moved towards Hugh Sinclair. The coldness with which he had been speaking had made clear to her so many things which she had never understood before.

'You were against the plan, were you not?' she asked quietly. 'You did not want to take me in.'

He shrugged. 'I had no strong feelings about it, either way. Since it amused Amelia, I allowed her to have what she wanted. I was not likely to be troubled by the child. But it was not my intention to have you foisted on the world as our own. What I'd had in mind was that you should be brought up to be Amelia's companion, perhaps eventually to marry one of the upper servants.'

Lucy could only stare at him, chilled to the marrow at the cold distaste in his voice.

'I have always regretted,' he went on with a frown, 'that I was not there to prevent the world from jumping to the conclusion that you were our child. But immediately after our return to London, I was forced to leave again to attend to my estates in Worcestershire. By the time I realised that London Society believed the child to be ours, it was too late to make the truth known. We should have been a laughing-stock.' His voice hardened. 'And the truth must not come out now. It would be disastrous to my career in Parliament and to our social standing.'

'Why did you never tell me the truth?' Lucy asked bitterly.

It was Amelia who answered her. 'How could we, without risking it all coming out? You were always such a reckless, wilful child . . . Oh, I never meant to deceive people! But you were so much admired by everyone in London, and I was so proud when they assumed you to be mine, and said how much you resembled me . . .' She paused to wipe her eyes.

'And then, later, I couldn't tell the truth, Lucy. Lady Stanmore had asked to be your godmother, and Sir William Lovelace your godfather, and I went ahead and had you christened as Lucy Sinclair, and—and I am not sure but that that was an illegal act, quite apart from fobbing off the child of a Scottish peasant on Society . . .'

Lucy gripped the table in front of her. Shallow, acquisitive Amelia had seen a pretty child, and had set about acquiring that child just as she was used to acquiring pretty ornaments to grace her apartments. And Hugh had allowed her to have what she wanted, for it absolved him from having to give her love. Neither of them had ever felt any real love for Lucy herself.

'No one need know!' she heard Amelia saying eagerly. 'The maid who attended me at Strathraora is dead, and so is the sewing-woman who became your nanny. No one knows, apart from your natural mother, and she promised never to speak of it.'

'But we will know, won't we?' Lucy returned with passion. 'We'll know that I am not a Sinclair, but some poor peasant woman's daughter.'

'I never think of it,' Amelia assured her eagerly. 'At least, not very often. Of course, if you had grown up to be common looking, or vulgar in your manners . . .'

Her husband cut through Amelia's sentence, his voice sardonic and with a note of hardness in it. 'I would advise you to forget what you have learnt, Lucy. It is to your advantage as much as ours that the truth should not come out. You would hardly like to lose your place in Society, would you?'

She shook her head in a dazed gesture. It was useless for herself and the Sinclairs to pretend that things could ever be the same again, that she would be able to resume her old life and forget that she was not a Sinclair.

While she had accepted him as her father, she had been able to accept Hugh Sinclair's cold generosity as no more than her right, a substitute for the love he had never given her. But how could she think of it as anything but charity from now on?

And every time Amelia said, as she so often had in the past, '*Dear child, I know that Society finds your unconventional ways refreshing, but don't you think you're going a little far this time*?' Lucy would sense that what she really meant was, '*Be careful that your vulgar birth does not give you away*.'

No, things could never be the same again. Even if she were to return to London, she would always be conscious of the fact that her friends would cut her dead if they had an inkling of the truth.

She addressed Hugh Sinclair, speaking with difficulty. 'I—don't believe any of us could sustain a pretence. I'm well aware that you must have resented my presence in your house in the past . . .'

'You dramatise the matter. I'm not saying that it pleased me to have the world think of you as mine. It placed me in a very awkward position. Fortunately my estates were entailed, and would naturally go to my eldest male cousin upon my death, but the world would expect me to bequeath my personal fortune to you. As it is, I've made more than generous provision for you, but I know that my lawyer thought it shabby behaviour by a father towards his only child, and the world will think so too after my death. However, it is no fault of yours that the situation arose as it did. As for resenting your presence in my house—you may believe me that I do no such thing. If anything, I am grateful that you have been there to occupy and amuse Amelia.' He gave her his cold, unemotional look. 'So you may be easy on that score.'

Lucy took a deep breath. 'In spite of what you say, *I* cannot go on as if nothing had happened. Something has happened. I am no longer the person I thought I was. I cannot go on behaving as though I were Lucy Sinclair . . .'

'Good lord, would it be such a hardship?' he interrupted impatiently. 'I've never denied you anything!'

'No, you've never denied me anything,' she agreed forlornly, and thought—*except love*. But then, it was probable that he would not have loved a natural daughter either. People had never seemed to matter to him. His only interests appeared to lie in books, and in his estates, and in his Parliamentary career.

Almost as if he sensed what she was thinking, he went on in an implacable voice, 'You *will* go on behaving as though you were Lucy Sinclair! I'll not let you plunge me into a scandal, just because you are too squeamish to accept what you've always accepted!'

'I—don't know. I have to think . . . ' She thrust her fingers through her locks. Her mother's name—she deserved to be told that, at least. But before she could form the question, Hugh Sinclair was speaking again.

'One good thing at least has come of your knowing the truth, Lucy. I suppose you overheard Alistair Munro blackmailing me . . .'

'*Blackmailing* you?'

'Did you not recognise it for what it was? Well, now that you know the secret he threatened to disclose to you, he has lost any power he had over me.' A chill smile curved his lips. 'Munro has nothing to gain by telling anyone else. I'll waste no time in sending for him, and informing him how the tables have been turned.'

'Alistair *knows*?' Lucy faltered.

'Yes, of course he does. It was his father, Iain Munro, the tacksman at that time, who found you and your mother on the road from Ross. Iain swore to keep the secret, but it appears that on his deathbed he rambled away about the matter to his son. But surely you must have overheard?'

She gave him no time to finish. She stumbled unseeingly from the room and went up to her bedroom. Sinking into a chair, she caught sight of her reflection in the mirror opposite. Suddenly and shockingly it came to her that she had lost her identity, and that she had nothing to put in its place, for she had forgotten to ask who her mother had been.

Other thoughts came crowding in, jumbling together in her brain. The most shattering of them all was the knowledge that Alistair had been aware she was not a Sinclair. He had known it when he came to London, and that was why he had called to see her.

'*Have you no compassion at all for your own people*?' he had asked her, and he had meant it literally. He had obviously assumed at the time that she knew about her origins. And when he realised that she was in ignorance, he had kept quiet, no doubt even then perceiving that he might be able to use the knowledge to blackmail Hugh Sinclair . . .

Now, by confronting the people she had always regarded as her parents, she had removed that weapon from Alistair's hands. He would be powerless after this to stop the clearance of Bencraig.

Another thought occurred to Lucy, and a sound of bitter humiliation escaped her. How often had she not reminded him that she was the laird's daughter, and his social superior! She winced at the thought of his secret laughter, remembering the mockery in his eyes on those occasions. Had he shared the joke with Fiona later? He must have done so, for she could have learnt only from

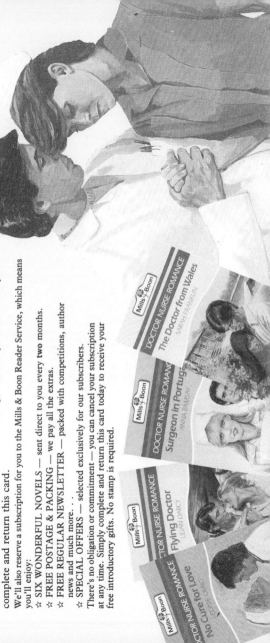

him that the Sinclairs were not Lucy's true parents . . .

The door opened and Kirstie came in, carrying a scuttleful of coal. Lucy waited for her to stoke the fire and leave, but instead the woman settled down on her knees and began to rake out the coals.

'You may leave that,' Lucy ordered in a muffled voice.

'You father particularly asked me to attend to your fire first, miss, and it will not draw, for the grate is clogged. I still have the other fires to attend to before I finish for the day.'

'Very well, then, but please be as quick as you can.'

The sight of Kirstie working at the fire, her swollen hands becoming covered in soot and coal-dust, intruded into Lucy's thoughts, and she struggled to marshal them into coherence.

She had been given a stark choice by the Sinclairs. In reality, it was no choice at all. She could either forget what she had learnt, and retain all the trappings of being privileged Lucy Sinclair in the eyes of the world, or she could—*what*? No, there was no acceptable alternative. She did not belong with the Sinclairs, and yet she did not belong anywhere else.

With sudden self-knowledge, she understood why she had not pressed Hugh and Amelia for information about her real mother. It was because, in her secret heart, she did not really wish to know. She was afraid. Afraid of being brought face to face with someone for whom she felt nothing and who would demand sacrifices of her. Or of being forced to look at some coarse, poor creature and feel ashamed of the woman who had brought her into the world.

She stared in front of her. How had she felt, that peasant woman, when she had given up her baby? Had she wept for her child during the years that went by? Very likely not, Lucy thought drearily. She had probably been relieved that she had been spared the burden of feeding and caring for the child. It was strange to think that if they were to meet, she and her mother would be total strangers . . .

Her glance fell on Kirstie again, and a dawning certainty began to creep over Lucy. She tried to dismiss it, but it would not go away. All the strands unravelled too neatly, forming a perfect pattern. Hugh Sinclair had specifically instructed that Kirstie Macleod and her family should be offered work in the house. Since when had he ever troubled to remember the name of any domestic servant? It would need very unusual circumstances for him to recall her existence after so many years.

A series of pictures flashed through Lucy's memory. There was herself, questioning Amelia about Kirstie Macleod. Amelia had dropped the mirror she was holding and accused the abigail of pulling her hair. She had, if was now clear, desperately been covering up the shock she had received. And afterwards she had done her best to steer the conversation away from Kirstie.

Another picture took its place in Lucy's mind. Hugh Sinclair's cold eyes gleaming as he told his wife, 'A staff will be engaged for you in Sutherland.' He had obviously been contemplating an exquisite punishment for Amelia, planned with secret, sadistic delight. She had placed him in the intolerable position of having to acknowledge a peasant's child as his own. And after all those years, he had been given a chance of getting his own back by arranging for the two women to be thrown together under the same roof. But her very shallowness had come to Amelia's rescue, for after her initial shock she had put the matter from her mind.

Hardly recognising her own voice, Lucy heard herself blurt out, 'You are—my mother?'

Kirstie's hands upon the fire-irons grew still. 'Ay,

miss,' she said without surprise, almost as if she had been waiting for the question and felt relieved now that it had been asked.

The room seemed to rock about Lucy. If she had been given time to imagine an encounter with her true mother, it would never have been like this. Neither would she have imagined her own instinctive reaction.

'*You gave me away*!' she wailed like a stricken child, and burst into tears.

Kirstie sighed heavily. She dropped the fire-irons in the grate with a clatter, and then she was at Lucy's side, placing an arm about her shoulder. 'A pity it is that you ever found out.'

Lucy clung to her as she wept. She could not help remembering how she had felt instinctively drawn to Kirstie from the beginning. 'I won't have you working as my servant,' she sobbed.

'It's glad enough I am of the work,' Kirstie said prosaically.

'I shall take you away!' Lucy heard herself form the reckless words, and it came to her that she did indeed have a choice, and had just made it. 'Somehow I shall earn a living for us . . .'

'No,' Kirstie said quietly but firmly, moving away from her. 'You do not belong in my life. There is no place for you there.'

CHAPTER EIGHT

ONCE AGAIN, logic deserted Lucy as her mother's uncompromising words rang in her ears. She acknowledged that, by uttering them, Kirstie had absolved her from all responsibility and had set her free to make the more advantageous choice of remaining privileged Lucy Sinclair. Her mother was not demanding sacrifices of her after all.

But no matter what her mind told her, her heart registered only a bitter sense of rejection. 'There was no place in your life for me twenty-three years ago either, was there?' she accused starkly.

Kirstie's look of resignation held an unutterable sadness. 'I was after doing my best for you. It's no easy thing for a woman to give her child away.'

'Do you think it's easy for that child to learn that she had been given away? That her mother would sooner continue to work as her servant than share her life in any way?'

'You could not share my life,' Kirstie said tonelessley. 'You speak of taking me away, and of earning a living for us. Even supposing you could do so, are my two other children to be cast off, abandoned and forgotten by me?'

'I—I didn't think . . . ' Lucy drew a painful breath.

Her relationship with Fiona was only just beginning to dawn on her, and this was the bitterest knowledge of all. Now she understood fully the girl's hatred and envy and contempt, and her savage sense of grievance.

How the acid must have bitten into Fiona's soul as she herded and milked goats, and contemplated sitting down to nothing but oatmeal for supper, and thought of the unknown half-sister who had been taken away to London where she lived the life of a lady. No wonder Fiona had tried to escape from the trap of her own life by contemplating running away to Edinburgh with someone, anyone—or, failing that, becoming Neil Buchanan's 'housekeeper'. And then, as a final, bitter slap in the face, to have that same privileged half-sister arriving at Strathraora, and being told to wait upon her as her personal maid.

A strangled sound escaped Lucy. 'Do . . . both Willy and Fiona know that I am their sister?' she asked.

'Half-sister,' Kirstie corrected, almost as if she were deliberately determined to emphasise the barrier between Lucy and her other two children. 'Willy knows nothing. Fiona overheard Alistair and myself talking about the matter. She it was who told you?'

Lucy nodded. 'She hinted. And I forced Mother and Father—Amelia and Hugh Sinclair—to tell me the whole truth. Except that I forgot to ask them—Kirstie, who was my father?'

'A poor man, but an honest one. His name was Farquhar Robertson. You have no need to be ashamed that you are his daughter.'

'I am not . . . ' She paused. It had not been shame that had stopped her from insisting to be told about her parents, and she did not want Kirstie to know that it had been fear. She went on slowly, 'It is a strange coincidence that you should have come to my room when you did.'

Kirstie looked away. 'It was no coincidence. Mr Sinclair sent for me and asked me to attend to your fire. He said I was to . . . make myself known to you, but the words were hard to find . . .'

Lucy drew a ragged breath as she recognised the reasoning behind his actions. Even if she had insisted on being told her mother's identity, he would have found a way of side-stepping the question. For he must have made up his mind that the truth, when she learnt it, should strengthen his argument that the masquerade be continued. So Hugh Sinclair had set out cold-bloodedly to nip in the bud any sentimental feelings Lucy might develop towards her mother, by accentuating Kirstie's position of servitude. He had intended that Lucy should be ashamed to claim kinship with a woman on her hands and knees, raking out the fire.

A fierce anger tore through her. 'Please don't go away,' she begged Kirstie. 'There is so much more I wish to ask you. I shall not be long.'

Her hands were clenched tightly as she left the room. Hugh Sinclair, she thought, might be a gentleman in the eyes of the world, in position and wealth he might be the superior of Kirstie Macleod—but as a human being, he was not fit to touch the hem of her faded, patched petticoat!

He was not in his study, and when Lucy hurried to the drawing-room she found him still there with Amelia. The expression of glazed boredom with which he had been listening to his wife's conversation changed to one of wary enquiry when he saw Lucy.

He was about to speak when Amelia forestalled him. 'Oh, Lucy, such tremendous news!' she cried excitedly, as though nothing of any moment had occurred to disrupt all their lives. 'And would you believe it, your father neglected to give it to me until a few moments ago—he says he forgot! So like a man, particularly when he must have known how it would raise my spirits! It almost makes up for having had to come to this bleak, mournful place . . .'

Lucy cut through her sentence, her eyes hard upon

Hugh Sinclair. 'My mother has just presented herself to me, exactly as you had planned.'

A cold smile twisted his lips. 'Good! I trust it has made perfectly clear to you the difference which exists in your stations?'

'Indeed it has! How clever of you to have had the forethought to install her as a chambermaid!' Lucy's voice broke. 'Such a poor, shabby little figure, with her swollen hands.'

'Oh, Lucy, dear!' Amelia exclaimed with the shallow kindness which came so easily to her. 'Don't be upset! I shall do something for poor Kirstie. I must confess that I was quite shocked when I saw how old and worn she looks now. I know—I shall go through my wardrobe and see whether some of my older gowns cannot be made over for her.'

Lucy felt herself seized by a wave of bitterness. 'The blue velvet might do, perhaps! That would be very suitable for scrubbing floors and raking out fires!'

'Why, Lucy, I . . .'

'She is my mother! Does it not strike you that it may be offensive to me to hear you talk of her as no more than an object of charity?'

Amelia's mouth trembled. 'I meant to be kind! And to tell the truth, Lucy, I cannot think of her as your mother! Surely, now that you have had time to think matters over, you can see for yourself that you are worlds apart, that you are far more my daughter than poor Kirstie's? Good lord, child, she is a servant!'

'As I would be a servant,' Lucy pointed out grimly, 'if you had left me where I belonged, or if you had not allowed people in Society to believe that I was your child!'

Amelia grasped her hand. 'My dear, you must not talk so! You must forget that she is your mother, particularly now that we have been invited to stay at Dunrobin!'

'Dunrobin?' Lucy frowned.

'Dunrobin Castle, the seat of the Countess of Sutherland,' Hugh Sinclair answered her smoothly. 'One of Elizabeth's cousins was to leave London for Scotland soon after I did so, to entertain a gathering at Dunrobin. We dined together one evening, and when he learnt that we would be in residence here he invited us to join them. We shall do so next week.' A slightly mocking look flickered into his eyes. 'No doubt the rural charms of Strathraora are beginning to pall, and you would welcome an occasion for picking up the reins of Society once more.'

Lucy's expression was grim, since she understood only too well. His strategy had been extremely clever. She had no doubt at all that, were it not for this present crisis, he would have remained silent about the invitation to Dunrobin Castle, which he would have considered a waste of time to accept. But now he was using it as a step in his carefully planned campaign.

First Lucy's mother was to be presented to her as a servant of the most menial kind, the difference in their positions cruelly underlined. Then, by way of complete contrast, she was to be borne off to Dunrobin Castle in the role of privileged guest, demonstrating very clearly to her all she would lose were she unwise enough to claim kinship with Kirstie Macleod.

Amelia was already chattering eagerly about the impending visit. 'There is so much to be done before we leave! Hugh, I do wish we had known that we were to be invited to join Lady Sutherland and her husband, for I might then have brought my best furs. Oh, and how I regret, now, that I had not waited for my new gowns to be delivered! I had a presentiment that they would be needed. Harriet will have to get to work, refurbishing and remodelling . . . ' She looked up at her daughter's face.

'Lucy, we shall have to inspect your wardrobe, too, and see what is to be done about adding a little variety to the gowns you brought with you. I do hope that Kirstie has taught Fiona to sew. She herself used to sew beautifully but now, with her hands so badly deformed, it would be quite useless to look to her. However, something must be done, for nothing is more boring or provincial than to be seen in the same gown night after night.'

All at once, the inanities seemed like a tidal wave threatening to engulf Lucy. She made a despairing little sound as she ran from the room, and hurried upstairs.

But Kirstie had not waited for her, and suddenly the house seemed like a prison. She went downstairs again, took a cloak from a hook in the hall, and stepped outside. Evening was falling, and a mist was rising with the setting of the sun. It cloaked the slopes of the hills in a soft grey and muffled the valley in an eerie silence. Without conscious decision, she left the gardens of Strathraora House and began to trudge aimlessly down the lane. The lonely grandeur of the landscape, the feeling of melancholy which she had sensed before when the hills enclosed her, gripped her by the throat.

Then the realisation came to her that she belonged in this landscape. Her roots were in these hills and glens. No matter what the Sinclairs had made of the small child they had taken into their home, they had never erased from her heart the call of this wild homeland of hers. It had always been there, bred in her bones and buried beneath the layers of sophistication she had acquired as Lucy Sinclair, the toast of London Society.

The smell of peat smoke reached her nostrils, and the strange sense of belonging seemed to heighten. It was almost as though she had subconsciously retained the memory of that familiar and pungent smell all through the years she had been Hugh and Amelia's daughter.

The smoke was rising from the clachan, and Lucy turned mechanically towards it. As she did so, she saw in the distance a small figure wrapped in a plaid, tramping ahead of her. It was instinct rather than anything familiar about the bowed figure that made her recognise Kirstie, and she began to run. 'Wait! Please wait for me!' she called.

Kirstie could not have heard, for she continued to walk towards the clachan. Lucy sped to catch up with her, and as she did so, Kirstie glanced at her. 'You should not have come,' she said quietly.

'I wanted to talk to you. Why did you not wait for me, as I asked?'

Kirstie sighed. 'There was no more to be said between us.'

'Yes, there was!' Lucy hesitated. 'What shall I call you?'

'You'd best call me Kirstie, miss.'

'I can't. You're my mother. And don't call me "miss"!'

Kirstie did not reply, but continued to walk towards Bencraig.

'Are you going home?' Lucy questioned.

'Ay, miss. The ewes have to be milked.'

'May I go with you?'

'You'd best not, miss.'

'Stop calling me "miss"!' Lucy bit her lower lip. 'Please let me go with you!'

Kirstie paused, and looked away. 'It will be dark soon. The strath can seem haunted in the darkness. You'd best away home.'

'I want to see where you live,' Lucy insisted.

Kirstie shrugged, and strode on again. There was an indefinable grace about the bowed head with its neat, greying braids that brought tears to Lucy's eyes.

'At least you shall not be my servant while we remain

at Strathraora,' she muttered fiercely. 'I'll tell Hugh Sinclair that I won't have it so!'

'You would not be doing me a service, child,' Kirstie told her firmly. 'Pride is a luxury that the poor cannot afford. Cleaning your bedchamber, calling you "mistress", means we shall be able to buy black pudding to eat with our potatoes during the hungry months ahead.'

'I'll give you money!'

'It is Hugh Sinclair's wish that I work for you,' Kirstie interrupted. 'In Strathraora it is important to obey the wishes of himself and his factor. The day is coming when we shall be plucked from the land in the way a wild flower is pulled up to make room for the potato. There is nothing we can do to stop it. All we can do is strive to delay the evil day. Alistair tells me that we have just won such a delay, but . . .'

'Oh, dear God!' Lucy cried in an anguished voice. 'Hugh Sinclair will not delay now! I have ruined everything! He postponed the clearance only because Alistair threatened to tell me the truth about my birth, but now that weapon has been rendered useless! And it is all my fault!'

'It is the fault of my poor, wild, reckless Fiona!' Kirstie sighed. 'Well, all we can do now is hope not to incur the laird's anger, so that when the time for eviction comes he will not have our house-timbers and our possessions burnt for good measure.'

Kirstie's words had evoked a vivid picture in Lucy's mind of the tenants and cottars she had seen on her arrival in Sutherland, plodding desolately away into nowhere against a background of their burning houses. She could not endure the thought that the same fate might befall Kirstie.

'I shall come and live with you in your cottage!' she cried recklessly. 'Even Hugh Sinclair's conscience wouldn't allow him to evict you then!'

Kirstie shook her head. 'No. Even supposing you were to be foolish enough to throw away everything the Sinclairs can give you, and that by your doing so we were to save our home, you could not come and live with us. You have been reared to be a lady. You know nothing of stacking peats, of threshing barley or shearing ewes. You would be a charge upon us, an extra mouth to feed, a source of resentment to Fiona and an intolerable added burden to Willy.'

Lucy surveyed her through a glitter of tears. It gave her a desolate, shut-out feeling to know that Kirstie wanted nothing from her, and that she was making it clear she had nothing to give Lucy. In spite of her mother's slight body and her look of weary resignation, there was a kind of strength about her which Lucy instinctively wanted to lean upon. From Kirstie, intuition told her, she would be able to draw an emotional security that Amelia had never given her. But she was to be denied even that. Everything Kirstie had to give was mortgaged to the family she had acquired after she had allowed Amelia Sinclair to take away her firstborn . . .

They had reached the clachan by now, and one or two people were about, driving their animals into the byres. They stopped and stared, began to hail Kirstie in the Gaelic and then grew dumb when they obviously recognised her companion. Lucy found herself being accorded a respect which was completely devoid of any warmth.

'This is my cottage,' Kirstie said, and opened the door of one of the small dwellings.

Lucy had never tried to imagine what the interior of these cottages would be like, but she supposed that somewhere in the back of her mind there had been a cosy, romantic image gleaned from a novel she had read. The reality was a crude shock.

In the centre of the small living-room, a peat fire sent smoke wavering up to a hole in the roof. A large iron cooking-pot was suspended over the fire from a crook and chain. In one corner was a rude bed; an earthen seat stretched along beside the fire, and a battered old chest served as an extra seat.

Kirstie was watching her. 'Do you still have a mind to join us, child?' she asked ruefully.

'No!' The word was torn from her. To live like this, without comfort or refinement, without dignity, without any of the things that made life bearable . . . No, she could not do it!

Kirstie touched her hand gently. 'Ay. I understand the way of it,' she said.

Lucy turned to the door and blundered outside. It had grown completely dark now, with no moon and the stars obscured by clouds. She felt no fear at the thought of finding her way home in the dark; only a great sense of sadness and personal failure.

She was startled, far more than frightened, when a large figure suddenly loomed up in front of her and arms enclosed her in a rough embrace. Alistair Munro said something in the Gaelic, his voice a caress. Then his mouth sought hers in the dark.

Just as the smell of peat smoke had stirred something in her mind, so his kiss this time had a strangely familiar quality, although it was nothing at all like the previous times he had kissed her. Or perhaps it was because of the difference. She knew only that it was as though she had always been aware somewhere deep within her that it would be like this, that she would be moved to an aching, joyous response, that she would fling aside all the years of careful schooling in the conventions and cling to him with a wildness which seemed to be part of these hills and glens.

He lifted his head, but did not let her go. His fingers

moved upon her throat. *'Thàinig oirnn do dh'Albainn crois,'* he muttered, his voice sad and at the same time savage.

She stiffened, and then pain and betrayal washed over her. He would never have spoken to her in the Gaelic, for he knew that she did not understand it. In the dark, he had seen her emerge from Kirstie's cottage and had assumed she was Fiona.

Lucy drew away from him. 'You have made a mistake,' she said tonelessly. 'You were not kissing Fiona.'

He was silent for a moment, so that she could not assess his immediate reaction. Then he said, 'I apologise. It was an easy mistake to make in the dark. You had best let me see you home, Miss Sinclair.'

'I shall see myself home. You came to look for Fiona, I believe. Kirstie will know where she is.' Lucy moved past him, hesitated and stopped. 'What you said just now in the Gaelic—was it private, or may I know what it meant?'

'It was not private. It meant: "A cross has been laid on us." ' His voice was sombre now. 'Hugh Sinclair sent for me, and told me you know yourself to be Kirstie's child and therefore I no longer have power over him. So the clearance of Bencraig is to go ahead, and the people will have to bear the cross of destitution and starvation.'

There was nothing she felt able to say, and she shook her head hopelessly. After a while, as she walked towards Strathraora House, she found that other matters were being pushed to the background, while her mind returned obsessively to that scene between them in the darkness. If only it were possible to erase the memory of what had happened, for none of it had really happened to herself. It had all been for Fiona—the caressing words, the warmth of his hands on her body, the hungry, possessive kiss. Even his anguish over the looming clearance of Bencraig had been meant to be shared with Fiona.

When Lucy reached the house, the door was opened by Willy Macleod. 'Ach, miss, you should not have gone out alone in the darkness, I am telling you!' he exclaimed impulsively.

'Why, Willy . . .' She made an involuntary movement towards this shy, awkward young half-brother of hers, but froze when she saw him blush a fiery red. He did not know of their relationship, she remembered, and since she had discovered that she lacked the courage to throw in her lot with her real family—even had they wanted her—he had better remain in ignorance. So all she said was, 'It was kind of you to be concerned, Macleod. Are Mr and Mrs Sinclair at dinner?'

'Ay, miss. Will I tell Mr Armsworth that you are home?'

'Yes, please, Macleod.' She handed him her cloak to be hung up in the hall and made her way to the dining-room, where the Sinclairs were engaged in eating their first course.

'Where have you been, Lucy?' Amelia exclaimed. 'You might have given some thought for my nerves before you disappeared like that without leaving word! And you have not changed . . .'

Her husband interrupted her, with a sardonic look at Lucy. 'My dear Amelia, has it not yet occurred to you that she owes us no filial consideration? She is, in fact and in law, a free agent and may do as she pleases. She may even refuse to continue living with us, and stay with her natural mother instead.'

'Oh no! She couldn't do that!'

'She is of age. We couldn't stop her.'

'But we must! What would we tell people? How would we explain?'

Hugh flicked a slight smile in Lucy's direction. 'It must be her decision.'

Lucy stared down at her hands. *He knows*, she thought with mortification and self-contempt. He knows that I have not the courage to do anything but continue the masquerade of life as Lucy Sinclair.

Armsworth entered at that moment to serve Lucy with soup, and a discreet silence was forced upon the three of them. She felt assailed by a mixture of loneliness and loss, and it was a moment before she fully understood the reason for that feeling. It had a great deal to do with Kirstie, but it was also because she was seeing Hugh and Amelia clearly now, untrammelled by feelings of duty and respect. Amelia was nothing but a spoilt and self-centred woman, incapable of any real emotion.

And Hugh exploited people. He had exploited Amelia by marrying her for her fortune, and he had exploited Lucy by using her to keep his wife contented and occupied. Now he was bent on using her again—to maintain the public image he had built for himself, and Lucy knew she would have to allow herself to be so used, for the only alternative would be to embrace the alien and miserable existence of the people in the clachan.

A sudden resolution came to her, and when Armsworth withdrew from the room, she addressed Hugh Sinclair. 'In spite of your taunts, you are anxious for me to continue playing my part in Society as your daughter—not because you have any affection for me, but because it would give rise to a great many embarrassing questions if I were not to do so.'

He was watching her. 'Go on, Lucy.'

'I am prepared to do as you want, Father . . . ' She broke off. 'Do you wish me to continue calling you that?'

'It would certainly raise eyebrows if you did not,' he

returned drily. 'Particularly as you have just indicated that you are content to have matters remain as they have always been.'

'There is something you must do for me in return,' Lucy went on. 'You mean to clear the land of your tenants. I want you to promise that, whatever you may do about the remainder of your estate, you will allow the clachan of Bencraig to continue undisturbed.'

He made an impatient sound. 'If progress had been stopped for everyone who disliked change, Lucy, we should still be living in caves!'

'I shall not leave here, Father, until I am assured that my mother and her neighbours will not be uprooted from their homes!'

He said nothing for a while, and only Amelia's little cry of protest disturbed the silence. 'Very well,' Hugh conceded at last. 'The clachan of Bencraig shall remain as it is.'

Lucy inclined her head. 'Thank you, Father. I shall be ready to leave with you and Mother for Dunrobin Castle next week.'

Amelia immediately began to prattle about the visit to Dunrobin, and she was still engrossed in the subject when dinner came to an end. Hugh sought his study, and Lucy fled to her room.

She was astonished to find Fiona waiting for her. She had assumed that the girl was either visiting neighbours or, perhaps, bringing the ewes home for Kirstie to milk. Lucy had certainly not expected to see her in the bedroom after that scene between them at lunch-time.

'I thought you had left the house, Fiona,' she broke the silence.

'No, miss. Harriet told me that you are to visit Dunrobin Castle, and I took the liberty of looking through your wardrobe and listing the clothes which need attention.'

Fiona's new-found humility made Lucy feel awkward and self-conscious, especially in the light of her knowledge that they were half-sisters. She would very much have preferred it if Fiona had refused to serve her any longer, but now that she had seen what the crude cottage in the clachan was like, she could understand why her half-sister was not eager to return to it, much as she might resent having to wait upon Lucy.

The girl did not refer by so much as a change of expression to that scene which had taken place between them earlier, even though Kirstie must surely have told her what had happened. It was only when she had brought in hot water for Lucy to wash, that Fiona allowed the careful mask to slip.

'Which nightgown will I lay out for you, miss? The one with the embroidered bodice, or the white silk, or the one with lace sleeves?' There was envy in Fiona's eyes as she catalogued the choice.

A reckless surge of bitterness and anger flowed through Lucy. 'You fool!' she exclaimed fiercely. 'What are embroidered bodices and lace sleeves? You have so much more than a choice of pretty nightgowns! Yes, I know now why you hate me, so let us drop the pretence!'

Jealousy flared openly in Fiona's eyes. 'It isn't fair!' she cried. 'Why should you have been the one who got everything?'

'I did not get everything,' Lucy corrected her drearily. *I did not get Kirstie's love*, she thought. *I did not get Alistair . . .*

'If only I'd had your chances!' Fiona flung at her in a bitter voice. 'The best I can ever hope to do for myself is to marry Alistair Munro. And, even then, I shall always be poor!'

Lucy stared at her. 'Do you not love him?'

A moment later she knew that her expression must have betrayed her, for she saw Fiona's mouth curve in a smile, and a gleam of malice entered her eyes. 'I do believe that, for all your riches, you truly envy me! It seems I have something after all which your money couldn't buy!'

Lucy turned away. 'You may go, Fiona. I don't need you any longer.'

She lay awake for a long time that night. It was as well, she thought, that Alistair Munro belonged to Fiona, and that she herself would never have to choose between the life to which she had been brought up and that to which she belonged by birth. Yes, it was a good thing that neither Kirstie nor Alistair wanted her. All the same, she found herself sobbing hopelessly into her pillow.

The following days, while she waited to leave Strathraora House, seemed endless. Amelia had plunged herself into preparations and plans for their visit to Dunrobin Castle, and had pressed an army of local women to help with an orgy of sewing.

Hugh Sinclair was also busy, closeted for long periods in his study with Neil Buchanan. To Lucy's surprise and relief, nothing more had been said about the possibility of her marrying the factor, and the man appeared to have lost interest in her.

But the day before they were to leave for Dunrobin Castle, he waylaid her in the gardens, where she had gone for a walk. 'Miss Sinclair, I wished to speak to you in private. I did not wish you to leave for Dunrobin perhaps believing that I have been wilfully negligent in my attentions of late. It is just that I have been kept so busy . . .'

Dismayed, she realised that he was about to make her a proposal, and she forestalled him quickly. 'Yes, you have been very busy with your discussions with my father. I cannot think why that should be so, since he promised me that his land would not be cleared. I hope you have not been trying to persuade him to have fresh Writs of Removal served upon the people?'

'Indeed, no. Your father is not a man who allows himself to be persuaded once he had made up his mind in a matter. No further Writs will be served.'

Lucy's gaze travelled towards the clachan. She wondered whether Alistair knew that she was responsible for the crofters' reprieve, and whether he would make an attempt to seek her out before they left for Dunrobin. She had daily been yearning for a sight of him, but he had been keeping his distance.

' . . . other estate matters which required discussion,' she heard Neil Buchanan go on, and forced herself to pay attention. He stopped, and tried to take her hand in his, but she was quick to place both hands behind her back.

'Miss Sinclair—Lucy . . . ' he said earnestly. 'You must be fully aware of my feelings . . .'

'Yes, Mr Buchanan.' She was seized by angry contempt for him as she recalled his treachery in the matter of the *ceilidh*, and her anger grew as she recalled something else. 'I believe I know only too well what you have in mind,' she went on. 'I overheard you talking to Fiona one day, and you made it very clear that you were scheming to marry me. You also said, I remember, that such a marriage would benefit her as well.' Lucy made her voice smooth as silk. 'Did you, perhaps, have it in mind to offer her a post as *housekeeper* once you had married me?'

She saw him flush. 'I meant, merely, that if you were to become my wife, she would be able to retain her post as your maid.' He gave an angry laugh. 'Someone has clearly been making mischief. I did offer Fiona work as my housekeeper, and if she chose to read something else into that, I cannot be held responsible.'

Lucy gave him a direct, withering look. 'You have

never, of course, felt in the least attracted to Fiona!'

His flush deepened. 'She is very beautiful, and she would go with any man who could offer her the things she wants. But once I had met you, I did not give her a second thought!'

'I am sorry, Mr Buchanan,' Lucy cut him short. 'I cannot marry you, and Fiona has nothing at all to do with my reasons. Now, if you will excuse me, I must go inside and start changing in time for dinner.'

She hurried away from him before he could protest. Thank heavens, she thought, that she would not have to see him again after today. They meant to travel south when eventually they left Dunrobin Castle, and it struck her with a painful pang that she would probably never return to these hills and glens.

When she arrived in her room, Kirstie was there alone, folding up clothes that were to be packed. Lucy's glance went automatically to her mother's poor, swollen hands, to see whether they were worse or better today.

'I have sent Fiona to help Mrs Bannerman with the putting away of the household silver,' Kirstie told her in a quiet voice. 'I wished to say my farewells to you.'

'Fare—Farewells?' Lucy echoed the bleak word. She blinked rapidly, conscious of an overpowering need to reach out to her mother. A great tenderness for Kirstie had been growing inside her; it frightened her, for it promised her no peace of mind in the future.

'Yes, child. My cleaning has been done, and I must away to the clachan.' She held out one of her distorted hands. 'May God always be with you.'

Lucy looked into her mother's worn, dignified face, and her composure deserted her. She took Kirstie's hand and brought it to her lips, tears streaming from her eyes. Her mother lifted her free hand and touched Lucy's hair.

'Ach, do not greet! Better it is for you to forget me,

and make the best of what the laird and his lady can give you.'

'And—you? Will you—forget me?'

Kirstie's eyes slid away from hers. 'I have another daughter.' Gently she freed her hand and turned away, and through a blur of tears Lucy looked for the last time at her before the door closed finally behind her.

She poured water into a bowl and washed her face, and she was less distraught by the time Fiona came in to help her to change for dinner. The girl folded Lucy's discarded gown to pack it, and spoke abruptly.

'You would not consider taking me with you to Dunrobin Castle, to act as your maid?'

Lucy have her a startled look. 'You would leave Kirstie and Alistair, to wait on me? Why?'

'Because it would give me a chance to make something of my life!' Fiona said passionately. 'I might meet someone of influence and power . . .'

'You mean a man, don't you?'

'Yes, a man!' Fiona agreed defiantly. 'Why not? Someone who could offer me some of the things *you* have always taken for granted!'

'I thought you loved Alistair?'

'I do. But love is a luxury only the rich can afford. *Will* you take me with you?'

Lucy shook her head slowly. Kirstie, she sensed, would never forgive her if she were to offer her beloved, wayward daughter such temptation. 'I am sorry . . .'

Fiona flung the gown she was holding on the floor. 'I understand!' she shouted. 'I must not be allowed to compete with you in any way, must I? I must be kept down, where we both belong! You have the power to do something for me, and you refuse! Well, I'll not lift a finger in your service again! Finish your own packing!' She stormed to the door, banging it behind her.

Lucy sighed deeply. Even if she had not been thinking

of Kirstie, it would have been impossible to take Fiona to Dunrobin. Hugh Sinclair would never have permitted it, for it was obvious that he wished to put distance between Lucy and her natural family. And Fiona was so volatile that she might well have blurted out, in a temper and in front of witnesses, that Lucy was her half-sister.

She thought of Alistair, and her heart twisted. Did he guess how shallow were Fiona's feelings for him? If he did, would he still consider himself irrevocably 'promised' to her? The answer was not important, for she herself would not see him again. Instinct told her that he had deliberately been keeping away.

She squared her shoulders and went down to dinner. She had half-feared that Neil Buchanan might have been invited to this last meal, but only Hugh and Amelia joined her at the table.

'I can hardly believe,' Amelia said excitedly, 'that tonight is to be the last one spent in this gloomy house! I have not been truly warm since we arrived!'

'Do not exult too soon,' her husband warned in a dry voice. 'I dare say Dunrobin Castle will be quite as draughty. It is a great, Gothic extravagance, by all accounts.'

'Well, at the very least the company will be congenial, even if one has to wear one's furs indoors. Oh Lucy, that reminds me—have you borrowed my seed-pearl brooch?'

'No, Mother.'

'I last wore it pinned to my sealskin stole, and it should have been put back inside my jewellery case, but I cannot find it. I must remember to ask Harriet to have a thorough search made. Hugh, were you given any indication of the functions planned to take place at Dunrobin Castle? Or who else would be among the guests? I do hope no particular friends of the Davenants have been invited. It would be so awkward if they have . . .'

Amelia talked incessantly about their forthcoming visit, and Lucy felt as relieved as Hugh Sinclair looked when at last the meal came to an end, and she was able to escape.

Before returning to her room, she took the opportunity of saying goodbye to Willy Macleod. As she shook hands with the blushing youth who still did not know she was his half-sister, she knew that this was the last she would ever see of her real family. Weighed down by sadness, she climbed the stairs.

In the morning, the household was engulfed in the furious throes of imminent departure. The servants carried trunks and boxes to the waiting carriages, and Harriet flitted between Amelia's room and Lucy's as she helped both women into their travelling clothes.

At last everything was ready. The furniture had been draped in holland covers once more and the fire in the hall had been banked down. Only Mrs Bannerman was to stay behind in her own quarters to look after the house.

Amelia was about to take her place in the carriage when she checked, and exclaimed, 'I forgot all about my seed-pearl brooch! I meant to ask Harriet to search for it.'

'Mrs Bannerman will find it and keep it safe,' her husband assured her. 'Let me help you on board, Amelia.'

'It is quite my favourite piece! I couldn't possibly rest easy until I have it in my possession again.' She turned to Lucy. 'Do hurry to the other carriage and ask Harriet and Armsworth to search my room for it.'

'My dear,' Hugh begged with barely veiled irritation, 'leave the brooch behind, and if it should be lost to you, I shall replace it.'

'No, it must be found!' Amelia insisted.

Lucy climbed down from the carriage, promising to help Harriet to search for the brooch. She thought both Hugh and Amelia were making an unnecessary fuss about the matter, and longed only to get away so that she might begin to try to put memories of Kirstie and Alistair behind her. At last, after a prolonged search, the brooch was found where it had become lodged between two drawers in the bedroom.

Hugh Sinclair was fuming, his mask of politeness gone, by the time Lucy handed the brooch to Amelia. 'For the love of God,' he snapped. 'Climb aboard so that we may be on our way!'

Deliberately, Lucy did not look back at Strathraora House or at the clachan of Bencraig. She kept her gaze fixed upon the enclosing hills, their snow-laden summits shimmering white in the wintry sunshine.

She became aware, suddenly, of some kind of commotion, and of a moving blur speeding past the carriage. The coachman shouted something; the horses reared and whinnied and then slowed down as they were brought under control.

Hugh Sinclair had just begun to turn down the window of the carriage when Lucy caught sight of Alistair. He sat upon his horse, his face haggard, his eyes stark with a frozen and terrible rage. He leapt to the ground and pulled open the carriage door, unceremoniously bundling Hugh Sinclair from it, hurling a string of words in the Gaelic at him as he did so. The force and the fury in his voice told Lucy that they could only have been obscenities.

'Take your hands off me!' Hugh Sinclair protested impotently.

Alistair gave him a contemptuous shake and released him, and Amelia screamed as her husband fell in an undignified heap on the ground.

'Call off your men!' Alistair shouted at him. 'If you have no pity, at least show a little restraint! Give the people a breathing-spell so that they may save their house-timbers before Bencraig is cleared!'

'Bencraig?' Lucy cried. 'No, you're wrong! He promised! He said that whatever happened, Bencraig would be left alone!'

'His factor moved in with an army of helpers half an hour since,' Alistair told her harshly. 'A Warrant was read to the people, telling them to leave their homes immediately, and the heather is being burnt at this moment. The fires will spread to the cottages.'

Lucy jumped from the carriage and stared in the direction of Bencraig. A pall of smoke rose from the hill. The recent mild weather had melted the last of the snow which clung to its slope, exposing the heather, and this was now a blanket of flames.

'*Kirstie*!' Lucy cried, and turned passionately on Hugh Sinclair. 'You promised! You never meant it, did you? Of course you didn't! How could I have been such a fool as to believe you? Bencraig had to be the first to go! It had to be razed, and Kirstie driven away so that I would never find her again! If Mother had not lost her brooch, I would probably not have known what had happened until it was too late!'

Hugh met her eyes, and his own were hard as pebbles. 'Buchanan shall pay for this. I told him to wait until noon. Well, the thing is done. Come, we must not keep them waiting at Dunrobin Castle.'

'Kirstie!' Lucy cried again, and began to run towards Bencraig. Hugh Sinclair caught up with her, and took hold of her arm.

'Listen to me!' he said, his voice like ice. 'If you go back there, if you go to your mother, I'll wash my hands of you. I'll have my men drive you from my land with as little mercy as if you had never left Kirstie Macleod! You will become one of them again.'

She was barely listening. The only thought in her mind was of Kirstie, indomitably trying with her poor swollen hands to defend her cottage against Buchanan and his men.

Lucy broke away from Hugh Sinclair, and as she ran she knew that, come what might, she had finally and irrevocably made her choice.

CHAPTER NINE

EVEN IN THE midst of the emotions swirling within her, Lucy found herself wishing prosaically that she had been dressed in something more appropriate for running over rough ground. Her travelling ensemble and matching elegant boots had not been designed for such exertions. She stumbled, the hem of her gown catching at the toe of her boot, and was unable to stop herself from falling heavily.

The force of it drove the breath from her body and brought tears to her eyes. She sat up, rubbing a grazed elbow, and watched dully as the carriage bearing Hugh and Amelia Sinclair proceeded on its way to Dunrobin Castle. He had meant every word he had said! Then a breeze brought the smell of burning heather to her and cleared her mind of everything but Kirstie's plight.

She stood, and saw that Alistair was riding towards her, his face gaunt with anger and reckless determination. She said nothing as he helped her up in the saddle. Then he was spurring his horse towards the burning clachan of Bencraig.

Her blood froze as they neared the clachan, and the sound of human misery and despair reached them: women weeping, children screaming in terror, all mixed up with the blasphemous rage of men watching helplessly as their world was plundered and sacked before them. The hysterical barking of dogs and the fear-crazed bellowing of cattle added to the noise and echoed in the valley.

Confusion was everywhere as they rode into Bencraig. Some of the people had defiantly barricaded themselves inside their homes, but a minority were complying with the orders of Buchanan's men to vacate their cottages. An old man and his wife stood resignedly beside a pitiful pile of belongings, and both were weeping.

A passion of rage and pity tore through Lucy. In that moment she knew that the daughter of Hugh and Amelia Sinclair had ceased to exist. Here in this ravaged part of Scotland was where she belonged. These were her people—their humiliation and despair were her own.

Alistair dismounted and helped her from the horse. He shouted to the crofters in the Gaelic, and the tone of his voice told her that he was whipping them up into active resistance. Men began to use their plaids to beat at the burning heather.

Lucy saw that a well-built man wearing a dark frock-coat and with an air of prosperity had appeared among the people. He picked up a chair from a pile of belongings stacked outside someone's cottage and mounted it, using it as a platform, and his voice rang out, resonant and filled with authority. Many of the crofters stopped beating at the flames and gathered to listen to him in an attitude of respect. As she pressed closer, she heard him declaim,

'Resist the factor's men and you resist the will of God! It has been ordained that you should leave your homes; it is part of the Heavenly Father's mysterious but ever-caring scheme for all of you. Only eternal damnation can be yours if you continue to pit yourselves against the might and right of your masters here on earth, who themselves are but tools of the Master of all Creation!'

Lucy shook her head in disbelief. He was obviously their minister, and respect for his calling was achieving what fear of Buchanan's men had failed to do. Many of them were obediently ignoring the fires and stood listening to him with heads bowed, as they must have been used to doing when in the kirk on Sundays.

Suddenly Alistair was there, his voice ringing out above that of the minister. 'You are a hypocrite and a knave, McKenzie! Get back to your comfortable manse, and to your rich food provided by Hugh Sinclair—the only master you truly serve!'

'You blaspheme . . . ' the minister began to roar at him. With a contemptuous gesture Alistair stooped and jerked away the chair, so that the man toppled to the ground. With his authority and dignity in shreds, he picked himself up and scuttled away.

Alistair began to lead the crofters in their resistance, abandoning Lucy. Human chains were formed, spreading out from the burn in all directions. Sacks were soaked and passed on in relays to the men in front fighting the fires in defiance of the factor's hired henchmen.

Lucy's glance went to Kirstie's cottage, and a moment later she caught her breath. Neil Buchanan himself came lurching out of it, bearing Fiona in his arms, almost as though she were a trophy. The girl did not appear to be objecting, and she offered no visible protest until Kirstie suddenly emerged from the cow-byre. Only then did Fiona begin to scream, and beat her fists against Buchanan's back.

In spite of all the other noises, Alistair must have recognised her voice, for Lucy saw that he was cleaving a path for himself through the confusion of people and animals, shaking off restraining hands and sending flying any of Buchanan's men who blocked his path. There was murder in his eyes as he passed Lucy.

Neil Buchanan had set Fiona on the ground and was holding her fast while he kissed her. The next moment he was jerked roughly away from her, and then Alistair's fist crashed into his face. The man fell to the ground, and Fiona ran, loudly sobbing now, into Alistair's arms.

Lucy had fought her way over to the cottage, and with a glance, examined her mother. Kirstie looked haggard and spent, and yet there was something unflinching about her. Lucy had a child's instinct to touch her for mutual comfort and reassurance; instead, she kept her hands stiffly at her sides as she moved towards her. 'I've come to be with you,' she said.

'Ach, such foolishness,' Kirstie returned in a weary voice. 'Go home, child.'

'Hugh Sinclair's home is no longer mine.'

But Kirstie was not listening. 'I must see and make sure that Fiona was not hurt.'

As Lucy trailed after her, she heard Kirstie address the girl in the Gaelic, and even though she herself did not understand a word of it, her meaning was clear. Kirstie's eyes were full of tender concern; her bracing and yet gentle voice was that of a mother telling her child, 'All will be right now, for I am here.'

Lucy felt as if a door had been shut in her face. Fiona raised her head from Alistair's chest and looked at her with eyes that held undisguised loathing. 'Have you come to watch the fun? Does it amuse you to see Sinclair's men bring us to ruin?'

A ruin, Lucy thought, which you sought to escape. If you could have evaded Kirstie, you would have allowed yourself to be carried away to safety by the factor . . .

Automatically, she looked to where Buchanan had been brought to the ground, and then she stiffened. He was crouching on his knees now, his pistol drawn and trained upon Alistair. Kirstie had seen it too, and gave a cry. With the speed of lightning, Lucy moved so that she stood between Alistair and the factor. Alistair was almost as quick, for the next moment he was jerking her aside. But she ducked under his arm and ran to confront the factor.

The pistol dropped from Buchanan's hand, and he rose unsteadily, staring at her as though she were a ghost. 'Miss . . . Sinclair . . .'

'Yes, Mr Buchanan!' A glimmering of an idea was stirring to life. 'As you see, there has been a change of plan. My father will be most displeased with you. You were told to wait until noon, were you not?'

She saw Buchanan shake his head, as if to clear it. 'The men I hired were eager for sport,' he muttered defensively. 'Why are you not on the way to Dunrobin?'

'As I said, there has been a change of plan. My father was taken unwell, and he asked me to tell you to call off your men.'

'Your father sent you here, into danger?' he asked in disbelief.

She smiled sweetly. 'Had you waited until noon, as you were ordered to do, there would not have been the least danger. Now, please command your men to put out the fires.'

'But the heather must be burnt. It is the only way to encourage the growth of cotton grass and deer hair for the sheep that are coming. Miss Sinclair, are you sure you are not—not . . .'

She drew herself up to her full height. 'Not *what*, Mr Buchanan? Will you call your men off, and start beating out the fires, or shall I return and tell my father that you choose yet again to disregard one of his orders?'

Her training as the daughter of Hugh and Amelia Sinclair was obviously giving her an authority which Buchanan dared not argue with, and the fact that he had been knocked unconscious must also have affected his powers of reasoning, for he lurched away, shouting orders to his men.

Sullenly, deprived of their sport, the factor's men

began to work side by side with the crofters to beat out the flames. Lucy followed Kirstie and Fiona to the burn, where she soaked sack after sack until her movements became entirely mechanical, leaving her mind free to continue its own thoughts.

She knew it would not take long for Buchanan to learn she was not a Sinclair after all, and that she had been cast adrift by the man whom he thought of as her father. But at least she had gained a breathing-spell for Kirstie and her people. Buchanan would go to Strathraora House, and when he found no one there but Mrs Bannerman, he would know that he had been tricked. But, even so, he would be bound to ride all the way to Dunrobin Castle for further orders from Hugh Sinclair.

With all the fires conquered at last, the crofters began to drift slowly to their homes. But there was no elation in their eyes, no look of victory on their sombre faces. It was as if they knew that they had been given only a respite before their inevitable fate overtook them.

Lucy realised, at once, that she was alone. A terrible chill of desolation overcame her as she stood there with the smell of burnt heather in her nostrils, and gazed round her. The door of each cottage was closed, shutting her out.

I don't belong here, she thought. But where *do* I belong?

She sat down upon a boulder, wrapping her skirts tightly about her for warmth. Rage, and fear for Kirstie, had sustained her for so long, but now she felt empty and drained as she contemplated the future.

Her reckless action had cut her off from the only world she knew, and had done nothing to gain her entry into the world in which she belonged by birth. Did she even want to enter it, she wondered. But what else was there? All she had taken with her from the Sinclairs' world were the clothes she was wearing. It struck her now with overwhelming force that she, who before had always had every material thing she craved, was completely destitute.

A shadow fell across her. She looked up into Alistair's face. His mouth was cast in tender lines, his eyes warm but strangely melancholy. 'Kirstie's child,' he said softly.

'Am I?' Her voice was bleak as she remembered her mother's rejection.

'Ay, you are that.' He stooped, forcing her to her feet. 'Kirstie has ever had courage and an indomitable spirit. You have it also.'

'Fiona is Kirstie's child too,' Lucy said involuntarily. 'And yet . . .'

He looked away from her. 'Ay, fine I knew she would have gone with the factor in her fear.'

'And—it alters nothing?'

'No.' He brought his gaze back to her face. 'You cannot stay here on the hillside, Lucy.'

'You—you have never called me Lucy before,' she said unevenly.

He did not respond to that, but merely said, 'You will take cold if you stay here.'

'I don't know where to go,' she admitted quietly, and looked away. A wind had risen and was sweeping across the mournful hills with a sound like a lament, flattening the clothes against her body.

'You must take shelter,' Alistair urged again. 'Go to the house of your mother.'

The tears which she had been fighting rose to her eyes at his words. She tried to blink them away, but he had seen them. He lifted a hand, and brushed them away. She felt his slightly unsteady touch against her skin, and without conscious thought she covered his hand with her own and brought it to her mouth, parting her lips against his palm. He looked down at her, his eyes shadowed and unreadable.

'Go to Kirstie,' he said abruptly, taking her arm. In silence they walked towards Kirstie's cottage, where he left her at the door. She watched until his tall figure was out of sight before she knocked diffidently.

The door was opened by Willy Macleod. He stared at her in astonishment for a moment. 'Oh, miss, we have you to thank! You tricked the factor!'

'Don't call me "miss", Willy. My name is Lucy. May I come inside?'

She saw his colour rising. 'It—it wouldn't be fitting, miss . . .'

'Don't grovel, Willy Macleod!' Fiona's furious voice cried from inside the cottage. 'Have you not guessed the truth? She is no better born that you or I! She is Mother's daughter, too!'

The muscles of Willy's face grew slack with shock. Kirstie pushed him out of the way and drew Lucy inside the cottage. 'You will share our meal, and afterwards Willy will fetch a carriage from the stables at the big house and drive you to Dunrobin Castle. If you have quarrelled with Hugh Sinclair, then you must beg his pardon and ask him to forgive you.'

'No!'

'We will talk about it later. Sit down, now, and eat.'

The meal was a frugal one of oatcakes toasted upon the fire, washed down with what Lucy supposed must be ewe's milk, for it had an unfamiliar taste which she found unpleasant. They ate in silence, with Fiona casting sullen, resentful glances at her while Willy watched her with bewildered eyes. Hungry though Lucy was, she found it difficult to swallow the food. After watching her for a while, Kirstie rose and brought a small crock of honey from a shelf, offering it to her in silence.

Fiona exploded vindictively, 'The honey was being

saved for medicine against the grippe, but *she* must have it instead!'

'Whisht, child!' Kirstie commanded sternly. 'Any guest is entitled to the best one has to offer.'

Lucy pushed the crock of honey away. 'I don't want the best,' she said, her voice thick with unshed tears. 'I am not a guest.'

Fiona led out a peal of mocking laughter. 'How, then, should we treat you? As a member of the family?'

'Yes. I—should like to stay here . . .'

At this Willy choked on his food, and Fiona exclaimed bitterly, 'So that when you travel to Dunrobin Castle in the morning you might divert them with tales of how the common people live?'

'I am not going to Dunrobin Castle. I meant that I wished to make my home with you.'

'Oh, by all means!' Fiona cried derisively. 'Willy sleeps down here in the boxed-in bed, and Mother and I share the only other bed upstairs. But one of us could no doubt sleep on the floor to accommodate you! And then—let me see—you would not expect to help with the shearing of the ewes, would you? Or with the spreading of muck in the fields, or with the ploughing or the cutting and stacking of peats! And I cannot picture you tramping blankets in the washing-pool! So what will you do with your time, my fine lady? Languish by the fire all day while Mother and Willy and I work to feed you with the kind of common fare you clearly despise?'

Lucy stared wretchedly into the smoking fire as Kirstie rebuked Fiona. 'You have made me ashamed for you!'

'But how dare she, Mother? How dare she talk of flinging away all the chances given to her, of turning her back on Dunrobin Castle and the Sinclairs—all to make her home with us?'

'Whisht, Fiona! Go now, you and Willy, and look for

the ewes that the factor's men scattered into the hills.'

After they had gone, there was no sound in the room other than the crackling of the fire. Kirstie broke the silence. 'Fiona was right. You must go away, Lucy. You do not belong here.'

'I don't seem to belong anywhere . . .'

'You belong with the Sinclairs, who have brought you up. You must go back to them.'

'It would be impossible, even if I were to bring myself to beg for their charity. Hugh Sinclair promised me that Bencraig would be left undisturbed, that the land would not be cleared. He tricked me. It was planned that we should be well on our way to Dunrobin before the Warrant was read to the people. But we were delayed, and Buchanan's men went to work earlier than they should have done.'

She made a weary gesture. 'When Alistair stopped us with the news, I had to come and make sure that no harm came to you. Hugh Sinclair gave me an ultimatum. If I went to Bencraig, he said, he would cast me off. And so—I am no longer Lucy Sinclair.'

There was something almost like ruthlessness in Kirstie's face. 'You must appeal to Amelia Sinclair. She is a stupid woman, but a kind one. She would give you enough money to live comfortably in some town like Edinburgh. Whatever you do, wherever you go, you cannot share our lives. There is no place for you here.'

Lucy's voice cracked. 'Don't—Don't you care anything about me?'

She found Kirstie studying her with an expression which was dispassionate and at the same time regretful. 'My caring for you was done with many years ago, child. No one can mourn for ever, and the poor cannot afford to mourn for long. The struggle to survive fills so much of our lives . . . ' Kirstie's voice hardened. 'I have done what I could for you, Lucy, without taking any account of my own feelings. I gave you away at a time when you were all I had, so that you might grow up in a way of which I could only dream. And now you are after throwing it all away for a foolish sentiment.'

Lucy covered her face with her hands. She felt Kirstie's hand move gently over her hair, and she caught it and held it between her own, bringing the swollen fingers to her lips. Her eyes were wet with tears.

'It is growing dark,' Kirstie sighed. 'You could not stay here, even supposing there was room. Go now, to Strathraora House. Mrs Bannerman will be there even though the house is shut up, and she will prepare a room for you for the night. In the morning Willy will escort you to Dunrobin Castle, where you must humble yourself to Hugh Sinclair.'

Lucy rose and stumbled to the door. She half-turned, and found Kirstie watching her with sad but unrelenting eyes. Blinded by tears, she pulled open the door and went outside. A blast of cold air met her, as cold as her own future. She walked slowly away from the clachan.

A fine rain was falling across the strath, and the hills wore a shroud of grey. The wind sang a melancholy tune as it sped down the valley, whipping her clothes against her legs, tugging at her hair. Driven by a sudden impulse, she turned her footsteps towards Alistair's cottage. It was raining harder now, lashing her face, painfully stinging her skin, and her skirts were clinging wetly around her legs by the time she reached it.

She put up a hand to the door, and felt it move at her touch. Uncertainly, she stepped inside. The room was dark and gloomy, relieved only by the flickering of the fire in the hearth, and at first she did not see Alistair, sitting motionless before the fire.

He did not move even when she drew hesitantly closer. He was staring into the flames, his profile harshly sculpted, his eyebrows drawn down at the corners, as if his thoughts gave him pain. She cleared her throat . . . 'Alistair?'

He turned his head to stare at her, then rose. 'Lucy! What are you doing here? Is anything amiss at Bencraig?'

'No.' She attempted a smile. 'It was just—I had nowhere to go.'

He frowned at her. 'Why did you leave Kirstie?'

'There was no room for me there.'

'Kirstie turned you away?' he asked with disbelief.

'She was right to do so.' Lucy shivered, and moved towards the fire, holding out her hands to the blaze. 'I knew all the time that I did not belong there. It was only when you told me to go home to my mother that I fooled myself into believing there might be a place for me in Kirstie's life.'

'You are her daughter . . .'

'Fiona is her daughter also, and she resents me bitterly. And Willy is painfully in awe of me. Even if there had been room for me, how could we all have lived together in those circumstances?'

He came to her and removed her wet pelisse from her shoulders. His fingers brushed against her throat as he did so, and a spasm shook her at his touch. Something crackled between them; an intensely charged atmosphere that reminded Lucy of the moment just before a rampaging electrical storm broke.

He moved away abruptly to the other side of the room, where he spread her pelisse out on a sofa to dry. 'What do you mean to do now?' he asked.

She fought to speak naturally. 'Kirstie wants me to throw myself on Hugh Sinclair's mercy, but I cannot bring myself to do that. Tomorrow, I shall try to think of something. But as for tonight . . .' She stopped, and looked about the room.

'It would not be wise or proper for you to stay here alone with me, Lucy,' he said quietly.

The blood drummed in her ears at the thought, but she forced herself to give him a wan smile. 'Would it be wise and proper for me to sleep in a ditch?'

He did not return her smile. 'Sit down by the fire while I think.'

She obeyed, and he drew a chair up to the fire for himself. She had to fight an undermining feeling of belonging, a sense of rightness in sharing his hearth like this.

Alistair broke the silence. 'I shall ask old Morag Donaldson to come and stay here with us. Her daughter will be glad of the extra space in her cottage. But I cannot ask Morag to come out in this weather, so we must wait until the rain ceases, Lucy.'

He rose and lit a fir candle, and went through into what she remembered was the kitchen. A little later, she could hear him moving about, and she shook off the languor that had been creeping over her and went to join him. He was standing before the fire, stirring something inside a cooking-pot.

She smiled at the look of concentration upon his face. 'What is that?'

'Broth,' he answered.

'Did you make it?'

'Ay.'

'I don't know how to make broth, or anything else,' she confessed humbly.

'No, I did not suppose that you did.' His voice was dry.

'I'm quite useless,' she said soberly. 'Fiona is right. I'm like—like some sea creature which has been removed from its natural environment, which has never learnt to walk and has forgotten how to swim. I wish . . . ' Her mouth trembled. *'I wish I were Fiona!'*

She had never meant to say it. The cry had been torn from her by her desperate need, by his physical nearness and by the bitter memory of how everything else had ceased to exist for him when he saw Fiona being carried out of the cottage by Neil Buchanan.

She heard him make a sound deep in his throat. She was not aware that either of them had moved, so naturally did they come together. She had the odd feeling, as his arms enclosed her, that her whole being merged with his, fusing into one. When he let her go again, the shock was as devastating as if a limb had been severed.

'You'll marry Fiona, won't you?' she asked bleakly.

He moved away from her, his arms stiffly by his sides. 'Ay, I'll marry Fiona.'

She moistened her lips, staring at him with a pain which she knew was reflected in her eyes. She could not resist the agonising impulse to probe the wound even further. 'And nothing could possibly happen to make you change your mind?'

'I shall see and make sure that nothing does happen.'

'You must—love her very much,' Lucy said forlornly.

The lines of his face had taken on a gaunt look, and his eyes were empty. 'It is love of a kind, Lucy. She is a weak, wayward, reckless child who needs to be protected from herself.' He stared at a spot above Lucy's head, and added with deliberation, 'I promised Kirstie I would marry her and look after her.'

Lucy stood motionless. So it was not love which bound him to Fiona, but a promise extracted from him by her mother. And, without putting it into words, he had come as close as he probably ever would to admitting that what he felt for Lucy herself was far more than physical attraction.

'You promised Kirstie . . . ' she echoed. 'Why?'

'Because, at the time, I had no way of knowing that

. . .' He stopped, and went on, 'I had ever been fond of Fiona, and had I not still regarded her as a child at the time I would doubtless have thought of wedding her, even without Kirstie asking it of me. It was no sacrifice to do so, and it meant such a great deal to Kirstie. I owe her far more than I could ever repay.'

'In—In what way?'

'Two years ago my mother became very ill. It was feared to be the smallpox, and no one would come near the house. One could not blame them. But Kirstie did not hesitate. She insisted on moving in, and without a thought for herself she fought like a demon to save my mother.'

Yes, Lucy thought, Kirstie *would* do something like that. But oh, to have demanded in return a commitment from him to marry Fiona!

'My mother could not be saved,' she heard Alistair go on, 'even though it was not the smallpox after all. But people, once frightened, are not easily reassured, and out of respect for their fear Kirstie and I stayed here alone for weeks, to show them that we did not intend passing on any infection. It forged a strong bond between us. She told me of her fears for Fiona should anything happen to herself.'

'And so—you will marry Fiona to repay a debt!' Anger washed over Lucy. 'You will sacrifice yourself, throw away your whole future, because of a promise to Kirstie! I have learnt a good deal about Fiona . . .'

'Then you will have learnt that, like an unreasoning child, she will blunder into any kind of danger if she thinks she has spied the promise of an easy life and pretty trinkets. Ay, Lucy, I know Fiona too.' He smiled grimly. 'I know that she toyed with the notion of going to the factor, and I know also that she will have tried to persuade you to take her to Dunrobin Castle. I would not have allowed her to do either.'

Bitterly, Lucy burst out, 'And I—I count for nothing, do I? Not with Kirstie, and not with you! You will never say it, so I shall do so—I love you, Alistair!'

A spasm twisted his mouth. 'Ay. But you are strong, Lucy.' The silence which followed between them seemed to spin into an eternity. He broke it abruptly, his voice as matter of fact as if she had never interrupted with that outburst.

'For all her waywardness, Fiona minds what I say. Even when I gave my promise to Kirstie, we were living within the shadow of the land clearances, and Kirstie knew that if Fiona were faced with hardship and adversity she would use her beauty to find a way out. But with me, she will be protected against her own nature.'

'It—isn't fair—that Fiona should get everything—because she is wayward . . .'

He took her chin in his hand, his forefinger moving gently along the line of her lower lip. 'And would it be fair, Lucy, if I were to break my promise and reject her for you? For the privileged sister who was given chances Fiona would sell her soul for? The sister she already resents and envies so bitterly?' He shook his head. 'That, Fiona could not bear. It would lead her to the kind of reckless behaviour that would break Kirstie's heart.'

Lucy turned away from him. The wind had dropped and the rain had begun to ease off. She moved out of the kitchen into the other room, and stood by the fire, staring unseeingly into the flames.

After a while Alistair joined her. 'The rain has almost stopped. I shall go and fetch Morag now.'

'Yes.' She raised her eyes to him. 'Will you—tell me something? That evening when you kissed me as I left Kirstie's house. Do you remember? You had mistaken me for Fiona . . .'

'I did not mistake you for anyone.' He looked into her eyes and then glanced away. 'When I said that a cross had been placed upon us I was quoting one of our bards, and I did not have the clearance of the land in mind.'

The cross of a doomed and hopeless love, she thought with anguish. It would have been better if they had never met.

'The other times I kissed you,' he went on, 'did not count. But that night it was real, and I should not have done it. It was a longing too strong to fight. You looked so forlorn and defeated as you left Kirstie's cottage . . . So I allowed myself to weaken, and it was as I knew it would be. Just as I knew it would be.'

He lifted a hand and touched her face, his fingers moving along the smoothness of her cheek and lingering for a moment upon her mouth. 'And that is all there is ever to be. You understand, Lucy?'

He made his own rules, and lived by them. He would not deviate from what he saw as honour and duty. 'Yes,' she said with pain. 'Yes, I understand.'

He left her then, without a further word.

It was as I knew it would be. She remembered the strangely familiar feeling of his hands upon her body and his mouth claiming hers. It would have been unendurable if it had all been meant for Fiona.

A sound escaped her, half-way between a sob and a bitter laugh. To think she had once vowed to fight Fiona for him, and had even imagined the girl might have secrets in her past which would cause Alistair to cast her off! Fiona's very weaknesses kept him committed to her.

Lucy's glance roamed about the room. Fiona would live there with him one day soon. As tacksman, he held a lease, and could not be evicted like the crofters. How could she have forgotten that he would naturally take in Kirstie, too, and Willy Macleod? Whether he could afford it or not, he would take them in.

It was a bitterly ironical thought that she had burnt her bridges to no purpose. Whatever happened, her family would have the security of Alistair's home and the protection of his status as tacksman. While she herself would have to dwell alone in a no man's land, wanted by no one, mattering to no one.

CHAPTER TEN

LUCY AWAKENED slowly, the faint, unfamiliar scent of wood smoke in her nostrils. Drowsily, she lay and waited for her long-accustomed morning ritual to begin. But there was no discreet footfall of a servant, no gentle drawing back of the curtains, no steaming dish of chocolate with which to soften the beginning of a new day.

Memory came flooding back. She was in the house of Alistair Munro, and far removed from the life of luxury she had known as the daughter of Hugh Sinclair. Anguish and a sense of desolation swept over her as she remembered fully how alone she was now.

She rose and went to the window, flinging the shutters wide. Mist curled over the hills, draping itself about the crests, sliding down along the slopes to hover over the strath like an outstretched hand.

The beshawled figure of an old woman appeared round the side of the house. Morag Donaldson had come readily to Alistair's cottage the night before, but she spoke no English and seemed to have very little concern left for the world. Her seamed old face had been incurious about the circumstances which had brought her to sleep in Alistair's house; she had nodded and smiled, and if she was aware that Lucy had been brought up as Hugh Sinclair's daughter, she was totally uninterested in the reasons for her seeking sanctuary with his tacksman. Now, like some small industrious ant, Morag was scooping up kindling and muttering to herself. Lucy closed the window and sat down on the bed, staring in front of her. What was she to do now, where to go?

She might conceivably obtain a position as a governess in Edinburgh. She was well skilled in such useless social accomplishments as singing and dancing, she was fluent in French, could paint modestly well in water colours and was able to play the pianoforte tolerably well. She had been educated as a lady, so the only way she could possibly earn her own living would be by passing on her own skills to others. Her mouth set grimly. She would change her name and try to put the past behind her. There was no other way.

She went over to a table on which stood a basin and ewer. The shock of the icy water as she began to wash reminded her even more forcefully of the way in which her circumstances had changed. Life was going to be cold and bitter from now on.

Alistair was in the kitchen, stirring porridge in a pot on the stove. The sight of him, large and masculine, his black hair falling forward over his brow, his movements impatient as he performed his domestic tasks, brought a painful tightness to her throat. She longed to take the work from him, to serve him in some way. Instead, she leant against the table.

'I've decided to seek employment in Edinburgh,' she said quietly. 'Would it be possible for you to convey me there? I believe you possess a pony trap . . .'

'Yes, I could take you to Edinburgh,' he answered without expression. 'But not until the end of the week. I have to attend a set in a few days' time.'

'A set?'

'An auction,' he explained. 'My lease is due for renewal, and I have to bid for it. It is no more than a formality, but it has to be observed.' He stirred the porridge with more concentration than the task seemed to warrant, and finally looked up to meet her glance. 'How will you live until you find employment?'

She stretched out her hand so that the light fell upon the stone of her ring, a birthday present from the Sinclairs. 'I shall have no need for such adornments from now on,' she said lightly. 'It may as well support me until I can support myself.'

He moved away from the stove and studied her, his eyes sombre. 'A pity it is that I ever went to London, Lucy, and that I ever thought to appeal to you to help your people. You would have been the better for believing yourself still to be the child of Hugh Sinclair.'

And never to have known Kirstie? she thought. *Never to have known you, or the pain of loving? No, Alistair. The court balls and assemblies, the luxury of Lucy Sinclair's life, none of that could ever have compensated for not knowing you . . .*

Her smile was a little uneven, and her voice shook slightly as she replied, 'Do you remember that day, Alistair? You'd terrorised the servants, and when you came into my drawing-room I could see why they had been too afraid to throw you out! You looked so wild and out of place in Hugh Sinclair's house . . .'

'Ay, fine I remember,' he said softly. 'You were so grand yourself, so cool and disdainful, and you scorned to shake me by the hand. And I wanted to put my arms round you and force you to acknowledge me . . .'

He broke off. His jaw was tightly clenched, as though he had already said too much and feared that he might say more. For a moment their eyes locked in a gaze which held torment and hopelessness, and then he turned away. 'We'd best have breakfast,' he said curtly. 'Will you set the table while I go and look for Morag?'

She found bowls and placed them on the table, and afterwards she crossed to the stove, giving the porridge a tentative stir. She heard the outer door opening, and half-turned, just as Fiona's voice rang out.

'*Ciamar a Tha*, Alis—'

Fiona's mouth closed like a trap, and her eyes became glittering slits as they rested on Lucy. '*You*! What are you doing here?'

Lucy scraped the ladle against the edge of the pot, playing for time. 'I had nowhere else to go last night, Fiona,' she began at last.

'Do not lie to me, you shameless baggage!' Fiona spat the words out. 'Nowhere to go, with all the rooms in the big house empty?'

'I could not go there, Fiona. I have said farewell to the world of the Sinclairs.'

'You expect me to believe that?' Fiona's face was contorted with passion. 'You really expect me to believe that you have given up all the wealth and the privilege of being the Sinclairs' daughter, so that you might come and share our misery in the clachan?'

'I have quarrelled with Hugh Sinclair,' Lucy said wearily. 'Please calm down and let me explain.'

'I know fine what you are about!' Fiona shouted. 'You want my man, and you think you have seen a way of persuading Hugh Sinclair to buy him for you . . .'

'Fiona!' Alistair's voice cut like a whiplash through her tirade. He stood framed in the doorway, his brows drawn together in a scowl. 'What you have just said is not only degrading to Lucy; it is also an insult to me.'

'Well, I refuse to apologise!' Her eyes flashed defiant fury at him. 'If anyone should receive an apology, it is I! I called here to tell you that Mother wishes to see you, and I find that the two of you have spent the night together!'

'In company with Morag Donaldson,' Alistair corrected firmly. 'Lucy stayed the night here because she had nowhere else to go. What is more, she will continue to stay here until I can drive her to Edinburgh.'

Like a child, Fiona seized on a fresh grievance. 'You have never taken me to Edinburgh!'

'Nor will I this time. Lucy is going there to seek work with which to support herself.'

'Why *should* she support herself?' Fiona demanded with simmering resentment. 'Mother says she has but to weep and beg for forgiveness for Hugh Sinclair to take her back.'

'I shall never do that,' Lucy said quietly.

Fiona hunched her shoulders. 'Well, I think you are worse than a fool, and you are making a great deal of trouble for us by not returning to your fine folk at Dunrobin Castle.' Envy now vied with hostility in her expression. 'I dare say you will meet someone in Edinburgh who will offer you marriage and a gracious life. The gods have ever favoured you, have they not? And they say there are many opportunities to be had in the city.'

'The only opportunity I expect, or want, is the offer of work as a governess,' Lucy told her.

Fiona responded with a snort of contempt and disbelief, but she had no further opportunity to voice her hostility, for Morag Donaldson entered the kitchen at that moment. She dropped her armful of kindling by the stove with a triumphant grunt and broke into a spate of Gaelic. She was still talking as Alistair took her arm and led her to a seat near the stove.

During a brief lull in her monologue, Alistair asked shortly, 'Why does Kirstie wish to see me, Fiona?'

'There is a dispute among the men in the clachan over timber for the repairing of their houses. You must decide the matter.'

He nodded and took his place at the table, and they ate in silence. Immediately after breakfast, he left the cottage with Fiona. The girl gave Lucy one last look of hostility and resentment as she followed him. Lucy crossed to the window and watched them walk towards Bencraig. Fiona's hand rested possessively upon his arm.

With a kind of painful pleasure, Lucy picked up a shirt which Alistair had made an attempt to mend and which he had obviously given up in despair. With small, loving stitches she set about repairing the worn patches on it.

Morag had fallen into the abrupt sleep of old age when Kirstie called at the house. Lucy had been expecting her, and yet she was taken unawares by the rush of emotion which filled her at the sight of her worn face and weary eyes. She bent her head over her mending. For a while Kirstie watched her in silence, and when Lucy glanced up it was to see a look of perfect understanding in her mother's eyes.

'It cannot be, child,' Kirstie said quietly. 'He is not for you.'

Lucy felt her lips trembling. 'I know . . .'

'He would have wed Fiona by now, had Willy and I not needed her help so sorely. There are times when my hands are that swollen I cannot work.'

Lucy said nothing, but kept her head bent over her mending. After a while, Kirstie spoke again. 'You must go away, Lucy. Willy is to set off for Dunrobin Castle this morning.'

Her head jerked up. 'I won't go with him!'

'Ay, I know that, foolish child. I have written to Hugh Sinclair, reminding him of his duty to you. I have asked him to come back for you.'

'He would never do that! He is a cold, proud man. He cares nothing for me.'

'We shall see.'

Lucy shook her head. 'I am to leave for Edinburgh at the end of the week. I shall find employment there as a governess.'

Kirstie smiled faintly. 'You would not last above a week as a governess. You are too proud to learn servility. You have been brought up to command, not to obey.' She rose, and looked down at Lucy. 'Go away from here. Go as soon as you can. Changes are coming; there is unease in the valley. The men of Bencraig go on repairing their houses as though it still mattered. They repair their ploughs as though there will be ploughing to do in the spring. But in their hearts they all know that there is to be no tomorrow for them in Strathraora.'

And you, Lucy thought, are concerned for Fiona's tomorrows. You are afraid that if I stayed, Alistair might break his promise to marry her. How little you know him . . .

Aloud, she said quietly, 'I shall leave at the end of the week.'

Kirstie moved to the door. And as Lucy watched her go she accepted, finally, that Fiona would always have a place in Kirstie's heart into which she herself would never be allowed to intrude.

That afternoon news reached Lucy, through Alistair, that two other villages had been forcibly cleared of Hugh Sinclair's tenants. 'McKenzie, the minister, proclaimed it a merciful dispensation of Providence,' he said, his voice raw with bitter rage. 'It was God's way, he said, of bringing the people to repentance, rather than have them damned to eternal hell-fire.'

During the hours that followed, she could see the bands of people thus brought to repentance, as they wandered pitifully across the glens in search of sanctuary. Her anger rose to match Alistair's, and mixed with it was fear.

But Bencraig remained unmolested. Had Hugh Sinclair changed his mind about clearing its people from the land? she wondered. Could it be that he felt some affection for her after all, and that after his anger had died he felt concerned that she should not be caught up in violence?

Time moved on remorselessly, eating away the precious few days that she was to spend under Alistair's roof. She seldom saw him, for he spent most of the day out of doors, and often returned late to the house. In the evenings Morag, who had slept the day away, eagerly engaged him in conversation, and he obviously deemed it both safe and wise to give all his attention to her.

On the day before Lucy was to leave for Edinburgh, Alistair journeyed to a nearby town to bid for the renewal of his lease, so that Lucy was alone with Morag when Neil Buchanan called at the cottage.

At sight of the factor, Morag cowered into a corner. Lucy's heart gave an uneasy lurch, but she forced herself to address him steadily. 'Well, Mr Buchanan?'

'Miss Sinclair.' He bowed, and she flushed at what she took to be mockery. But then he went on in a silky tone, 'I doubt if it would please your father to know that you are living under the tacksman's roof. The old woman looks near-blind to me, and is very likely deaf as well.'

Lucy's flush deepened, but for a different reason now. She dismissed his insinuations, for there were other matters to occupy her thoughts. Surely the man must know by now that Hugh Sinclair had cast her off?

'I bring you a letter from your father,' he continued. 'It requires a response, and one of my men will be calling for it at midday.'

She took the letter he was holding out to her, striving to retain an impassive front. The longer he remained in ignorance of the truth, she sensed, the safer they would be in Bencraig.

'Thank you, Mr Buchanan.' Her tone dismissed him.

He stood his ground. 'Miss Sinclair—Lucy—I'll be frank with you. You know that I wish to marry you, and it is a match which would have your father's blessing. He has promised to turn over to me all the revenue from his Scottish estate if we married.'

She studied him with a thoughtful frown. It seemed that, for some reason, Hugh Sinclair was continuing to pretend that she was his daughter.

Her silence had obviously encouraged Buchanan, for he took a step closer to her. 'The reason why you turned down my proposal before is quite clear to me now. You have formed an infatuation for the tacksman. But you know that a match between you could never be, and I am willing to forgive the fact that you have lived here with him . . .'

Shaking with rage, she gave him a push that sent him tripping over the threshold. Then she slammed the door in his face and bolted it.

He gave an angry laugh. 'Think about my offer, Miss Sinclair! If the whole truth about your shameless behaviour were to come out, I very much doubt if anyone else would consider taking you!'

Still trembling, she sat down and broke the seal on the letter. As she began to read, it was almost as though Hugh Sinclair were there in the room with her, talking to her in his cold, unemotional voice.

> You will, by now, have experienced life on the level of your own kind. I know you only too well to imagine that you have been anything but wretched and uncomfortable. It was never my intention to cast you off, but merely to frighten you and to force you to discard your foolish, sentimental notions about your family.
>
> Bencraig must and will be cleared. The people have had the Warrant read to them and they know that they must go. I want to make it plain to you that, whatever you may decide, Bencraig will be cleared,

for the sheep are already on their way.

No one here at Dunrobin Castle knows the truth about your birth. I have merely told them that my daughter was unwell and had had to be left at Strathraora House, and Kirstie Macleod assured me in her letter that none of my tenants knows the truth either. The people merely believe that you and I have quarrelled. Join us here at Dunrobin, and no more will ever be said about the matter. At noon, one of Buchanan's men will arrive with a carriage to convey you here. Whether you decide to come or not, the clearing of Bencraig will begin shortly after midday.

Lucy refolded the letter and moved to the window, staring outside to where Bencraig nestled amid the blackened heather. It was not often that life offered one a second chance such as had just been extended to her.

And it was not as though Kirstie would be destitute. She and Fiona and Willy would be taken in by Alistair. Lucy smiled bleakly to herself. She knew the advice which Kirstie would give her: *'Go back to where you belong.'*

But Kirstie would be wrong. How could she ever again belong to the London Society which she used to accept as her rightful setting? If she returned to the Sinclairs, it would be an act of cowardice, because she had been unable to face life without the luxury they could give her. But, then, would there be anything particularly praiseworthy in embracing a life of servitude as someone's governess, and under false pretences at that, hiding behind a false identity and a manufactured past? I belong nowhere, she acknowledged the truth once again. My choice is merely in which world I am to become an outsider . . .

She had still not decided what to do when Alistair came home. One glance at his face drove her own dilemma from her mind. He had the dazed look of a man whose world had crashed about him.

'Alistair! What is it? What has happened?'

He gave her an unseeing look. 'They did the one thing I did not expect,' he muttered. 'The one thing I could do nothing to fight against . . .'

'What happened?'

He spoke in harsh, staccato bursts. 'I was outbid. By someone acting for Buchanan. Everyone knew what was going on. But they were within the law. God in heaven, there was a Munro here centuries before a Sinclair set foot on the land . . . We are as much part of this strath as those hills out there!'

She went to him, touching his arm. 'Alistair . . .'

With a groaning sound, he caught her to him and held her tightly. 'It was a charade, to deprive me of my land! Buchanan is to be made a gift of it. It is to be his reward for clearing Hugh Sinclair's sub-tenants from their homes.'

He put her away from him and groped in his pocket, drawing out a crumpled document. It seemed to her that the action and the words which he began to read out from the warrant brought with it a sharp, physical pain.

'You are ordered by decree and sentence to remove yourself, servants, goods and gear forth and from the said land.' He flung the document on the floor, and the harshness in his voice intensified. 'Bidding for one's land has ever been a formality. But Hugh Sinclair used the letter of the law to rob me of my land. Land which my forefathers have held for generations.'

The full implication of what had happened struck her for the first time. 'Oh no, Alistair . . . ' she whispered. 'And Kirstie? What is to become of her now?' Her glance sought the clock upon the mantelshelf. 'Bencraig is to be cleared in one hour!' She dug in her pocket for the letter which she had received from Hugh Sinclair, and thrust it at him.

As he read it, she saw his expression crystallising in a look of fierce resolve and reckless action. 'No,' he said with quiet menace. 'By God, *no*.'

He thrust her aside and went to the door. She ran after him, afraid of what he meant to do. He had seemed fully capable of challenging Buchanan and all his hired men single-handedly. But he was already running towards the clachan, beyond the reach of her voice.

Lucy was about to set off after him when a carriage swept up and the driver sprang from it, blocking her way. 'I am to take you to Dunrobin Castle, miss,' he addressed her respectfully. 'Mr Buchanan says it is the master's orders. He is waiting to have a private word with you before you leave.'

So neither Hugh Sinclair nor Buchanan had had any doubts that she would fall in with their respective demands. The thought slipped into her mind and was immediately crowded out by fear for Alistair and concern for Kirstie.

'Get out of my way!' she ordered tersely.

'But, miss . . .'

'Out of my way!' She pushed him aside and ran towards Bencraig.

Alistair was addressing the people in the Gaelic when she reached the clachan. She could understand nothing of what he said, but his meaning was made clear by the harshness of his voice, by the grim look in his eyes and by the growing hardening of determination among the crofters. They were to resist Buchanan's men to the bitter end.

Lucy pushed her way through the crowd to where Kirstie was standing. 'It would be madness to resist Buchanan this time!' she said urgently. 'He'll come better prepared than he did before. He is a cruel man

—he would enjoy using violence. Someone may be hurt, and it would be to no purpose, for he cannot fail to win!'

Kirstie shook her head. 'We will resist, Lucy, even though we cannot win. We are not dogs, to be driven from the land by the crack of Buchanan's whip. We may lose our homes and our livelihood, but we will keep our pride!'

The crowd began to disperse. Lucy stood by helplessly as the men, led by Alistair, armed themselves with picks and hoes and anything else that could be used as a weapon. Women and children hurried away to barricade themselves inside their houses, and Lucy bowed to the inevitable and followed Kirstie's hurrying figure.

Inside her mother's cottage, Lucy watched as Fiona and Kirstie gathered their possessions and put them outside, ready for the time when Buchanan would have beaten them into submission. Fiona's eyes were filled with fear and desperation. She looked at Lucy, and her face twisted. 'What is she doing here?' she asked her mother sharply.

Kirstie stared at Lucy as though, for the first time, she had become fully aware of her presence. 'You must leave us, child! Away now! I know that Hugh Sinclair has sent for you. These are our affairs, and not yours. Go now, to your own people!'

Lucy knew that her words had been deliberately hurtful and meant to shock her into leaving, and yet she felt as if she had been slapped in the face. She left the cottage, her shoulders bowed, and walked to where the men were waiting for Buchanan. She could feel tension building up like a threatened storm.

Alistair saw her, and frowned. 'You should not be here! Go back to my house, Lucy!'

'And sit and wonder what is happening to you and Kirstie?' she demanded, fear cracking her voice. 'If this is not my fight, at least let me witness the fate which is to befall the—people—I love . . .'

Before Alistair could say any more, a shout went up. Buchanan was coming with his men.

Contrary to Lucy's prediction, the factor had clearly not expected resistance of any kind this time. A look of surprise crossed his face when he found himself confronted by a solid body of men, forcing him to halt.

'Have you all taken leave of your wits?' he shouted. 'You know you cannot stop what must be done, for the law is on our side!'

'The people have nowhere to go. How are they to live?' Alistair demanded.

Buchanan shrugged. 'Rather than make trouble for yourself, Munro, you should be packing up your possessions and seeing after your own affairs! Step aside, man, and let us through!'

'I know your master cares for no one, as long as he himself grows richer!' Alistair hurled at him. 'But if the people are to lose their homes, they must be compensated!'

'As to that,' Buchanan called out, 'Mr Sinclair has empowered me to offer compensation, so stand aside!'

'How much compensation?' Alistair demanded, gesturing to his men to hold the line before the advance of Buchanan's hirelings.

The factor shrugged. 'The allowance is three shillings for the timbers of each cottage to be burnt.'

Lucy saw the flesh upon Alistair's face tightening with the force of his fury, so that the bones stood out prominently. He raised the pick-axe with which he had armed himself, and growled, 'Come one step closer, Buchanan, and you are a dead man!'

The factor withdrew slightly, his eyes glittering with rage. 'You will pay for planning this resistance, Munro! You are breaking the law, and you know it!'

'It is a law which deserves to be broken,' Lucy cried passionately, 'if it can authorise the payment of such paltry compensation for people's losses!'

Buchanan's malevolent gaze went to her. 'As for you, my fine madam, you will live to regret the refusal of my offer! You thought I remained in ignorance of what passed between you and your father, did you not?' His voice quivered with spite. 'My cousin honoured me with his confidence. He told me of the last chance he was giving you. He said that if you refused to go to Dunrobin, that if you persisted in ranging yourself with these people, I was to show you no mercy! "Drive her from my land," were his instructions. "Drive her into the sea if necessary, but never let her be heard of again!" Oh yes, you will be sorry that you did not accept me, that you deprived me of all the revenues from Strathraora!'

He signalled to his men to withdraw, and they turned away. 'He will be back with more men,' Alistair said levelly. 'But we shall resist until fair compensation has been paid.'

The crofters voiced their approval, and then dispersed to prepare for the inevitable struggle. Alistair turned to Lucy. 'This is no place for you,' he said in a grim voice.

'Isn't it? You heard what Buchanan said. It is clear that Hugh Sinclair regards me as an embarrassment to himself. I have no doubt at all that Society will be told I have died in Scotland. That is why he does not wish me ever to be heard of again. Whether you and Kirstie like it or not, my lot has been cast with yours!'

He sighed. 'Go, then, and take shelter with Kirstie. I mean to ride to all the neighbouring clachans and summon help. We are together in this, for what happens in Bencraig today will happen in other villages tomorrow.'

'They could put you in prison for doing that,' she

pointed out fearfully. 'They will say that you incited the people to riot . . .'

'I know,' he returned carelessly. 'There is no help for it.' His expression hardened. 'I should have done that long since, instead of seeking to persuade Hugh Sinclair to show some pity.'

Lucy had turned away to walk to Kirstie's cottage when his voice stopped her. She looked over her shoulder at him. His expression was nakedly revealing, his eyes dark with wanting and needing, the cast of his mouth tender.

'*A ghràidh mo chridhe*,' he said softly.

'What does that mean?'

His lashes shuttered his eyes. 'It means—Thank you for the mending of my shirt.'

Unable to answer, knowing instinctively that it meant far more, she moved towards her mother's cottage.

Kirstie merely sighed when Lucy told her what Buchanan had said, and then went on preparing for whatever lay ahead. It seemed to be part of her strength that she accepted what could not be altered, without lamenting over it.

Men from neighbouring clachans began to arrive, in trickles at first and then in a steady stream. They gathered grim-faced behind a barricade at the foot of the hill to wait for Buchanan's men, but as the afternoon wore on and the factor made no appearance, the tension left them. Someone had brought bagpipes and began to play a lively air, so that it occurred to Lucy that an ignorant outsider might mistakenly suppose they had gathered for a *ceilidh*.

The light was just beginning to fail when the music stopped abruptly, and a shout went up that Buchanan was coming. Lucy, watching anxiously through the windows of Kirstie's cottage, saw at once why it had taken the factor so long to return. He had come back at the head of an army of sheriff's officers and underlings.

'Give yourself up, Alistair Munro!' a voice shouted into the silence that had fallen. 'I have authority to arrest you! Come quietly, and tell these people to comply with the law!'

'We shall continue to resist,' Alistair called out, 'until adequate compensation has been paid for the loss of the people's houses and their pasturage!'

The sheriff's officers began to advance. Pandemonium broke out: men cursed and screamed as the swinging butts of the officers' muskets caught them on the head, dogs barked frantically, and children in the cottages shrieked with terror. A volley of shots fired over the heads of the crofters added to the cacophony of sound.

Fiona was weeping with fear. Kirstie held her tightly, and Lucy stood alone by the window, involved in what was going on, yet knowing herself to be a mere onlooker.

A shout of despair went up as the officers and Buchanan's men succeeded in breaking up the ranks of the crofters. And then a madness seemed to take hold of the invading forces, the mania of a mob driven by a wanton thirst for destruction.

They fell viciously upon the houses. Pots and pans, meal-kists, presses and stores of food supplies were flung into the burn, with weeping women stumbling after to recover what they could. One by one the cottages were being set on fire, forcing their occupants to flee into the night. Straining her eyes, Lucy could see by the light of the flames that Alistair and a few indomitable crofters were fighting on against the overwhelming odds, but the majority of the villagers ran to their cottages to make sure that their families were safe.

Fiona screamed as the door of Kirstie's cottage came crashing down, and three of Buchanan's men lurched inside, bent upon destruction. Kirstie said something to them in the Gaelic; her voice was dignified, her eyes unflinching as she faced them. Something like shame flickered in their eyes, and they allowed the three women to leave the cottage unmolested.

The sky was now alight with the glow of burning buildings, the air thick with smoke and with noise. People squatted despairingly upon the bare hillsides and watched their houses burn.

Lucy left Fiona and Kirstie, and ran through the crowds in search of Alistair. Arms enclosed her, holding her in a hard grip, and she looked up into Neil Buchanan's face. It was difficult to remember the ingratiating charm he had employed towards her in the past, for now it was a cruel mask, his eyes glittering slits of malice and triumph.

'Looking for your Highlander, are you?' he inquired mockingly. 'Let me take you to him!'

His hand was upon her arm, forcing her through the darkness to the barricade the crofters had erected at the edge of the village. There, his face deathly pale, his body still, Alistair lay sprawled on the ground.

Lucy put a hand to her trembling lips and heard Buchanan's laughter ringing harshly in her ears.

'I didn't say he was alive, did I?'

CHAPTER ELEVEN

NUMBLY, LUCY fell on her knees beside Alistair's motionless body. The wail of a lone piper playing a lament on the hillside seemed to fill the valley. The light from the burning houses flickered upon Alistair's features and she leant forward and touched his face with trembling fingers. At first she thought she had imagined the slight movement of his lips, that it had been a trick of the firelight. And then his pale eyelids flickered momentarily, unmistakably.

'He's—alive,' she breathed.

'Only just,' Buchanan corrected. His voice became wary. 'You realise it was an accident, of course. The men were ordered to fire over the heads of the crofters. Munro's shooting was an accident.'

He turned away from her and shouted to his henchmen to finish up and move out. Their work was done.

By the light of the fires, Lucy gently drew Alistair's shirt back from the wound in his side. She ripped the flounces from her petticoat to stem the bleeding, and all the while her lips moved in a prayer that he might live. She was only half aware of Buchanan's men and the sheriff's officers departing, and of the people of Bencraig pitifully trying to salvage what they could from their burning houses.

She heard Fiona's voice raised in hysteria, calling out to Alistair, but she did not pause in what she was doing. Then Fiona was there on her knees beside her, sobbing bitterly and about to throw herself upon him.

After her initial shock, Lucy's mind was sharp and hard as flintstone. She had no pity to spare for Fiona's fear and grief. Nothing mattered but Alistair. He must not be allowed to lose more blood. She pulled Fiona away from him, and when the girl resisted, she slapped her face.

'Leave him to me!' she cried grimly, ignoring Fiona's howl of rage and pain. 'If you want to help, fetch Kirstie and Willy, but do not touch him again!'

A bitter wind began to blow through the strath, and children wept with fright and cold as they clung to their mothers' skirts and searched hopelessly for shelter. Lucy knew that Alistair would never survive a night in the open.

She paused in dressing his wound, and glanced about her, concentrating on the chances of finding shelter for him. There was no use in trying to have him taken to his own house. Even if he survived the journey, Buchanan would doubtless have posted one of his men there, for it belonged to him now. It was his gift from Hugh Sinclair for the rape of Bencraig.

But, somehow, a place would have to be found for Alistair to spend the night. Lucy gazed back at the burning clachan. Here and there, men were succeeding in the grim fight to seize their house-timbers from the destructive tongues of the fires. But of Kirstie's cottage, she could see, there was nothing left worth salvaging.

Fiona came running towards them again, followed by Kirstie and Willy. Kirstie knelt beside Alistair and removed the dressing that Lucy had fashioned, her fingers gently probing the wound. 'I fear he will not live,' she said in a quiet voice.

'He shall live! He shall!' Lucy's hands were tightly clenched.

'The ball is very deeply lodged.'

'Then it must be removed!'

'Child,' Kirstie said gently, 'he would not survive such an operation.'

'He must not die!' Fiona wailed. 'What would become of me? He said he would see that I was never in want!'

Lucy only half heard her. She was looking with despair into Alistair's face. Already it had the unreal quality of someone whose hold upon life was slipping away. 'He shall not die!' Her voice cracked. 'I shall not let him die!' She turned her head. 'Willy!'

'Yes, miss?'

'That byre over there—the one which is no longer afire. To whom does it belong?'

'To Iain Duncan, miss. He has gone to get help to dismantle it. He will rebuild it in another place.'

'Stop him! Tell him the byre is needed for shelter for Alistair.'

'Ach, miss, Iain Duncan is that contankerous and mean, he'll not care about anyone but himself. He wants the byre dismantled so that he can stack its timbers for easy carrying.'

She thought rapidly. Then, tearing the diamond ring from her finger, she held it out to Willy. 'Offer this to Duncan in exchange for the byre!'

He blinked stupidly at her. 'But, miss . . .'

'Take it! Tell him its value is fifty guineas.'

She felt Kirstie's hand closing on her arm. 'Lucy, this is foolishness! The ring is worth a fortune! You could live for months upon what it would fetch! You must think of yourself. To sacrifice it for an old byre . . .'

'It is not merely an old byre!' Lucy interrupted passionately. 'It is shelter for Alistair, a chance for him to survive! His *only* chance. Go now, Willy, and quickly, and then return so that you may help me carry Alistair inside.' He obeyed without further argument.

Lucy saw that Fiona was regarding her resentfully. 'Alistair is not your concern,' the girl muttered. 'If anyone is to save him, it should be I! I shall nurse him myself, and take care of him . . .'

Her voice broke as she glanced down at him, lying so still and white. 'He—He looks to be already dead,' she sobbed, and Kirstie embraced her, murmuring soothing words of comfort and reassurance.

Lucy bent over Alistair once more. The small flame of life that flickered within him had burnt so low that for one fearful moment she thought it had indeed gone out altogether. But his pulse was still beating faintly, and she mouthed a little prayer.

Willy returned shortly with the news that her offer had been accepted. The byre was hers. He had brought a timber plank and two friends back with him. The three young men carefully transferred Alistair's body to the plank and carried him into the byre. It smelled strongly of the sheep it had lately housed, but all that interested Lucy was that its walls kept out the biting winds, and that the straw inside was warm and dry. Fir candles were lit. Then, under Kirstie's direction, Willy and his friends went to fetch the things that had been salvaged from her cottage.

Night had fallen completely now. Fiona sat in a corner of the byre with her head upon her knees, sobbing that Alistair was dying and that she had lost everything. For once, Kirstie was too preoccupied to offer her usual comfort. Grave-faced, she examined Alistair's wound and listened to the faint beating of his heart.

'He is very weak, Lucy,' she said quietly. 'He cannot hope to live unless the ball is removed, and how can that be done when the shock of such a thing would kill him? We have nothing to give him, not even a dram to soften the pain or clean the wound. We have no medicines, no proper food with which to keep him alive if he should survive the night. We must resign ourselves . . .'

'No!' There would be no resignation, no admitting of defeat, while the merest thread of life remained to him. Lucy's face was set determinedly as she turned to Willy.

'I want you to come with me, please. I mean to find medicine for Alistair.'

'Ay, miss.' Even in her desperate urgency she registered the fact that he would never be able to adjust to the knowledge that he owed her no deference or obedience. He stood before her, ready to do her bidding without question.

She gave one last lingering glance at Alistair's face. 'Look after him,' she whispered fiercely to Kirstie. 'Don't let him die!'

Sadly, Kirstie nodded. It was clear that she thought Alistair would die, and that she had built no hopes upon Lucy being able to find medicine which would save him.

But Lucy's hurried steps were purposeful and determined as she walked across the darkened valley with Willy at her side. A clouded moon barely lit their path. The merciless wind whipped at her skirts, but she would not allow herself to be hindered by it. They moved quickly, urgently, towards Strathraora House.

The house was in darkness, its gloom silhouetted against the dully-lit hills. Lucy pounded upon the front door, and a scraping, scuffling sound finally emerged from inside the house. Then the door was opened by Mrs Bannerman, a shawl draped over her nightgown.

The housekeeper's hand flew to her mouth. 'Why, Miss Lucy!'

'Mrs Bannerman, please let us enter.'

'I—I cannot, miss.' The woman's voice quivered with agitation. 'I dare not let you in. I've had word from the master this day. My head is after spinning, for he said you are not to be allowed to set foot inside the house —and himself your own father, too! He said you were sure to come here for food and shelter . . .'

'Did he, indeed!' How little Hugh Sinclair knew her. She would rather die of exposure than take anything from him again for herself. But Alistair was a different matter. She would beg or steal, sink her own pride, if it would help to keep him alive.

'You may tell him that I forced my way in,' she said tersely. 'Move aside, Mrs Bannerman, and allow me to enter.'

The old habit of command still came easily to her, she discovered, and Mrs Bannerman's obedience now was automatic and involuntary. She wrung her hands in agitation as Lucy and Willy entered the hall.

'I need some things urgently,' Lucy said. 'Brandy, medicine, and clean sheets for dressings. No, don't fret, Mrs Bannerman. I shall find them for myself, and then you may truthfully tell the master that I stole them.'

As she moved hurriedly through the house, Lucy thought of the calculation and ruthlessness of Hugh Sinclair. From what Mrs Bannerman had said, he had not publicly unmasked her. No doubt he was afraid that, if he did, the story might reach London. But he was allowing his servants in Scotland to believe he had cruelly cast his own daughter adrift, for what did he care for the good opinion of these people? They were not important or powerful; they could do his public reputation no harm.

Bitterness and anger engulfed her as she moved from one empty room to another, remembering the people of Bencraig huddled on the bleak hillside. This vast house, used only about once every twenty years by the Sinclairs, would have provided sanctuary for so many.

But it helped nothing and no one to ponder the unfairness of life. Even now, Alistair might be dying. That thought drove everything else from her mind, and she concentrated on collecting the things he would need in his struggle for survival.

From the cellar she appropriated three bottles of Hugh Sinclair's best brandy, well aware that he would regard it as theft. He would probably be glad of an excuse to have her tried in some obscure Scottish court and transported, to where she could no longer be an embarrassment to him. No matter. The brandy would soften the pain when they removed the ball from Alistair's wound.

She found clean sheets, and took what she thought would be of most use from the medicine store—laudanum, hartshorn, and an elixir against fever. Then she called Willy to help her to carry the things, and they took their leave of a distressed Mrs Bannerman.

The lone piper was still playing his lament as they neared Bencraig, expressing the grief and hopelessness of the people who huddled on the hillside while they waited for daybreak. Fear clutched at Lucy's heart. What if she were too late; what if Kirstie had been unable to keep Alistair alive?

But when they entered the byre, she knew from Kirstie's reassuring glance that he was still clinging to life. Tension drained from her like an ebbing tide, leaving only determination. She glanced about the byre. Kirstie knelt beside Alistair, and in a corner, Fiona had fallen asleep.

The fir candles threw a flickering light over Alistair's face. His eyes were open, but clouded with pain. They cleared momentarily when he recognised her, and his lips made a painful effort at speech. She leant closer to him to hear what he said.

'Look after—Fiona. She has not—your strength . . .'

Tears clouded her eyes. 'You are not going to die!' she said harshly. 'I have brought you some brandy. You will drink some of it, Alistair; as much as you can swallow, for we mean to remove the ball from your wound, and I am afraid of giving you a large dose of laudanum in your weakened state.'

She raised the bottle to his lips, and he drank from it. There was silence in the byre as they waited for the alcohol to take effect and numb his senses. Without discussing it, all three of them knew that Alistair's survival depended utterly upon the forthcoming operation.

'Will you do it?' Lucy asked Kirstie in a low voice.

'Ach, my fingers are too swollen, child. They could not hold the knife steady. And Willy, I fear, would be no less clumsy than I. You had best remove the ball.'

'I—don't know if I can!'

'You must,' Kirstie told her firmly. 'Bring the candles closer to Alistair's side.'

Fiona was still sleeping soundly, her even breathing constrasting with the harsh, painful gasps coming from Alistair. It struck Lucy that Fiona did indeed love Alistair in her own limited way. When there was danger, when there was no hope of rescue from any other quarter, she clung to his strength. If he were no longer there, she would be lost, for Kirstie was getting old and she had her physical limitations. So, terrified of a future without him, Fiona had cried herself to sleep and left it to others to try and save him . . .

'It is time,' Kirstie said.

Desperately trying to keep her hands steady, Lucy picked up the knife. 'Hold the blade to the flame of the candle,' Kirstie ordered.

Lucy obeyed, and then heard Kirstie remark with doubt in her voice, 'Some say it helps to prevent infection.'

While Lucy was preparing the knife, Kirstie poured brandy on a piece of clean linen and wiped the edges of Alistair's wound with it. He ground out, in the Gaelic, what could only have been oaths, but he offered no resistance.

'Now, Lucy,' Kirstie said. 'Use the tip of the knife and probe the wound. See if you can reach the ball.'

Blood gushed anew from the wound as she touched it, and she had to fight against a wave of nausea. An agonising, immeasurable span of time seemed to pass as she explored with the knife and listened to Alistair's alternative groans and curses, before she encountered the resistance of metal.

'I've—found it,' she reported unsteadily.

'Now use the knife to loosen it and bring it to the surface.'

Again, fresh bleeding started so that it was impossible to see what she was doing. She tried to keep panic at bay and concentrate on what she was doing. Alistair's body arched in a convulsive spasm and then grew still.

With the bloodstained knife in mid-air, Lucy looked at Willy, who had been holding Alistair by the shoulders to restrain him. 'He has gone,' her half-brother muttered.

Her glance moved slowly, like that of an automaton, to Alistair's face. In the candle-light it had a waxen hue. A raw, savage cry was torn from her lips.

'Stop that!' Kirstie ordered sharply. 'You are fools, both of you. He has but fainted, for he could no longer take the pain. Work quickly now, Lucy, and dig out the ball!'

He was alive—Kirstie had said so! Lucy tried to close her mind to everything but that thought as she struggled to prise the ball from the wound. At last she brought it to the surface, and as she handed it to Willy, she saw Kirstie placing her ear against Alistair's chest.

'Ay, there is a heartbeat,' she reported.

Lucy looked at her in numb shock. 'You mean—

you did not know? When you said he had merely lost consciousness . . .'

'Dead or alive, it would not have helped him if you had stopped digging for the ball. Now, Lucy, bind up his wound. I am going to try and find feathers to burn, so that we may revive him for long enough to give him more brandy mixed with honey and milk.'

Alistair did regain consciousness for a brief moment, but drifted off again almost immediately after he had swallowed a mouthful of the draught. Lucy made him as comfortable as she could, and sat down beside him.

She stayed by his side all that night, refusing to try to sleep, intermittently placing her ear to his chest for the sound of a faint but reassuring heartbeat. Towards morning, he seemed no longer to be so deeply unconscious, for he was shivering with cold. She wished she had thought to bring some warm woollen blankets from Strathraora House, for those salvaged from Kirstie's cottage were old and threadbare. Lucy lay down beside him and tried to warm him with her own body.

Daylight dawned harshly, with a cold sun shining from a clear blue sky, cruelly exposing the ruins of the clachan. It brought no comfort to the wretched people who had spent the night on the hillsides. They were beginning to round up what animals had not been scattered, to gather together their possessions and to prepare to leave.

Lucy had taken a pitcher and had gone to the burn to fetch water with which to sponge Alistair's face. She discovered that a rumour was rippling through the strath, warning that Buchanan's men were on their way to raze whatever was left of Bencraig, and to drive the people away—by force if necessary. The rumour was probably true, she thought. Somehow, she would have to defend their byre against Buchanan's men.

When she returned, Fiona was weeping beside Alistair, who was now conscious but seemed to be rambling. 'How—How ill he looks,' she sobbed. 'He does not know me . . .'

'Please move aside, Fiona,' Lucy said. 'I wish to sponge his face.'

Fiona's fear was replaced by jealousy. 'It is for me to look after him!' she cried.

'Very well.' Lucy watched as Fiona moistened a cloth and wiped Alistair's face. 'His dressing will need to be changed,' she pointed out afterwards. But Fiona blenched when she saw the wound, and she was more than happy to allow Lucy to take over.

Kirstie and Willy returned from outside, and Kirstie reported sombrely, 'Buchanan's men have been spied in the distance. Willy must dismantle the byre, for we shall have need of the timbers.'

Lucy looked at Alistair, who had been slightly revived by the cold water. His face was still deathly pale, his eyes unfocusing, and he muttered a few feverish words. 'He cannot be moved yet!' she protested.

'He will have to be, Lucy. It would not benefit him if the byre were to be destroyed by the factor's men. What he will need more than anything else is shelter.'

'If we are to move on,' Fiona suggested, 'could we not go to Edinburgh? I have been told that life is easy there, and I have no doubt that we would be able to obtain work . . .'

'Ach, whisht, child!' Kirstie broke in impatiently. 'What foolishness! We know nothing of city ways. When we have breakfasted, Willy must see to the dismantling of the byre.'

She sighed. 'The ewes did not yield much milk this morning. What there is will have to be saved for Alistair. For the rest of us, there are some cold oatcakes brought from the cottage. They will have to suffice.'

Anxiety gnawed at Lucy. It had not been possible to

bring food supplies from Strathraora House, for with the household and servants gone, any food on the premises belonged to Mrs Bannerman. It did not seem to her that ewes' milk would provide much sustenance for a man fighting for his life.

An idea came to her, and she said, 'Willy, before you dismantle the byre, go to Alistair's house and see what you may rescue of his livestock. A milk-cow, in particular, would be valuable, and also some hens.'

Willy nodded, but when he returned from his mission, he brought with him only Alistair's horse and some of his clothes. Buchanan had indeed posted a man at the house, he reported.

'He said I could take only clothes belonging to Alistair. All else was to be confiscated. I knew he did not have the law on his side, but what could I do? He was armed with a pistol.' Willy grinned and gestured towards the horse. 'I saw the beast in the paddock and secretly loosened the gate. When I left, I found that he had indeed strayed into the lane, as I had hoped.'

Buchanan, Lucy thought angrily, obviously considered himself quite safe in laying claim to Alistair's possessions, for the factor believed he would die of his wound. But it was fruitless to waste time and energy on anger, and she began to help with the preparations to leave the strath.

With the assistance of some of his friends, Willy dismantled the byre, stripping down the battens, salvaging anything which could be used later in the building of a shelter. Alistair's horse, and all other mounts owned by the crofters, were loaded with household goods packed in plaids and blankets. What the animals could not carry was packed into creels, to be carried on people's backs. At last they were ready to leave Bencraig.

Alistair was once again unconscious when they

strapped him carefully to the timber plank. Willy carried one end and a friend of his the other. Fiona, Lucy and Kirstie walked on either side, carrying what they could.

They gathered at the foot of the hill where the other refugees waited. Women and children were weeping. Many of the people, Lucy realised, had never been away from Bencraig in their entire lives. One old man refused to go. He ignored the arguments and pleas of his family, and long after everyone had given up trying to persuade him and had begun to walk away, Lucy turned her head briefly and glanced at him. He was sitting on the hillside, a dignified, resigned figure, preferring to die of exposure and starvation in his birthplace rather than be driven from it.

'Where are we going?' Lucy asked Kirstie as they stumbled along in the wake of the crofters.

'Nowhere. Anywhere.' Kirstie sighed deeply. 'Where is there to go?'

'There is the land by the sea . . .'

'The people fear it. So we shall keep on walking until it grows dark. Then we shall take shelter, and go on again in the morning, until we have left Hugh Sinclair's land behind us. After that—we shall see.'

As time passed, Lucy became barely conscious of the burden she was carrying. Her main concern was always for Alistair. 'Take care that you do not jolt him!' she repeatedly warned Willy and his friend. 'He cannot afford to lose more blood if his wound should open again.'

Fiona appeared to be quite content, now, to leave the nursing of Alistair to Lucy. Apart from sporadic flashes of anger or unrealistic hope, she seemed to be wholly given over to despair at the hardships with which they were being forced to cope.

It struck Lucy that, in an ironical way, she herself had been brought up to contend far more readily with adversity than Fiona had. For although she had never lacked material things, she had equally never had someone in the background on whom she could lean for emotional or moral support. Fiona, on the other hand, had always had Kirstie, who would comfort and protect and watch over her. Now they were facing a situation in which Kirstie was totally impotent, and Fiona had no inner resources on which to fall back.

For several days, Alistair seemed to hover between life and death. When the fever claimed him, Lucy removed her pelisse and covered him with it, and during those icy nights when he shivered uncontrollably, she found that there was only one way in which to keep him warm, and that was to mould her own body as closely as possible against his.

On one such occasion she realised suddenly that he had stopped shivering and was having a moment of lucidity. She tried to pull away from him, but he moved his hand and laid it against her breast, and in the moonlight streaking in through the ill-fitting timbers she could see his eyes looking deep into hers. She gazed back at him, seeing everything about him with a sharpened clarity—the way his lashes curled slightly at the tips, the way his hair fell across his brow and the expression of loss and longing in his eyes.

'Lucy,' he whispered, and then his eyes closed and he slept briefly before the fever claimed him again.

The following morning, the fever appeared to have burnt itself out, but he seemed little better otherwise. The days became a kaleidoscope of grim hardship, of being numb with anxiety over Alistair, of never having enough to eat, of always being light-headed with fatigue.

'If we could only stay for long enough in one place' —Kirstie summed up what Lucy was feeling—'for Alistair to have time to build up his strength and recover from his wound. The people need his guidance.'

It was true. The people of Bencraig seemed to be wandering with a complete lack of aim, like flotsam upon a tide, to anywhere but the sea which they feared. They would erect crude shelters against the hillside, and when the landowners' tenants came, inevitably, to harry them into moving on once again, they obeyed meekly. Without Alistair to guide them or argue their case, they lacked purpose, and went in whichever direction they happened to be chased.

Wherever they wandered, destruction and devastation was all around them. They passed villages in which the houses were still smouldering. In one glen, a pall of smoke was so dense that it obscured the hills, and the smell of burning was all-pervading. Other bands of crofters wound their way aimlessly across country.

Fiona went to speak to one such group, and when she returned, the look of despair in her eyes had been softened by hope. 'They are bound for Golspie,' she reported, 'where they have been told they will be given potatoes and barley. They have merely to show a certificate, signed by their minister, stating that they are destitute. I think we should return to Strathraora, and ask the minister to give us a like certificate, entitling us to alms.'

Lucy would have been quite prepared to beg for what now seemed to her to be luxuries, because it was a constant battle to find suitable plants which Kirstie could boil into a broth.

Willy said, 'We have walked in circles, and cannot be far away from Strathraora. Nothing would be lost if we were to return there for a certificate.'

Lucy looked at Alistair, who seemed to be asleep on the litter but could equally well have been unconscious. The fever had not recurred, and his wound had been healing well, so why was he not making any other progress? A diet of potatoes and barley might restore him to health. . . .

Then she remembered something. 'Do you not recall what the minister, McKenzie, was preaching to us the very first time Buchanan attempted to clear the clachan? He said it was God's will and that we would be damned if we resisted. I have no doubt at all that he would deem it to be our just punishment to starve! He would not sign a certificate, and it would be a useless waste of time to return to Strathraora.'

'You don't know everything!' Fiona rounded on her. 'I say we must try for a certificate!'

Kirstie touched her shoulder. 'No, Fiona. Lucy is right. We had better go on, and search for a place to shelter the night.'

Fiona cast Lucy a look of hatred, and picked up her load again. All the countryside through which they were now passing had been turned over to tenants from the South, and had been made into vast sheep-walks. Lucy could understand the bitterness that ate into the hearts of the people of Bencraig and was clearly visible upon their faces, for the pastures upon which the alien sheep were grazing had, for generations, been the grazing-grounds of their own livestock.

They stopped in the shelter of a hill, and Willy erected a rough hut with the dearly-bought timbers, while Lucy and Fiona went off in different directions to seek edible plants for Kirstie to boil. They returned with creels filled with nettles, and a while later Lucy knelt beside Alistair where he lay in a corner of the hut. She tried to persuade him to take some of the nettle broth, but he seemed not to hear her. She raised his head a little and spooned some of it into his mouth. He swallowed it, but it did nothing to revive him.

Lucy looked up at Kirstie. 'What shall we do?'

'There is nothing we can do,' Kirstie answered

quietly. 'He needs nourishment. The nettle broth cannot build up his strength, Lucy.'

'Isn't there anything . . .?'

Kirstie shook her head. 'We have a few potatoes left, but they must be saved for seed. Even if we were to sacrifice them, they would not benefit a sick man. He needs meat broth, and we have only the two ewes left. We dare not sacrifice *them*.'

It was ironic that when they had last slaughtered one of the sheep, Alistair had been too gravely ill to be able to take anything but a mixture of ewes' milk, honey and brandy.

'There might have been some of the mutton ham left,' Fiona burst out, glaring at Lucy, 'if we had not had an extra mouth to feed all this time!'

'Hush, child!' Kirstie reprimanded sternly, but her eyes were sad and compassionate as they rested upon her younger daughter's face. Lucy guessed what she was thinking—that Fiona was fast surrendering to the hardship, the poverty and the hopelessness of being moved from her home. The girl had grown thin and listless, and roused herself only occasionally to direct a hysterical outburst at Lucy, or forsook her apathy for a storm of weeping. She needed someone of authority to tell her that everything would come right again, that there was hope. She needed Alistair.

For the first time in days, Lucy became consciously aware of her own hunger as she supped the unsatisfying nettle broth. Hunger had become so much part of her existence that she had almost ceased to notice the hollow feeling at the pit of her stomach, or the fact that her only gown hung about her body in a way which would have horrified Amelia Sinclair.

The thought of Amelia brought a flash of anger. She could visualise the kind of life the Sinclairs would be living in the opulent splendour of Dunrobin Castle, neither knowing nor caring about the hardships their dispossessed tenants were facing.

The anger was still there the next morning when she bent over Alistair and saw his gaunt face. A hard resolve formed in her mind.

'Willy,' she said abruptly. 'I want your help, please.'

'Yes, miss?'

'Stop calling her "miss"!' Fiona screamed. 'Stop fawning upon her, you great dolt!'

He flushed, and ignored her, and obediently followed Lucy from the hut. He said nothing as she strode away from the settlement of crude shelters and climbed the hill. Only when she had stopped and was regarding a flock of grazing sheep, did he venture a question.

'What is it you want me to do, miss?'

'I want you to help me to steal a sheep, Willy.'

'Miss!' He had turned pale. 'They would be after transporting us, for sure!'

'Not if they do not catch us,' she returned ruthlessly. 'Look, the sheep have become used to our presence, and there is no shepherd about. We shall take that one, grazing by itself. You go round and head it off.'

Willy nodded nervously at her command, and moved over to the sheep to bring it to the ground. Lucy steeled herself to help him without flinching as he took his knife from his stocking and slaughtered the animal, and then the two of them dragged the carcass into the shelter of some bracken. They said nothing to the others, but mounted a furtive guard over the patch of bracken, and when darkness had fallen they brought the carcass to Kirstie.

Fiona lost her control when she saw the evidence of what they had done. 'We shall all be thrown into prison! She has brought us nothing but trouble!' she screamed, glaring at Lucy.

'There are times, child, when one has to risk everything in order to survive,' Kirstie told her. 'Remove the fleece, Willy, and cut up the meat so that I may make a nourishing broth.'

Some of it was salted and cured, and what could not be preserved for future use was presented to others in their party, who reciprocated by making Kirstie gifts of potatoes and barley. No one questioned where the meat had come from.

Alistair seemed to improve almost from the moment he had swallowed the broth fed to him by Lucy. She had smoothed the blankets over him and had begun to move away, when his whispered voice reached her.

'Lucy . . .'

'Yes, Alistair?'

'It meant "*Love of my heart*".' He closed his eyes. *'A ghràidh mo chridhe.'*

She saw that he had fallen asleep, and she stared down at him with a frown, wondering whether he had been rambling or if she had perhaps misheard what he had been saying. Suddenly his meaning came to her. The Gaelic words had been the ones he had murmured to her shortly before Bencraig was cleared, and he had just translated them into English. Her own heart gave a painful spasm, and she struggled hard to make her face expressionless so that it would not betray her to the others.

Alistair looked markedly stronger by the following morning. The remainder of the broth had been re-heated, and he was able to take a second helping of it. Kirstie, Lucy realised, had been right; it had only been lack of nourishment that had been preventing Alistair's recovery.

For their dinner that evening, Kirstie made a stew of potatoes and nettles cooked with some mutton-bones. Alistair was offered more broth, but he waved it away and demanded some of the stew, and he would not allow himself to be fed.

'I could have sworn an oath,' he said when he had finished eating, 'that I tasted mutton.'

Lucy grinned happily at him. It was the longest, most coherent sentence he had constructed since he was wounded.

'It was mutton,' Fiona told him. 'Lucy put all of us at risk by stealing a sheep!'

'Did she, indeed . . . ' A ghost of a smile curved his mouth, and then he frowned. He closed his eyes and lay so still that Lucy thought he had fallen asleep. Suddenly, with a tremendous effort, he levered himself from the litter and stood up, swaying alarmingly. Perspiration beaded on his forehead.

'You are still too weak, Alistair!' Lucy cried. 'Lie down again!'

Grimly he shook his head. 'Must . . . get the use of my legs back.'

'Then lean on me.'

'*I'll* help him!' Fiona cried possessively, pushing Lucy out of the way.

The improvement in his condition continued rapidly after that. With Fiona offering him support at first, he regained strength in his legs by walking around inside the shelter, and even when he was able to go a little further afield without support, Fiona clung to his side.

With her days and nights no longer occupied in attending to Alistair, Lucy could see clearly the limbo into which she had cast herself. She shared the hardship and the poverty of the others, but she was not part of them. A camaraderie existed among the people of Bencraig, and it shut her out. It was not that they were hostile to her, as Fiona was. They treated her with politeness, even with respect, but there was a barrier between them and herself which would probably never be torn down.

One warm afternoon she left Kirstie's hut and made her way to a nearby burn. It was deserted. But before long, she knew, the shepherds of whoever leased this land would discover this small settlement and move them on again. How long could they go on living this gipsy life?

She sighed, and removed her gown. She bathed and washed her hair in the burn. Dressed only in her chemise, she glanced at her reflection in the water, and smiled ironically as she considered the contrast between her present circumstances and the expensive silk undergarment with its tucks and flounces, a relic of her past life. What would her old friends say if they could see her now, with her wet hair blowing in the breeze, and with only one gown to her name? She knelt, and began to wash her gown, rubbing it against a stone. Aferwards she spread it in the sun to dry, and tried to bring some order to her hair with her fingers.

She felt the ground vibrating under someone's footfalls, and looked up, into Alistair's face. Their eyes locked for a moment, and the hunger and longing in his gave way to an expression of bleakness. He looked away.

She tried to speak steadily. 'You should not have walked the long distance from the shelter.'

He made an impatient gesture. 'I'm tired of being fussed over. It is necessary to take charge of the people. They have been drifting for too long without any purpose.'

'I know. They have very little food left. They have slaughtered most of their livestock, and some have eaten their seed potatoes.'

'Foolishness!' he growled, sitting down beside her. 'Hugh Sinclair has allotted a piece of land for them by the sea. The people are afraid of the sea; they do not understand its ways. But they must go there, for it is the only place from which they cannot be moved on again.'

'You told me once that they couldn't eke an existence from the sea.'

'They must! They shall!' In his intensity, he gripped her bare shoulder. 'I have thought of a plan . . .'

His voice tailed off, and he stared down at his hand resting against her sun-warmed flesh. Almost involuntarily, it seemed to her, his fingers began to move against her bare skin, warm and slightly unsteady, setting a pulse beating in her throat. She heard his breath coming unevenly, and raised her eyes to his face. It was totally revealing, every guard down, naked with longing and desire. His free hand slid along the soft silk of her chemise to her waist, and he bent his head to hers. With his face so close to hers that she could feel his uneven breath upon her cheek, he stopped and drew away, and rose to his feet.

'We had best go back,' he said in a dour voice.

She felt like a starveling who had been offered food, only to have it snatched away again. Reaching for her still damp gown, she pulled it over her head. Then, without speaking, she fell into step beside Alistair and they walked back towards the settlement.

Noise reached them long before the crude shelters had come into view, and they began to hurry. Lucy was forced to run to keep up with Alistair. The people were being moved on again, forced by the tenants' shepherds to dismantle their camp and take down their shacks. Men and women scurried to and fro, thrusting possessions into creels, tearing down timbers, collecting their livestock.

Lucy was burning with an impotent rage against Hugh Sinclair and all the other landowners who had caused the degradation and misery which seemed to be their daily lot as she witnessed the dull despair on the faces of the people.

But there was nothing despairing in Alistair's voice as it rang out, strong and clear. 'It was time, and more, that we moved on! But this time we make for the land by the sea!'

They watched him without response. Then someone muttered, 'We know naught of fishing.'

'Who said anything about fishing? We will not turn to the sea, but to the land by the coast! We will cultivate it, and we must hurry so that the ploughing can be done before it is too late in the season.'

A voice called bitterly, 'And how long, once we have made the coastland fertile, will it be before the laird sees its new value and takes it from us? We have no leases, no deeds or titles! Better that we wander and starve than that we should enrich the laird further by the toil of our hands!'

'Ay,' several other voices agreed.

Alistair regarded them grimly, his arms folded across his chest. 'Have you heard aught of Canada?' he demanded.

''Tis over the sea,' one man responded.

Alistair nodded. 'It is that. It is also a country of few men and no lairds. I have read about it in the *Inverness Courier*. It told of mountains and rivers and streams, of forest-land there for the taking, of grasslands in plenty and only wild deer and game birds to feed on them. A land, in short, waiting for a landless people like ourselves to claim it!'

Lucy stared at him in surprise. Was he suggesting that they should abandon the notion of taking up their land by the sea, and travel to Canada instead? But they had neither the money nor the resources for that.

'Even supposing we should want to go so far away,' she heard her own doubts being expressed by one of the crofters, 'how could we journey to Canada? We, who have no money for passages, and scarce enough food to stave off starvation?'

'We shall work to earn the money!' Alistair's jaw-line was set at a determined angle. 'We shall take up the land by the sea, and all the work we do will be for our own benefit alone. We will labour as one community; we will pool all the seed and the equipment we own. And when we have gathered in our harvest, we will buy passages for Canada, where each man will be his own master ever afterwards!'

Lucy could see that he had captured their imagination now. 'What manner of crops can be grown in Canada?' one man wished to know.

'The same as here,' Alistair said. 'Wheat, oats, barley and potatoes.'

The crofters discussed the matter among themselves. Then one of them called out, 'It is too far away, Alistair! If we were to go to Canada, we should never again be able to return home.' Others nodded in agreement.

'*Home*!' Alistair echoed scathingly. 'And where is your home, Fergus McDugan? Is it this bleak hillside from which you have just been made to remove your shelter? Is it the land by the coast which you fear so much? Or is it that burnt wasteland at Bencraig from which you were forced by your laird's factor? You have no home—any of you! But you do have the chance to make a new home for yourselves!'

The crofters shifted uncertainly. 'We have lived all our lives here,' someone muttered.

'And is that a good reason for starving here? For we shall starve if we do not go at once to the coast, and clear the land and plant our crops. And while we wait to harvest them, we will plan the new life we are to build for ourselves in Canada—the new community, the new Bencraig!' Alistair's eyes were alight, and a spontaneous cheer rang out when he continued,

'That is what we shall call our settlement in Canada —New Bencraig!'

CHAPTER TWELVE

LUCY WAS no stranger to the sea, for she had accompanied Amelia Sinclair on several visits to the Sussex coast, and even if no one else in their party was able to identify the different smells in the air, she recognised the sharp, salty tang of the ocean. For the past few days now the sky overhead had been filled with wheeling, screeching gulls.

The people's first euphoric enthusiasm for Alistair's plans had not lasted long. As their surroundings became more alien, their fears and uncertainties about the future were mirrored in their faces, and they began to drag their feet and voice every objection they could think of to continuing on to the coast. Alistair cursed them and reassured them in turn, and all the while he dangled before them the promise of the New Bencraig they were to build in Canada.

Within Lucy, the knowledge had been growing that there would be no place for her in that new Bencraig any more than there had been in the old one. She expressed her feelings to Alistair that evening when they found themselves alone together, searching for firewood.

'I shall stay and help with the work at the sea,' she told him. 'But I'll not leave for Canada when the time comes. I'll travel with you for part of the way and then take the road to Edinburgh. I'll seek employment there.'

'No!' His voice came out harshly. He threw down the

branches he had gathered and took her hands in a hard, painful grip. *'No!'*

'You will marry Fiona,' she said bleakly. 'What would there be for me in Canada?'

He shook his head in a blind gesture. 'An ocean—all those thousands of miles—separating us . . . That would be too hard to bear! Never knowing how you were, or where you were, or whether you were starving.'

Her voice shook. 'I don't belong anywhere, Alistair.'

His face was starkly etched, his eyes shadowed with pain. 'You belong with Kirstie,' he growled. 'You are her daughter.'

Lucy sighed. 'She does not need me. She has never needed me.' She freed her hands and walked deliberately away to join the others.

The evenings seemed colder here near the coast, and the people were making camp against a windswept, inhospitable hillside. Beside the smouldering fire which Willy was trying to coax into a blaze, Kirstie prepared their meagre meal while Fiona huddled close to it for warmth. To see the three of them together like that, unified as a family group which could never include her, smote Lucy to the heart. Her feelings were intensified when Alistair returned with an armful of firewood and Fiona immediately jumped up to move to his side. She had become more possessive of him since his recovery, and she seemed to seize every opportunity to ram home to Lucy the point: 'You have less than I now, for you do not have Alistair.'

'Tomorrow we shall reach the sea,' Alistair was telling them. 'Our wandering will be over, and we must work fast if the people are not to drift into famine.'

Kirstie smiled faintly at him. 'It was a fine dream of yours, that, the building of a new Bencraig. But I'm thinking it was no more than a dream to spur the people into moving to the sea.'

'No! I shall make it come true! Between all of us, we have enough seed left to provide a good harvest. We must all work together, and share everything equally like one large family. All money earned must go into a fund to pay our passage to Canada!'

Willy's eyes shone. 'You are certain that fine crops can be grown in Canada, and that the land is there for the taking?'

'Oh ay.' Alistair nodded. 'Tonight we must retire early, so that we may make a start at dawn.'

The next morning, before they began the final stage of their journey to the sea, Alistair addressed the people. He spoke in the Gaelic, so that Lucy did not understand the words he was using, but the note in his voice told her that his message was one of optimism and hope, and she could see by the people's faces that he was giving them fresh heart.

But when, later that day, they reached the land allotted to them by Hugh Sinclair, a hush fell over the crofters and they stared about them with empty eyes. Lucy could almost imagine that she heard Sinclair's malicious laughter mingling with the screeching of the gulls.

The goal, the land to which they had journeyed with such hope, was no more than a strip of grey, sour soil which carried the brine for miles inland. A few stunted trees had managed to survive, but the land was a final slap in the face for the people, a cruel joke clinging precariously along the edge of a cliff and bordered by bogs.

The families from Bencraig stood silent, as if unified in mourning. The silence was broken by Alistair's curses.

'By God, Hugh Sinclair will not serve the people in this way! I'll not let him!'

Rage gave Alistair's face the appearance of having been carved from granite. He turned to his horse and began to remove the load the animal had been carrying. Lucy hurried to his side.

'What do you mean to do, Alistair?'

'See Sinclair, and force from him justice for the people!'

He hurled himself into the saddle and rode away, grim purpose in the set of his shoulders and the tilt of his head, his plaid flying in the breeze.

Listlessly, because there seemed nothing else to do, the people began to put up their crude shelters again, some of them clambering down the cliffs to search for driftwood. A red-faced man emerged from a stone cottage perched upon a headland, and addressed the people in the Gaelic.

For Lucy's benefit, Willy translated. 'He says he is the mussel bailiff, whose duty it is to see and make sure that no shellfish is taken from the sea.' Willy made a bitter sound. 'He says we may take as much herring and other fish as it pleases us to do.'

None of the crofters, Lucy knew, was even remotely equipped for sea-fishing of any kind. Some went in search of plovers' eggs, and others prised limpets from the rocks under the mussel bailiff's watchful eye, while the remainder submitted in defeat and made further inroads into their meagre stock of seed potatoes.

As the days passed, an atmosphere of marking time grew among the crofters. All their hopes were focused on Alistair's return. Lucy retained an image of him galloping away, and she thought that if hard resolve alone could force from Hugh Sinclair what he was unwilling to give freely, Alistair must surely return triumphant.

'He had a plan of some kind,' she repeatedly assured Kirstie and Fiona.

'Of what use are plans against someone like Hugh Sinclair?' Fiona brooded.

Kirstie said quietly, 'I fear that, in his rage, Alistair may have done something rash and dangerous. It is now almost a week since he rode away.'

'He would not allow rage to lead him into a trap. He knows only too well that Hugh Sinclair would seize on any excuse to . . . ' Lucy stopped, and slapped her palm to her brow. 'Oh God, how could I have forgotten? Sinclair doesn't need an excuse! A Warrant has already been issued for Alistair's arrest!'

'What do you mean?' Fiona demanded shrilly. 'What are you talking about?'

'Don't you remember? If Alistair had not seemed to be near death, he would have been arrested on the night Bencraig was cleared. The Warrant must still be in force, and Hugh Sinclair will have had Alistair taken into charge! *That* is why he has not returned!'

Fiona burst into hysterical tears, and Willy moistened his pale lips. 'What—What shall we do now, miss?'

Lucy held her head in her hands. 'The best we can, I suppose. Alistair would have wanted us to make an effort . . .'

Fiona turned on her with passionate fury. 'It is not for you to say what Alistair would, or would not have wanted! You have no right to speak for him!'

Lucy gave her a blank look. Alistair was all too probably languishing in some gaol, and yet Fiona could preoccupy herself with something so trivial and irrelevant. She opened her mouth to speak, but Fiona jumped up and began to pace the ground, words erupting from her like floodwater after a river bank had been swept away.

'You have always had everything, and how I despise you for having thrown it all away! But I—what have I ever had? Poverty and hardship and near starvation and grinding toil! That has been my lot! The one thing I could call mine, the only thing I had which you wanted, was Alistair. He loved me and not you, and that helped to make up for all the chances that you were given and that were denied to me! And now—now he has gone, and once again I have nothing, and—*it isn't fair*!'

'Whisht, Fiona,' Kirstie said, going to her daughter and laying a comforting arm on her shoulder. 'Lucy was right. We must make an effort. We'd all be the better for something to do. Since we'll have to stay here now, we might as well start to build some kind of home.'

Lucy stood up and wandered away into the dark. What a fool she had been, wrapping herself in a false sense of security! Why, oh why had she not remembered that a Warrant had been issued for Alistair's arrest? If only she had, someone could have gone after him to warn him.

She dug her fingernails into the palms of her hands, and found her thoughts straying to Fiona. She had believed that her half-sister's resentment towards her was weakening, now that they shared a common lot of poverty and hardship, but this evening Fiona had made it clear that her feelings were as strong as ever, if not stronger. Perhaps what she could not forgive, now, was Lucy's rejection of the chance of being reunited with the Sinclairs. She had scorned something for which Fiona would have given her soul.

The thought of the Sinclairs set Lucy wondering desperately whether it would be worthwhile if she were to visit Dunrobin Castle and plead with Hugh Sinclair on Alistair's behalf. Then she remembered that last message of his, conveyed to her by Buchanan: *'Drive her into the sea if necessary, but do not let her be heard of again.'* She smiled bleakly. They did not sound like the words of a merciful man.

The following morning, at Kirstie's insistence, Willy began to construct a sod hut on the cliffs, and most of the others followed his example. But the crude dwellings were daily ravaged by gales, so that their interiors quickly became mildewed by sea-spray and the exteriors frosted with brine. The sky seemed to be constantly shrouded by a grey cloud which hung in mourning over the barren settlement, reflecting Lucy's own feelings.

Fiona's grief for Alistair was loudly expressed at first, and seemed to veer between self-pity and resentment towards Fate. But after a few days she seemed to lapse into a state of dull resignation.

Lucy did her grieving silently and in private. She imagined Alistair, fettered in chains, on board some convict ship bound for the colonies. He would not accept his fate with humility. He would continue proud and defiant, and would be punished all the more for it . . . She shook her head. She would drive herself mad by constantly thinking about him. Determinedly, she turned her thoughts to the people instead.

Without Alistair's leadership, she had expected them to give up in despair, to squat upon the cliffs and wait for famine to overtake them. Instead, with a kind of mindless tenacity, they began to follow the community plan that Alistair had outlined for them—as though they believed it could actually accomplish something in this desolate wasteland.

They worked long, hard hours each day to clear and plough the land, but the arable soil was so thin that it was obvious scarcely anything would grow on it, and in any case their precious seed was constantly being blown into the sea almost as soon as it had been sown. As if their struggles with the earth were not enough to batter their spirits, other troubles overtook them. The few cattle they still possessed strayed homewards to the strath, and were impounded when they were found on the new sheep pastures. Fines were demanded before they would be released, but with the exception of Iain Duncan no one could pay them. Lucy watched with bitter irony as the dour old man drove back the two scrawny cows for whose freedom he had, against all advice, exchanged her diamond ring.

When it became clear that no matter how grimly they battled with the land, nothing was ever going to thrive there, the people turned in desperation to the sea for a living. But they knew nothing of the ways of fishermen and had no pier or harbour; neither had they boats in which to put to sea. Fishermen from the south, their boats at anchor as they stretched their nets, seemed to mock them.

Day after day ground by, with the people all but starving. The men waded waist-deep into the sea, spreading out a net which had been constructed by the women, and if they were lucky they gathered a harvest of a few herrings. More often than not they had to content themselves with stewing seaweed for such sustenance as it might provide.

No news came of Alistair. Fiona rarely mentioned him now; it seemed to Lucy that the girl had no emotion to spare for anything but her own despair over the wretched existence they were leading, and Kirstie was obviously concerned about her daughter.

Kirstie herself was growing frailer and more drawn. Lucy suspected that she starved herself so that there would be more for the rest of them to eat. The sight of her hollowed cheeks and shadowed eyes made Lucy so angry that she would have gone out and stolen a sheep again had it not been for the ever-watchful presence of the bailiffs appointed by the Association for the Suppression of Sheep-stealing.

Instead, her mouth set with defiance and determination, Lucy collected a creel and left the hut. As she made her way towards the cliff edge, she met Fiona. The girl looked at her with dull, uninterested eyes and Lucy hesitated, chewing at her lower lip. For Kirstie's sake, if for no other reason, she wished to bring a spark of animation back to Fiona, and she decided to play upon her vanity.

'How beautifully thick and dark your hair still is, Fiona, in spite of everything! The sea air is taking the colour from mine.'

Fiona stared at Lucy's hair, and a small smile began to play about her mouth. She tossed her head back, thrusting her fingers through her locks. Then a brooding look entered her eyes.

'What does it signify, now, whether my hair looks well or not? If only I had been given a chance in life . . . I am sure there are any number of girls not half so pretty as I who are living lives of luxury in Edinburgh!'

Lucy made no comment, and Fiona went on, 'Why, I've been told that Mairi McDougal, who used to live in the next clachan beyond Bencraig, was taken to Edinburgh by a rich friend of Mr Buchanan! And everyone used to say that she was not nearly as pretty as I! It was simply that she was given a chance, while I was not.'

Lucy studied her. 'Would you really have welcomed such a dishonourable alliance, Fiona? Would you have sacrificed Alistair for the sake of living in luxury in Edinburgh as some rich man's mistress?'

'I might well have considered it,' Fiona defended sulkily, 'had I known that Alistair would finish up being transported to New South Wales or to some other colony from which he will never return . . . ' Her voice tailed off as she met Lucy's glance, and suddenly her eyes flashed with angry defiance.

'Yes, and yes, and *yes*! I would have welcomed such a dishonourable alliance with open arms! To drive round Edinburgh's streets in a grand carriage, wearing pretty gowns . . . What honour is there in living like this, like an animal, without food, without hope?'

Lucy suddenly remembered that Fiona herself had, at the age of fifteen, tried to seduce one of Neil Buchanan's friends into taking her away to Edinburgh. Alistair or Kirstie would have put a stop to it, and the man must have taken Mairi McDougal instead. She gave her head a slight shake. It was not for her to sit in judgment upon Fiona because of the girl's dream of a life of luxury and gaiety in Edinburgh. The misery she herself was now enduring had been accepted by her of her own free will. But Fiona had had no such choice. *She* had obviously realised, from an early age, that the only weapon she possessed with which to claw her way out of poverty was her beauty, and her bitterness was not to be wondered at because she had never had a chance to use it to that end.

Lucy had begun to walk on again, and was surprised to find Fiona falling into step beside her. 'Where are you going?' the girl demanded.

'To gather mussels.'

'That is against the law.'

Lucy shrugged. 'So is sheep-stealing. Mussels are easier to steal than sheep, and the risk is not so great.'

Fiona hesitated for a moment. 'I shall go with you,' she said impulsively. 'Together we could gather twice as many.'

It was a perilous trail down the cliffs to the rocks, but once the descent had been made, the rewards were bountiful. They prised black mussels from the rocks and soon the creel was filled to overflowing. They were preparing to climb back up when the sound of a stone slithering down a slope drew their attention. The man must have been there all the while, hidden in the shadows of a rock, watching them.

Lucy's heart bumped uneasily when she recognised him as the mussel bailiff. Why had he not made his presence known before now? she wondered. And then she saw his expression as he stared at Fiona, and she understood. She waited for him to approach them.

His hooded eyes were still admiring Fiona, who instinctively and with a purely feminine gesture tossed back her hair so that it rippled like dark water.

'Do you not know that for the taking of these shellfish I have a duty to have you given in charge?' The man continued to stare at Fiona as he spoke. 'Mussels are delicacies for the rich man's table, and not for the likes of yourselves—pretty as you may be!'

Fiona lowered her lashes. 'We were so very hungry, sir. It is more than two days since any herring was caught, and we have scarcely eaten since then.'

The bailiff's eyes were appraising her. 'Ach, 'tis a shame that such lovely lassies should go hungry! This time I'll not abide by my duty, but allow you to keep the mussels instead.'

Fiona thanked him prettily. He said something to her in the Gaelic; she laughed and tossed her head and made a retort Lucy could not understand, but which she knew instinctively to be provocative.

As they walked away from him, Fiona explained, 'He tells me he has a fine big salmon for which he has no use, if I should have a mind to collect it from his house this evening!' Her eyes were very bright.

Lucy frowned apprehensively at her. 'You don't imagine that he has offered you a salmon because he is sorry for you?'

'No, I am not a fool!' Fiona laughed. 'I know fine why he has offered it to me—impertinent devil!' But she continued to wear a flushed, complacent look. Her former apathy had been pierced by the reassurance that she was still attractive to men.

Kirstie's tired eyes lit up when she saw the mussels.

Their meal that evening had a festive air; it was the first time in weeks that their hunger had been completely appeased.

But, after the meal, a reaction set in. They had grown used to hunger and had accepted its pangs as part of life. But tonight, after the nourishing and satisfying supper, the thought of tomorrow's inevitable starvation suddenly seemed too much to bear. They grew silent and brooding as they contemplated their empty wooden bowls, and Lucy knew that each shared the same thought. Fiona stood up abruptly and went outside. Lucy, too, rose and in silence she helped Kirstie to wash the bowls and put them away, knowing that tomorrow they would be filled once more with nothing but thin potato broth.

But the following morning Fiona, who had risen early before anyone else was up, entered the cottage with a large salmon wrapped in seaweed. She handed it to Kirstie, explaining guilelessly, 'I found it trapped in a pool where the river joins the sea. Was it not lucky that I went for an early walk?'

Kirstie and Willy exclaimed over the salmon, and began to calculate how best to preserve part of it. But Lucy was regarding Fiona grimly. As soon as she could contrive to do so, she cornered the girl and demanded with angry contempt, 'Do you hold yourself so cheap, Fiona? A mussel bailiff!'

Fiona's face was contorted with passion. 'Yes, a mussel bailiff! The difference between eating and starvation! And if you tell anyone, I shall never . . .'

'Have no fear,' Lucy interrupted scornfully. 'I would not dream of inflicting such pain upon Kirstie!'

That evening Fiona disappeared after supper again, and in the morning she handed Kirstie some gulls' eggs she said she had found while out walking. Lucy thought of Alistair, and how he had said, 'Fiona has not your strength. She would use her beauty as a way out of hardship.'

Afraid that her expression might betray her to Kirstie, Lucy muttered an excuse and went outside to sit on a rock. From there she could look down into a small firth that a fishing vessel had just entered; the men were at work on her sails. One of them saw her and waved, calling out something which made his companions laugh. Their cheerfulness, their energy and their sophisticated craft told her that they were fishermen from the South, come to harvest with ease the fish which the crofters succeeded in catching only in pitifully small quantities and with a great deal of effort.

She turned her back on the fishermen and watched, without interest, as a dot on the horizon grew larger and resolved itself as the figure of a horseman. It would be a shepherd from one of the sheep-walks searching for straying animals or come to tell them that more of their livestock had been impounded.

Then something about the horseman seemed familiar. It was probably no more than a figment of her imagination, a likeness conjured up by her hopeless fear and longing for him, but all the same she kilted up her skirts and began to run.

The horse slowed, and its rider threw up a hand as she drew near. 'Lucy!'

'Alistair?' she whispered shakily.

He drew his horse up, dismounted and took great strides towards her. She studied him hungrily, barely able to believe in the reality of him. How much larger he seemed than she remembered, how very blue his eyes beneath the straight dark brows . . .

'You . . . ' she began. 'I . . . We all thought—you had been arrested and perhaps transported!'

'No, I was detained by officialdom this long while, but not in the way you feared, and I had no means of sending word to any of you.' He gave her a lingering, intent look, as though he were trying to imprint her image on his mind. And then he did a strange thing. He reached for her hands and slid them underneath his plaid so that she could feel the vibration of his heart against her fingers. He gazed down at her with love and desire in his eyes, but overshadowing it was a great and inexplicable sadness. Or perhaps the sadness was caused by the knowledge that he could not draw her into his arms and hold her close, for to Fiona belonged that place.

A spasm shook her. She could not tell him about Fiona and the mussel bailiff without Kirstie learning of it also. But Fiona must be made to release him from his promise, and she herself would not scruple to use her knowledge as a threat to that end.

Uncannily, as though he had been reading her thoughts, Alistair put her aside and said in a heavy voice, 'Nothing has changed. Nothing can change for you and me.'

'What—What happened to you?'

''Tis a long tale, and the others must hear it also.'

She tried to dismiss the sense of foreboding which was slowly creeping over her, and to take comfort in the fact that he was here, safe and free.

His gaze was scanning the sod huts, and registering the fact that there was little livestock left. 'Things have been bad here, Lucy?'

'Quite bad.' She deliberately understated the matter, for she had a feeling that they would become worse.

He shrugged. 'Well, let us away, so that I may tell everyone what has happened.'

Fiona, Lucy saw angrily, greeted him with as much joyful rapture as if she had nothing whatever on her conscience, and hung on his arm as he went to summon the others to a meeting. Lucy found herself alone in the hut with her mother.

'I have spoken to Fiona,' Kirstie said unexpectedly, 'and she'll not visit the mussel bailiff again.'

'Oh . . . ' Lucy put her hands to her face. 'I thought I was the only one who had guessed.' She lowered her hands and looked at Kirstie. 'How did you know?'

There was pain in Kirstie's eyes. 'I know Fiona, and I am not a fool. One salmon may chance to be trapped in a pool, but gulls' eggs found so easily the very next morning . . . ' She shook her head. 'I forced Fiona to tell me the truth. There will be no further gifts of food from the mussel bailiff.'

Kirstie looked straight into Lucy's eyes. She spoke slowly now and very deliberately. 'I grow older and more tired each day. Fiona will not go on heeding me for long. But she will always heed Alistair. If you tell him about the mussel bailiff, I shall never forgive you.'

The blood was drumming in Lucy's ears. 'You mean —he must be held to his promise to marry Fiona, come what may?'

Kirstie's face was resolute. 'Fine you knew, Lucy, that he was not for you. From the start you knew he was promised to Fiona.'

'A promise from which you could absolve him! And you must do so!'

'I'll not absolve him.'

'But you know that she has been faithless!'

'Understand this, Lucy,' her mother interrupted in a voice as unyielding as granite. 'My poor, wee, flawed Fiona comes before anyone. I made my sacrifices for *you* when I gave you away. Now it is Fiona's turn.'

'I'll say nothing about the mussel bailiff,' Lucy promised dully. 'But—you speak of sacrifices. Tell me this: would you ever have made the sacrifice of giving *Fiona* away to another woman, even for her own good?'

Kirstie did not answer for a moment. When she did so it was with typical honesty. 'No. I could not have ceased grieving for Fiona.'

Lucy turned away quickly so that her mother would not see her bereft expression, and went outside to where people were gathering to hear Alistair's account of his visit to Dunrobin Castle.

He did not begin to speak until everyone was on the bare headland above the cliffs. His voice was expressionless as he reported:

'I have been away this long while because, to begin with, it was no easy matter to gain access to Hugh Sinclair. In the end I forced my presence upon him. He totally denied that he owed the compensation which I demanded on behalf of all of us. He said there was no proof that any of us had lost anything through the clearance of his land. He told me that Buchanan and the sheriff's officers would be prepared to swear on oath that my livestock had been surrendered to the people of Bencraig on my behalf, and that all of you had been given ample time to dismantle your house timbers and take your belongings and your animals to safety . . .'

An angry murmur from the crowd interrupted him, and he waited until it had subsided. 'After I left Dunrobin Castle, I went to demand that the committee of the Highland Destitution Board should take up our case against Hugh Sinclair. There were long delays while the committee met and considered the matter and took my sworn statements. I was assured, unofficially, that the Board *would* fight for compensation from Sinclair. And then, suddenly, everything changed and I was told that our case was not proven. Hugh Sinclair denied that he or his agents had behaved in any but a just manner, and he was believed by the Board.'

A hard, cynical note entered Alistair's voice. 'The

committee's change of heart was explained when I learnt that Sinclair had just made a large and very generous donation to their Relief Fund. Sooner than pay us the money rightfully owing to us, he chose to enhance his own reputation and to influence the Board's decision . . .'

Alistair's voice was drowned by a roar of rage from the crowd. Lucy saw that he was looking straight at her, and she shook her head in helpless anger. Hugh Sinclair could still hold the fate of the people effectively in his hands, even though they had been cleared from his land.

When Alistair was able to make himself heard again, he spoke with his gaze still fixed upon Lucy, and almost as if his words were addressed to her alone. 'I had one weapon left to use against Sinclair. I sent him a message, asking how he would like me to make public the fact that the girl whom the world has looked upon as his daughter was now living in near starvation. I received a message from him in reply. If his daughter, he said, who had been carried away against her will in revenge for the clearance of his land, were to be returned to him, he would pay full compensation for all losses we claim to have sustained.'

Lucy jumped to her feet. 'It is a monstrous lie that I was taken against my will, and he knows it!'

'Of course,' Alistair agreed quietly. 'His meaning, however, is quite plain. Your disappearance has obviously become a growing embarrassment to the Sinclairs. They are finding it harder to fend off questions about you. They want you back, and they also want a story to satisfy the curiosity and speculation among their friends. But I made it clear to him that the decision whether to go back or stay must come from you.'

Silence followed his words. It was broken by Kirstie. 'She must go back,' she said firmly. 'She has been offered a second chance. For the sake of all of us, she must go back to the Sinclairs.'

Lucy stared at her, dry-mouthed. If she had needed further proof that there could never be a place for her in her mother's life, she had just been offered it.

Unsteadily, she picked her way towards Alistair. Fiona had come to stand by his side, and Kirstie hovered close by. Lucy looked only at him as she faltered, 'You—believe Sinclair—would honour his promise to pay compensation if I went back?'

'Yes, I do believe it, Lucy. Once you have been restored to him, he would naturally want everyone who knows the truth to depart speedily for the other side of the world.'

'Then I'll go back,' she said quietly.

Fiona lost all control. 'No!' she shouted. '*No*!' It is too much to bear! Go back, will she, to her life of luxury and pretty clothes, while I . . .'

'Be quiet, child!' Kirstie ordered tersely.

'Mother, it's not fair!' Fiona wailed, tears rolling down her cheeks. 'Is she always to be the winner in the end—while I always lose?'

Kirstie moved to gather her weeping daughter in her arms, and stroked her hair as if she were a child. Her eyes sought Lucy's. 'You'll be the better for forgetting all of us, child, and living your own life where you belong, with the Sinclairs.'

Lucy turned away, and when she spoke, her voice sounded unfamiliar to her own ears as she told Alistair, 'I am ready to leave whenever you like.'

CHAPTER THIRTEEN

THEY SET OFF the following morning, with Lucy mounted on an old mare borrowed from one of the crofters. Willy had bade her a clumsy but obviously sincere farewell, while Fiona had merely given her a stony look and walked away. Kirstie had placed an arm briefly about Lucy's shoulder, and said in a sad voice, 'This is the way of it, child.'

They were riding abreast, with Alistair matching the pace of his own horse to her mare, and neither of them spoke. Lucy tried to comfort herself with the thought that she was helping the others to begin a new life, but she continued to feel more bleak and bereft than ever. She understood, now, the reason behind Alistair's strange greeting the day before. Obliquely, he had been saying farewell to her even then, for he had known that she would have no choice but to go back.

At dusk, they came upon a deserted shepherd's hut. 'Well stay here for the night,' Alistair said. 'It is shearing time, and its owner will be away, gathering in his flock.'

They dismounted, haltering their horses so that they could not stray, and inspected the interior of the hut. There was a crude table and one chair, and in a corner lay a palliasse stuffed with straw. Alistair found a candle and lit it, and then he unpacked the potato-cake Kirstie had baked for them.

They ate in silence, seated side by side on the palliasse. The fir candle threw flickering shadows, and in its light Alistair's face appeared grim and drawn.

He rose, and pulled out the chair, seating himself and resting his arms on the table. 'Go to sleep now,' he commanded brusquely. 'There is still a way to go in the morning, and you need to be fresh.'

'So do you. You have been spending a long time in the saddle.' She hesitated. 'The—The palliasse is wide enough for two.'

He looked across the room at her. The flickering light accentuated his sombre expression, and revealed an unnatural whiteness about his mouth. She saw his hands gripping the edge of the table.

'Go to sleep!' he repeated harshly.

She shook her head, and felt tears sliding down her cheeks. 'You—cannot love me. If you did . . .'

'God!' His voice came out in a violent whisper. 'Do you think I find it easy—any of this? But believe me, it would be the harder for both of us in the end if I allowed myself to forget . . .' He broke off, shaking his head. 'So lie down and go to sleep, Lucy, and do not torment me further!'

Against all her expectations, she did sleep, but her dreams were so terrifying and despairing that she felt hardly rested in the morning. In almost complete silence they began to prepare for the remainder of the journey.

When, at last, the crenellated walls of Dunrobin Castle came in sight, Lucy had to fight an almost overwhelming impulse to spur her mare in the opposite direction. Everything inside her screamed out against being returned to the Sinclairs, against living the lies which would be necessary to save their reputation, and most of all against saying goodbye to Alistair for the last time.

He leant across in the saddle and caught the reins of her mare, forcing her to halt. 'Get down, Lucy.'

She gave him a questioning look. They had reached

a belt of trees just outside the grounds of the castle, and there was still a fair distance to cover.

He gave no explanation, but dismounted and held out his hands to help her from the saddle. As she slid to the ground, he uttered a rough cry, and then his arms were about her, crushing her to his body. His lips touched her cheek, but when she moved her head so that her mouth could meet his, she sensed the tremendous restraint he was imposing upon himself. His lips brushed hers in the briefest caress, and then he held her away from him, his hands locked in her hair.

'Farewell, *a ghràidh*,' he said simply.

'Alistair . . . ' Her voice shook. 'This is all we are ever to have. Can there not be—more? Something to remember?'

'Ah Lucy, Lucy, can you not see that the more there is to remember, the harder it will be for both of us? Come now, let me help you back into the saddle.'

Her vision was blurred as they rode up to the drive in front of Dunrobin Castle, and Alistair handed their horses to an astonished servant.

The door was opened to them by a liveried footman whose eyebrows rose superciliously at sight of them. 'To the tradesmen's entrance with you, if indeed you have any business here at all!'

Before Lucy could react, Alistair was saying icily, 'You are impertinent! Tell Mr Hugh Sinclair that his daughter has arrived.'

The footman looked baffled, and uncertain whether to judge the two of them by their bearing or by their worn and travel-stained clothes. At last he capitulated. 'Very well—sir.'

He moved aside so that they could step into the vast hall, and called to one of the servants standing at the foot of the stairs to have the message conveyed to Hugh Sinclair.

What self-confidence Lucy might have had was rapidly ebbing as they waited in the grand hall under the curious gaze of liveried servants. Perhaps, she found herself thinking, Alistair had misinterpreted Hugh Sinclair's message, and the last thing he wanted was for her to re-enter his life.

Then, with a sick feeling at the pit of her stomach, she saw Hugh descending the stairs, closely followed by Amelia. The sight of them was like being plunged back, momentarily, into another world; a world in which gentlemen wore tight white pantaloons and neck-cloths starched so high that they had difficulty in turning their heads. A world in which ladies spent the forenoon in having their elaborate coiffures perfected by their abigails.

Amelia thrust her way past her husband. 'Lucy, it *is* you!' she exclaimed. 'But oh, how could you call here, looking like this!'

Her husband silenced her curtly. Lucy studied them—the man, with no emotion other than that of calculation in his cold eyes; Amelia with her fear of social disgrace; and felt as far removed from them as if she were an alien creature.

Hugh Sinclair was leading the way into a sumptuously appointed salon. As Alistair began to follow, the older man said curtly, 'You may wait outside for your money, Munro.'

Alistair regarded him coolly. 'Did you think I would leave Lucy in your custody without making sure first what you intended by her? I wish to be reassured about her future.'

'You are hardly in a position to make conditions . . . ' Hugh Sinclair began.

Alistair said nothing, but his expression made it quite plain that he would not be budged.

Amelia's easy tears had begun to flow. 'Lucy, I don't

know how you could . . . First of all joining those wretched people—and then coming here, looking as you do, without a thought for what people will say! The servants will gossip . . .'

'Be quiet, Amelia,' her husband put in impatiently. 'The servants, and everyone else, will speedily be informed that Lucy was borne away by the crofters against her will, and that she has now been restored to us.'

'Oh . . .'

Alistair stirred. 'I am waiting to hear your plans for Lucy's future.'

'I do not think I could bear to return to London . . .' Lucy began.

'Nor shall you be,' Sinclair told her with a chilly smile. 'You will marry Neil Buchanan, who is still prepared—in spite of everything—to have you. You will live at Strathraora with him. It will be the most acceptable explanation for your withdrawal from Society.'

'No!' Alistair's harsh voice interrupted him.

Lucy put out a pleading hand. 'I could not contemplate such a marriage!'

'You have no choice,' Hugh Sinclair cut her short. 'I cannot risk a repetition of your outrageous behaviour in London. It does not matter much what people here might think or say, or whether they fully believe that you were taken away against your will. So, you will marry Buchanan.'

'No,' Alistair said again. 'Come, Lucy. We are leaving.'

'If you do,' Sinclair reminded him, 'the people you profess to care so much for will continue to starve by the sea.'

'Then so be it.'

Lucy felt Alistair's hand on her arm, but she shook her head at him. 'I cannot condemn you and the others to such a fate. I cannot go back. I shall have to do as he says.'

Alistair made an angry sound of protest, but suddenly his eyes were blazing with triumph. 'Lucy—has it not struck you what power you possess?'

'Power?'

'Ay! What matters more to the Sinclairs than their reputation, and hiding the truth from the world?'

Her pulse began to race with excitement as she grasped his meaning. The expression on Hugh Sinclair's face also confirmed that his vulnerable spot had been exposed.

'She shall not marry Buchanan,' Alistair told Sinclair. 'And the people will not continue to starve. For it is true that you care above everything else for your reputation, and it is also true that she has it within her grasp to destroy that reputation!'

'And I shall do precisely that if driven to it!' she confirmed.

'You deceive yourselves, both of you,' Sinclair stated harshly.

'I think not.' A feeling of triumph surged through Lucy, and with it a ruthlessness she had never before realised she possessed. 'You have driven the people to near-starvation,' she went on. 'You have insulted them with the allotment of worthless land by the sea upon which they could not possibly exist. I want the most generous compensation from you—enough money to pay passages for all to Canada, and also to buy equipment and supplies once there!'

Hugh Sinclair was watching her with cold rage. 'And if I refuse?'

'If you refuse, I shall write to all your friends in London, to all your enemies in Parliament, and tell them how you foisted the child of a Scottish peasant on Society, how you allowed that child to grow up believing that she was yours, and how you thereafter cast her off to starve! I shall write of the atrocities which you, through your factor, perpetrated upon your tenants, and of all the wretched deeds which were done in your name!'

'And, while you are about it, Lucy,' Alistair put in grimly, 'write also about the despicable plan to marry you against your will to that same factor, so that you might be safely exiled in Scotland!'

Amelia gave a little shriek of horror. Her husband's face had darkened. He moved to stand by the window, his back to them. After a while, he turned and looked at Lucy. 'If I agreed to your demands,' he said curtly, 'it would only be on condition that you left for Canada too, and never returned.'

'A condition I gladly accept!'

Only the flickering of a muscle beside his mouth betrayed his fury at the humiliating knowledge that he had been out-manoeuvred. Amelia clutched at his arm and wept. 'Do as she asks, Hugh!' she implored. 'The wretched girl would ruin us otherwise!'

'Wait here,' Sinclair addressed Lucy and Alistair harshly, 'while I write a draft for the money. I wish to lose no time in ridding myself of both of you!' He left the room with Amelia in tow.

As they waited, Alistair turned to Lucy. 'I could not endure to think of you married to such as Buchanan,' he said soberly. 'But you were right, that day when you said you would not go with us to Canada. What will there be for you in the future?'

What indeed? she thought, any triumph she had felt at besting Hugh Sinclair diminishing.

Alistair will marry Fiona, she told herself bleakly. Kirstie has made it clear that she will fight to the last ditch to that end. I have given my word to go to Canada, but I shall not fit in anywhere in the new Bencraig . . .

A footman entered the room, breaking into her thoughts. Hugh Sinclair had not deigned to hand them his draft in person, but had sent a servant to deliver it. As they were shown out of the castle afterwards, Lucy knew, without even the faintest of pangs, that she would never again lay eyes upon the two people she had once believed to be her parents.

Alistair broke the silence between them. 'The people do not trust Hugh Sinclair, Lucy. They would not believe in the value of a scrap of paper bearing his name. We must go first to Ullapool and secure our passages to Canada, so that the people may have evidence that they are not to be tricked again.'

She nodded, and spurred her mare on. For her own part, she was glad of any delay in returning to the others, for she knew that neither Kirstie nor Fiona would welcome her back, even in spite of their change of fortune.

In Ullapool, Alistair obtained berths for everyone on an emigration vessel due to sail within a fortnight. He also bought two spare horses, which meant that their return journey occupied far less time. Lucy was preoccupied with her own comfortless thoughts, so that she was barely aware that the ramshackle settlement by the coast was now in sight.

'Someone is coming this way,' she heard Alistair say, and she looked up, straining her eyes. As the distance between themselves and the running figure decreased, she recognised Willy.

She and Alistair reined in simultaneously when Willy collapsed on the ground, his breath coming in ragged gasps. With fear clutching her heart, Lucy said, 'Kirstie! Something has happened to her, has it not?'

Willy shook his head. 'Fiona . . . ' he managed at last. 'She is not—with you?'

'How could she be?' Alistair demanded, frowning.

'Mother thought—she hoped . . .'

Alistair did not wait to hear more. He spurred on his horse and galloped towards the settlement.

Lucy hesitated, and said, 'Willy, what has happened? You thought Fiona might be with us, therefore she must be missing. But how . . .'

'Ay, miss. We do not know what happened to her.'

Her mind a jumble of incoherent thoughts, Lucy gathered the reins and covered the distance to the settlement. She found Kirstie and Alistair together inside the crude sod hut. Small, shrunken, the skin of her face clinging to the bones, Kirstie looked as though she had been carved from some yellow wood. Her eyes were empty as they fell upon Lucy, showing no dismay or curiosity at her return.

'You say Fiona has disappeared!' Alistair spoke sharply. 'When was she last seen?'

In a voice which did not sound quite real, Kirstie said, 'There has been no sign of her these past two days. I thought it possible she had set out to meet you, Alistair.' A tremor shook that unnatural voice. 'You do not think it possible you might have . . . missed her?'

'It is not possible at all, Kirstie.' Alistair's denial was gentle but firm. 'Has a search been made for her?'

'Ay.'

'Including all the cliffs and gulleys?'

'Everywhere has been searched.'

Alistair frowned. 'Was she likely to venture too far into the sea?'

'She has no love for the sea.'

Lucy spoke for the first time. 'Perhaps the mussel bailiff might know something?'

Kirstie turned fiercely on her, that unnatural calm forsaking her. 'And what would such a one as the mussel bailiff be knowing about my Fiona?'

Lucy bit her lip, realising that, even in her agony,

Kirstie still sought to cover Fiona's tracks. After a moment, she said, 'The mussel bailiff is employed to keep watch on the cliffs and the sea. If anyone is likely to have seen where Fiona went, it is he. I think we should go and speak to him.'

'Ay.' Alistair rose. 'Stay here, Kirstie, while Lucy and I go and question the man.'

As they walked towards the headland where the mussel bailiff's cottage stood, Alistair spoke quietly. 'Fiona sought favours from the mussel bailiff, did she not?'

'How—did you guess?'

He sighed. 'I could read it in Kirstie's eyes.'

The mussel bailiff was sitting outside his cottage, at work on the construction of a lobster-pot. Alistair demanded without preamble, 'When did you last see Fiona Macleod?'

The man's eyes narrowed. 'And why do you wish to know?'

'Because she has disappeared, and if I find that you had a hand in it . . .'

'Disappeared, has she?' The bailiff stroked his chin thoughtfully. 'So *that* was the way of it!'

Alistair stooped, taking him by the shoulders and forcing him to his feet. 'Explain yourself!'

The man stirred uncomfortably in Alistair's grip. 'I have not seen her for these three days past. She came to me to say that she would not see me again, having promised her Mam.'

'And that was three days ago?' Lucy put in.

'Ay. Myself, hoping to change her mind—for she was such a bonnie wee thing—I said to her, "There is a fishing boat come into the creek nearby, for the mending of its sails." '

'I remember it!' Lucy broke in.

'Ay, well. I said to Fiona, "It is my duty to board the

vessel, to see and make sure she has taken no lobsters or crabs. Come you with me, Fiona, and if there are lobsters or crabs among their catch, you shall have the pick of them." '

The mussel bailiff spat with remembered disappointment. 'There were no lobsters or crabs, or if there were, they had hidden them. What there was, was a bold young skipper with a smooth tongue and sheep's eyes for Fiona. From Edinburgh, he was, and didn't she want to know all about the place from him? To hear him tell it, there was money for the picking up of it from the streets of Edinburgh.'

That would have been, Lucy thought with dismay, precisely what Fiona wished to be told. Aloud, she asked abruptly, 'When did the fishing boat sail?'

The bailiff looked at her with sly amusement. 'How many days past since Fiona was last seen?'

'Two.'

'Ay, that was the way of it, then.' The bailiff nodded. 'That young skipper, he says to her, "A bonnie lass like yourself . . . Folks would pay good money to see you on a concert stage. You can sing and dance, I'll be bound. My sister could teach you the way of things; she is a fine dancer herself, and not a night goes by but some rich admirer is waiting for the performance to end so they can beg her to eat supper with them. And she not one half as pretty as you!" '

Lucy and Alistair exchanged glances. Then he addressed the mussel bailiff. 'What did Fiona say to that?'

'Oh, she laughs and tosses her head and pretends to treat it as a fine joke. But later that day, did I not see her climbing down the cliffs to the creek with my own two eyes? The skipper came to meet her and they sat on the rocks to talk. And isn't she now missing, with the fishing boat sailed this forty-eight hours since, and on its way to the Firth of Forth near Edinburgh?'

Alistair nodded grimly and took Lucy's arm. They walked away from the cottage, and after a while Lucy uttered the thought uppermost in both their minds. 'I dread breaking it to Kirstie . . .'

'Ay. Poor Kirstie.'

'What are we going to do about Fiona, Alistair?'

'Nothing.' His tone was flat and uncompromising. 'She has made her choice.'

'Kirstie would never accept that!'

'She shall have to. Even supposing we know where to look for Fiona in Edinburgh, we could not go there. We sail for Canada in a fortnight, and we must make haste to reach Ullapool.'

Lucy stopped, pointing. 'Down there is the firth where the fishing boat anchored.'

Alistair cast a long, sombre glance at the empty inlet. 'What I cannot forgive,' he said harshly, 'is that Fiona should have dealt such a blow to Kirstie, who would have died for her!'

Lucy sighed. 'Fiona was tired of being hungry and penniless. She was also desperately jealous because she thought I was to be restored to the position of the Sinclairs' daughter. And you were not there to prop her up with your own courage, Alistair. That smooth-tongued young skipper from Edinburgh appeared in Fiona's life at just the moment when she could least resist him.'

He turned his head slowly to look at Lucy. 'I have failed Kirstie,' he said quietly. 'I have failed to prevent what she always feared for Fiona. But oh, *a ghràidh* . . .'

We are free. The knowledge hung unspoken between them. His hand went to the knot on top of her head, pulling out the pins so that her hair cascaded to her shoulders. Burying his hands in it, he drew her towards him. His hands slipped down to her throat, gentle and caressing. He bent his head so that his mouth touched hers in a gesture which was not a kiss but which, with its deliberate restraint, stirred her far more than a kiss would have done, although she could not have said why that should be so.

'Come,' he murmured against her lips. 'Let us go and break the news to Kirstie.'

She understood, then, why his restrained gesture had moved her so. It was because, even at such a moment, he would not allow himself to overlook Kirstie's pain. He was not a man who could rejoice unreservedly in his own freedom when it had been gained at such a price.

I would not, Lucy told herself, have wanted him any other way . . .

EPILOGUE

It was to be the first wedding ever held in New Bencraig. A minister from a neighbouring settlement was on his way and would arrive in the morning, and everyone would stop working and attend the ceremony. For weeks now the women of the settlement had been baking and roasting, and the men had tuned their fiddles and practised at their bagpipes for the *ceilidh* that would follow.

Lucy sat on a grassy knoll from where she could see most of New Bencraig. The sun was beginning to slip towards the horizon, throwing long shadows across the valley.

The clearing of the land had been completed, and here in Canada there was no scarcity of timber, so that fine dwellings had been erected to house the families who had made the crossing from Scotland.

She still shuddered when she remembered the voyage on a crowded emigration vessel, the storms which had rocked them, and the sickness which had prevailed among the people, none of whom had ever before ventured on a sea-going craft. The voyage had almost robbed them of their spirits, so that when at last they had arrived, the very sight of the almost aggressively fertile valley and the realisation of what they had undertaken had daunted them and filled them with a sense of inadequacy.

On either side of the wide valley rose ranges of hills

clothed in thick, verdant forests where game abounded. The plain of the valley had been overgrown with less dense clumps of larch, silver birch and pine trees, and a wide stream undulated through it on its way to the river, offering both fresh drinking-water and a future means of irrigation.

But the older settlers, in particular, had been homesick and dispirited, and had gazed with dismay at the riotous growth that would have to be hacked down, uprooted and removed. 'We'll never clear this land,' they had lamented. 'It is beyond human possibility.'

'We *will* clear it!' Alistair had retorted. 'Stop whining like old women, and let us make a start!'

He had bullied, cursed, encouraged, praised and insulted the people into making the effort needed to create New Bencraig. He had stressed the advantages of their new territory—the plentiful game and fish on which to live until the land could be cultivated and livestock brought in, the abundance of timber—and he had refused to acknowledge any setbacks.

He had toiled without flagging, and gradually others had followed his example until the valley started to echo with the sound of timber being felled as the land was cleared. A spirit of hope and eagerness had begun to spread through the settlers, and now even the oldest among them had ceased to pine for Scotland's gentle mists.

Their cattle grew fat upon the lush grazing and yielded an abundance of milk, their poultry multiplied and thrived, and the children became healthy and brown in the sun which seemed to shine all summer through.

Lucy thought of the change that had occurred in her own relationship with the people of New Bencraig. Whether it was because of her part in obtaining the money which had made it possible for them to settle here, or because she had accompanied them to Canada to share in the creation of a new community, they had accepted her.

Even Willy, she reflected with a smile, hardly ever called her 'miss' nowadays, and he had been flattered rather than over-awed when asked to give her away in marriage. And Kirstie . . .

Lucy sighed deeply. Until today, her mother had seemed to accept Fiona's loss with a strong, hard, cold courage. Kirstie had neither wept nor demanded that a search should be made for her. Instead, she had behaved as though she had never existed. If she showed Lucy no warmth, she did not appear to resent her either, and she had accepted, calmly, the announcement of the forthcoming wedding.

But, this afternoon, Lucy had been putting the finishing touches to her wedding gown when Kirstie walked in. 'Fiona would wish to carry coloured flowers,' she had said suddenly, her voice indulgent and tender. 'But my Prayer Book would be more suitable.'

Shock and pain had goaded Lucy into crying out, 'It is my wedding, and not Fiona's!'

Kirstie had given her a strange, blank look. 'Ay, to be sure it is.'

Lucy shook her head at the memory. The scene had been so unlike Kirstie, who had not once mentioned Fiona's name since they left Scotland. It was almost as if a hairline crack had appeared in a hard surface, and Lucy could only hope that the crack would not widen, but would become almost invisible over the years.

She saw that the sun had disappeared behind one of the hills now, and she rose and walked over to the house Alistair had built for the two of them. The door swung open at her touch, and as she entered she inhaled the faint, pleasant odour of timber which had been baking in the day's sun. In the living-room, with its walls of polished pine and its window which looked out over the forested slope of a hill, she sat down. The sofa, like all the other furniture, had been bought at the trading store down-river from which they obtained all their outside supplies.

She gazed about her, recalling the many times in the past when she had told herself that there was no place for her anywhere; that there would be no place for her in New Bencraig. How wrong she had been! Her place was here, and so was her future—in this house, on this land, with Alistair.

The room was growing steadily darker, and Lucy was about to light the candles when the door opened and Alistair's tall frame filled it.

There was sufficient light for her to see how vividly his blue eyes contrasted with his skin, which had been burnt a mahogany brown by the sun. He wore breeches made of soft animal hide, and a homespun shirt open at the neck, with its sleeves rolled up to display muscular arms. She could not help remembering her first sight of him in kilt and bonnet and plaid, with the frayed ruffles of his shirtsleeves falling over his work-roughened hands. He would be wearing those same clothes again tomorrow for their wedding—except that Lucy had replaced the ruffles on his shirt and had skilfully patched his plaid.

'Lucy!' he exclaimed, moving towards her.

She rose. 'I was about to light candles.'

'You should not have come here,' he said sternly.

'I know.' She smiled at him. 'By tradition, I should be shutting myself away and indulging in a nervous crisis at the thought of my wedding night!'

His lips twitched. 'Would someone who once stole a sheep, and who used threats to extort money from Hugh Sinclair—forbye all the other things I have known you do—be in the least apprehensive about her wedding night?'

'No,' she said softly, looking into his eyes. 'I am many things, but not apprehensive.'

He reached for her and pulled her down on to the sofa. His hands moved over her body with tenderness, evoking a tumultuous response. She felt his mouth on hers, ardent and demanding, and she was aware that their hearts were pounding in a matching rhythm. His hands were no longer merely tender but had become urgent, moulding her body into an explosive need of fulfilment, and she made a sound in her throat, unbuttoning his shirt and moving her palm over the mat of hair on his chest.

His kiss became more insistent, but with a sudden movement he heaved himself away from her. She sat up, rearranging her gown with unsteady fingers. In the gloom she could see him go to the cupboard and bring out candles. Then he searched for a tinderbox, and a moment later candle-light guttered in the room.

He came to sit beside her again, but did not touch her this time. She laughed shakily. 'Are you superstitious, Alistair? I know it is supposed to be unlucky for bride and groom to spend the eve of their wedding together!'

'We have waited this long,' he interrupted. 'We'll not degrade what is between us for the sake of twenty-four hours.' He shook his head at her in mock reproof. 'Ah, Lucy, you were ever one for offering me temptation . . .'

She laughed softly. 'But not to much avail! Sometimes I think you are made of stone, my love.'

His eyes glinted at her. 'Only wait twenty-four hours,' he promised in a husky voice, 'and you will find what I am made of.'

She held his glance for a moment in the kind of communication which requires no words. Then she sighed. 'I wished to talk to you about Kirstie, Alistair. Something happened this afternoon which disturbs me.'

He frowned. 'She is not ill?'

'No. She suddenly mentioned Fiona. For an instant, it was almost as though she had made herself believe it was *Fiona* you will be marrying tomorrow. A moment later, she seemed not to recall what she had said. I fear she may break down during the ceremony.'

Alistair shrugged his shoulders in a sad gesture. 'Poor Kirstie. There has ever been something unreal and unnatural about her behaviour since Fiona left. She has never allowed herself to grieve, Lucy. For my part, I hope she *does* break down tomorrow, no matter how much it may shock and distress anyone else. Once she has wept for Fiona, she will begin to accept you as the daughter remaining to her.'

'Yes,' Lucy said slowly. 'I was wrong to hope that it would prove to be no more than a tiny crack . . .'

Such was the understanding between them that he did not need to ask for an explanation. They were both silent for a while, listening to the sound of the night insects striking up their chorus, interspersed by an occasional call from an owl.

Lucy stirred. 'I have sometimes wondered whether you and I were not indirectly to blame for what happened.'

'The blame was Fiona's,' Alistair returned uncompromisingly.

'I meant—If we had gone straight back to the coast after we left Dunrobin Castle, she might not have done what she did.'

'Ay, maybe,' Alistair conceded. 'For she would have known that you were not, after all, to return to a life of luxury. That was what she could not bear—the thought of endless hardship for herself, while you wore pretty gowns and had servants to wait upon you.'

'Yes. If she had known that Hugh Sinclair had finally washed his hands of me, she would have counted herself luckier than I. But, on the other hand . . . I wonder if *anything* could really have compared with the lure of Edinburgh and the promise of being applauded and admired.'

'Ay, she thought Edinburgh was the crock of gold at the rainbow's end,' Alistair agreed. 'Poor, wild, reckless Fiona . . . ' He reached for Lucy's hand and pulled her to her feet. His arms went round her, holding her close against him, and his mouth moved in a slow, burning trail along her cheek before claiming her lips.

'Come,' he said, lifting his head. 'I am walking you home.'

As the front door closed behind them and they stepped out into the star-studded night, it came to Lucy that it was the last time that door would ever close against her. From tomorrow night the only purpose it would serve would be to secure herself and Alistair against the world.

She groped for his hand, and said sincerely, 'I hope Fiona found the fame and the admiration and the wealth she went in search of. I hope she found everything she wanted in Edinburgh.'

'Ay.' His fingers curled around Lucy's. 'For all her selfish, reckless folly, how can I wish her aught but well? Had she not done what she did, you and I would have remained forever apart, *a ghràidh mo chridhe*.'

He had spoken the literal truth, Lucy knew. Nothing but Fiona's defection would ever have persuaded him to abandon her. The rules he made for himself and lived by would not have allowed him to do so.

She remembered in wonder how she had once regarded him as arrogant. Aloud, she said impulsively, 'You really are the equal of the highest-born gentleman, and far better than most!'

'Oh ay,' he returned, and there was surprise in his voice that she had ever thought to question the fact.

Please tick the appropriate boxes to indicate your answers.

1 How many Mills & Boon books have you purchased in the last six months?

1 ☐ 2-6 ☐ More than 6 ☐

2 Did you buy these books new or secondhand?

New ☐ Secondhand ☐ Both ☐

3 If you bought new books, how many did you buy?

(a) 1 ☐ 2-6 ☐ More than 6 ☐

(b) Where did you buy them?

Bookshop ☐
Newsagent ☐
Department store ☐
Reader Service ☐
Other (Please state) ☐

____

4 If you bought secondhand books how many did you buy?

(a) 1 ☐ 2-6 ☐ More than 6 ☐

(b) Where did you buy them?

Market ☐
Secondhand shop ☐
Jumble sale, fete etc. ☐
Other (Please state) ☐

____

(c) How much did you pay per book? ____________

5 What do you do with your Mills & Boon books when you have read them?

Keep them ☐
Throw them away ☐
Pass them to friends/relatives ☐
Give them to jumble sales etc ☐
Sell or exchange them ☐
Other (Please state) ☐

____

6 What age group are you in?

Under 25 ☐ 25-34 ☐ 35-54 ☐ 55+ ☐

POST TODAY ____________________

Name ____________________

Address ____________________

____

____________________ Postcode ____________

Thank you very much for your help. We hope that you enjoy your free book. Please send your completed questionnaire to:-

Mills & Boon Reader Survey FREEPOST,
P.O. Box 236, Croydon, Surrey. CR9 9EL
Your address details may be retained by us for mailing you with other offers.

NO STAMP NEEDED

SEC1